THE KILL CODE COLLECTIVE

A Midwest Mystery Works Medical Thriller

by

Julie Holmes

Rob Jung

Brian Lutterman

Chris Norbury

John Baird Rogers

First published in the United States by Hawk Hill Literary, LLC

The Kill Code Collective

For information contact Hawk Hill Literary, LLC, 13274 Huntington Terrace, Saint Paul, Minnesota 55124.

Cover design by Jun Ares

Interior design by Jennifer Adkins

ISBN 978-1-7366108-7-9 (paperback)

ISBN 978-1-7366108-8-6 (ebook)

LCCN 2026904017

First Edition

10 9 8 7 6 5 4 3 2 1

*For all the fans and fellow authors who
encouraged this experiment.*

*Julie, Rob, Brian, Chris & John
May 2026*

Chapter 1

Sierra/Quinn

Who the hell wears five-inch heels in snow? Minneapolis in winter was not the time to wear fancy heels outside, snow or no snow. That was just asking for frostbitten feet. Sierra Bauer, aircraft mechanic, squinted against the falling snow and waited for the passengers to deplane. The pilots had called in a problem —nothing major, but she needed to talk with them.

The woman wearing said five-inch heels and a long red woolen coat held up the line of passengers as she made her way down the airstair of the Range Airlines de Havilland Dash-8 turboprop. A man behind the woman moved to her side as she wobbled on the slick, boot-flattened snow and offered his arm, which she accepted. Fat white snowflakes dusted the man's slick dark hair. Sierra shook her head. *Yet another idiot thinking they can come to Minnesota in January—the dead of winter—and not wear a hat.*

Passengers flowed out of the plane, a queue moving toward the terminal where a ramp agent beckoned them to a door. A flight attendant hovered behind the last passenger as another woman navigated the steps of the airstair. The woman stepped off the airstair, trailed the line of passengers heading into the terminal, and stopped. She fumbled with her watch, swayed, then collapsed.

Sierra dashed in her direction, reaching her before any ramp agents could. She froze. *Ohmygod.* "Alice?" The older woman's face was gray, and she seemed to be struggling to breathe. "Alice, it's Sierra Bauer. Can you hear me?"

Alice gasped for air. "Sierra?" She pointed at her watch and struggled to speak before she became unresponsive.

Sierra shook her. "Alice, are you okay?" *Ohmygod, ohmygod.*

One of the ramp agents—rampies—showed up beside Sierra asking if he could help. She told him to grab the AED—automated external defibrillator—from the plane. Just in case.

He took off toward the plane. Two more rampies stared at Sierra like they didn't dare move. *Damn idiots.* She didn't have a radio with her, but one of the rampies did. "Give me your radio."

The woman handed it to her. Sierra called the ramp agent dispatch. "This is Sierra Bauer, one of the mechanics. There's a medical emergency on the Range Air ramp."

The voice responded. "Medical emergency?"

"Get someone out here ASAP. Call an ambulance!"

The pilots, a flight attendant, and two more ramp agents joined the spectators. Sierra gestured for them to move back. "Give us some space. Someone get some blankets."

Sierra checked Alice's pulse. Nothing. Alarm ratcheted her shoulders tight. "Crap." She started chest compressions.

"Here." The ramp agent who'd retrieved the AED from the plane knelt on the wet pavement beside her. He opened the case and prepped the pads according to the instructions.

Movement in the nearest windows of the terminal arm caught her attention. People stared, jostling to get a better view, but one man moved away from the crowd, movements highlighted by his fluorescent-green-and-blue Seattle Seahawks stocking cap. He held a red duffel bag in front of his chest—odd. When she zeroed in on him, he left the window, disappearing beyond the other onlookers.

Sierra stopped compressions and checked Alice's pulse. Still nothing. *Damn it.* "Hey, you," she said to the rampie whose radio she'd borrowed, "check with Dispatch, make sure any EMTs on the field are on their way." A siren in the distance made her question moot. "Scratch that. Make sure someone gets their attention."

Alice's face grew more ashen. The ramp agent beside Sierra hesitated, a pad in each hand. "We need bare skin, and it says she can't be wet."

It was snowing. How the hell would she not be wet? "Find something to put under her so she's not on the snow." Sierra resumed chest compressions. *Come on, Alice.* She swallowed the knot rising in her throat.

The small crowd gave way to the Airport Fire Department ambulance that pulled to a stop in front of the plane. The EMT firefighters rushed past the rampie who waved them in to where the woman lay.

"How long has it been?"

"Don't know." Sierra stood back, giving the EMTs room to work. She shadowed them while they moved Alice onto a collapsed gurney and off the wet pavement, telling them what had happened before they arrived.

One EMT cut Alice's shirt open. "She's got a device." He turned to Sierra. "Did she have a purse?"

Sierra grabbed the purse from the ground where it had fallen. She shoved the contents that had spilled out back into it.

"Look for a medical device ID card. Might be in her wallet."

Sierra dug through the purse and pulled out a long pocketbook, like the one her grandmother used. She opened it, scanned the contents for anything that looked medical, and found a card with a caduceus on it. She handed it to the EMT. "Here. Her name is Alice Holmgren. Her husband is a—"

"She's got an ICD. Implanted defibrillator." He handed it back to Sierra and returned his attention to Alice. "Give us some room."

They worked on Alice for a few minutes more while Sierra watched from a distance, chanting encouragement under her breath. After their AED delivered a third shock, the EMTs loaded the gurney into the ambulance, with one EMT climbing into the back and continuing CPR. The other EMT set the brakes on the gurney and closed the doors.

A shout caught Sierra's attention. She recognized the voice. Quinn.

Detective Quinn Moore, Minneapolis-St. Paul Airport Police Department, spoke with the EMT before she got into the driver's seat. He reached Sierra as the ambulance drove away, sirens screaming.

"Hey." Quinn laid a gloved hand on her shoulder. "Heard the call come in. Didn't think you were on the rescue team today."

Sierra wiped wetness from her eyes. "Yeah, well, apparently the universe decided I was having a slow day."

Quinn focused his brilliant blue eyes on her. Assessing, she knew. "Let's go inside." He led her down the hall past the ramp agent office and into the terminal. People milled around, the drone of conversation thick with speculation. An announcement for an impending boarding came over the speakers.

Sierra stopped before Quinn led her out of the gate area. "Hold up. I need to contact the maintenance office to make sure someone checks the pilot's write-up."

"They can figure that out without you, can't they?"

"I said I'd check it, and I didn't."

Quinn unzipped his coat and turned to face her, his APD badge on a lanyard around his neck. "The next crew will see no one signed it off, right?" He pulled her to the side, away from the passengers collecting near the gate agent desk. "What happened?"

Sierra blinked away tears and breathed slow and deep to stop the emotions threatening to choke her. "It was Alice, she collapsed on the tarmac, I tried, I couldn't …" She spoke it all in one breath to get it out.

"Slow down," Quinn said. "Alice who?"

"Alice Holmgren. The Holmgrens are family friends. We used to go to their cabin every summer, and they used to come to our place in the fall when the apples were ready. She … she taught me how to crochet. Her husband, Arthur, was my dad's mentor in pre-med studies. Oh my God, what am I going to tell Dad? She didn't look good when she got off the plane. I didn't know it was Alice until I got close. It seemed like a heart attack, but the EMTs said she had an ICD."

"A what?"

"An ICD. An implanted defibrillator." Sierra realized she still held Alice's purse. "Oh, crap. I should have sent this with her." She pulled out the wallet and read the card to Quinn. "Implantable cardioverter defibrillator. It's got her name and phone number, her doctor's name, model, serial number, and the manufacturer, Voyageur Cardiac Systems." Sierra knew a little about the devices, since her father was a nurse practitioner. Not a pacemaker, but similar. She didn't know Alice had heart issues.

"What did the EMTs say?" Quinn asked.

"Nothing to me. Did they tell you anything?"

"They didn't. You know the routine."

Sierra nodded. "If it was a heart attack and she had an ICD … That makes no sense. I mean, they're for managing arrhythmia that could trigger a heart attack."

Quinn sighed. "We don't know. I'm not a doctor, and neither are you. Let's go to my office, where it's quieter." He guided her toward the mezzanine.

"But her husband, Arthur, is a doctor. And their daughter, Olivia." Sierra tucked the card back into Alice's wallet and returned it to the purse. "I can't believe I still have her purse; I should have sent it with the EMTs. They'll want to know her name and stuff."

"I've got the contact information for the emergency services in my office. I'll give them a call."

"I'll have to call Olivia from your office; my phone is in my locker at the hangar. Then I need to get back to the gate."

Quinn placed a hand on the small of her back, a comforting weight. "Are you sure you want to go back after this? I think they'll be okay at the gate without you for the rest of the day. Besides, I should get your statement before I contact the family. Do you have her husband's number? If not, maybe your dad has it."

When they reached the Airport Police Department offices, Sierra waved to Yvonne Maxwell, the department's favorite administrative assistant, as they passed the front desk. "Hey, Yvonne. How did your granddaughter's concert go?"

Yvonne beamed. "Beautifully. Did I tell you she got first chair for the flutes?"

"Congratulations to her. And to the proud grandma."

"Thank you, I'll let her know." Yvonne nodded toward the purse in Sierra's hand. "That's not yours. I bet you don't even own a purse, do you?"

Sierra offered a small smile. "God, no. This belongs to a lady who collapsed on the tarmac. I forgot to give it to the EMTs."

Yvonne gasped. "I hope she's okay."

"Me too." Part of her was hopeful, but Sierra knew that if an AED couldn't jumpstart a person's heart, the odds of recovery dropped by the minute. She didn't need to add another airport death to her bingo card. It'd been years since the last one, and her coworkers still gave her flak about it.

"Yvonne, can you find out where they took her?" Quinn asked. "The airport fire department EMTs picked her up at the Range Air gate."

They left Yvonne to make the calls. When they reached Quinn's office, he gestured for Sierra to enter ahead of him, then closed the door. "You okay?"

Good question. It rolled through Sierra's mind again: Alice's fall, her efforts to save her before the EMTs arrived. Alice and her mom peeling and canning apples. Bonfires at the Holmgrens' cabin on Pelican Lake. The look on Alice's face when Sierra gave her a crocheted throw in her favorite colors. Her chest was tight, and she had to wipe her eyes again. "Not really."

"Then let's take a minute before I get official," he said, arms wide.

She stepped toward him. He knew her so well.

He wrapped her in his arms and she held on, soaking in the feel of him and the refuge he provided. He smelled like Quinn, with a touch of Stetson and something that reminded her of long cozy evenings with him curled in front of the TV watching their favorite shows. It settled her nerves. He was *home*.

He released her. "Better?" he asked.

She inhaled deeply, breathing out to a count of five. "Yes. I'm ready for official now. After I call Olivia."

"Wait until Yvonne finds out where they took Alice. Then you can tell Olivia where to find her." Quinn pulled a notepad and pen from a pocket. "This is only a formality. The incident happened on airport grounds, so someone will ask. Best to have your statement on hand. Tell me what happened."

Sierra did, from the point where the passengers started deplaning, to the moment Alice collapsed on the tarmac, through Quinn's arrival.

A knock at the office door preceded Yvonne's entrance. Her gaze shifted between the two of them. "I'm not interrupting, am I?"

"No," Quinn said. "Just finished taking her statement. What's up?"

Yvonne stepped aside and gestured to a woman about Sierra's age standing just behind her. "This is Olivia Holmgren. She was waiting to pick up her mother and got worried, so she checked here to see if we'd heard anything. Thought it'd be best to bring her straight to you."

"Thanks, Yvonne," Quinn said. "I'll take it from here."

Yvonne patted Olivia's shoulder and left the office.

Sierra crossed the office and embraced her. "Olivia. I'm so sorry."

"Sierra Bauer?" Olivia said as she pulled away. "Wow, I haven't seen you forever. What's going on? I was supposed to meet Mom."

"Olivia," Sierra said, "this is Detective Quinn Moore. Quinn, this is Olivia Holmgren."

Quinn stepped forward. "Miz Holmgren—"

"Just Olivia. Or Doctor." Olivia gripped the strap of her purse, knuckles white. "I'm looking for Mom. She was supposed to arrive over an hour ago. The airline agent said the flight…" She trailed off, eyes widening when she focused on the desk. "Is that Mom's purse? What happened?"

"Olivia," Quinn said, "your mother collapsed on the tarmac when she got off the plane, and it appeared she had a heart attack. Sierra performed CPR until the EMTs arrived. They weren't able to revive her before they took her to the hospital."

Olivia's eyes widened. Her complexion paled. "She what?"

Sierra guided her to a chair. Olivia dropped into it. "She collapsed when she got off the plane. I was right there. I tried."

"So she's still alive?"

"We don't know. We're waiting to hear."

Tears welled in Olivia's eyes. "She … she had a checkup last week. She was fine. She has an ICD. They checked it, updated it, made sure it was working. It was fine." She focused on Sierra. "Did someone try an AED?"

"The EMTs got there fast. They used one."

Furrows carved Olivia's forehead. "How long? How long before the EMTs got there?"

Crap. Sierra had no idea how long she'd done CPR before the EMTs arrived. It had felt like a long time, but it probably wasn't more than a few minutes. "I'm not sure. I didn't look at my watch when I started CPR. I focused on helping her."

"Her watch." Olivia waved at the purse on Quinn's desk. "Is her cell phone in her purse? She's got a smart watch. If something happened with her heart, her watch would have recorded it. That's why I got it for her before she got her ICD."

Sierra handed Alice's purse to Olivia, who dug through its contents. "It's not here. She must have had it in her coat pocket. Where did they take her?"

"Yvonne is checking on that. Dr. Holmgren, I need to ask you a few questions. It's just a formality," Quinn said as he sat behind his desk, notepad in front of him. "Do you mind if ask what your specialty is?"

"I'm a neurologist. I'm doing research on intracranial stimulation, for Parkinson's and epilepsy treatment." Olivia pulled a tissue from a small packet in her purse and dabbed at her eyes. "What am I going to tell Dad?"

Sierra settled in the other visitor chair quietly while Quinn continued to collect information. Olivia insisted her mother had been in good health, had just had her routine checkup. She had the ICD to manage an arrhythmia. No, her mother hadn't been sick recently. Her mother had been at a teaching conference; she was a professor of education at the University of Minnesota in Minneapolis.

A knock at the door interrupted the data collection. Yvonne entered, her visage somber. She handed Quinn a piece of paper and left in silence, easing the door closed behind her.

Quinn read the memo and frowned. The atmosphere in the office seemed to gain weight.

Sierra recognized the look. Bad news. "Quinn?"

He focused on Olivia. "Dr. Holmgren, I'm sorry to inform you that your mother has passed away."

"What?" Shock tightened Olivia's voice. "How can that be? She was fine last week. I can't believe . . ." Olivia closed her eyes and took a deep breath, blew it out. And another.

Sierra laid a hand on Olivia's arm. "Olivia, I'm so sorry."

Quinn wrote down information on a clean page of his notepad and tore it off to hand to Olivia. "Yvonne found out where they took you mother. I'm sure you have some things you need to do. I'm sorry for your loss. Here's my card. You or your father can call me with any questions."

"Thank you," Olivia took the paper and turned to Sierra. "It's good to see you again, Sierra."

"It's good to see you, too. I wish it was under different circumstances. Do you want me to go to the hospital with you?"

"Thank you. I'll be okay. I've got to call Dad."

Sierra gave Olivia another hug. "I'm so sorry. Let me know about the service. You have my number?" At Olivia's nod, she continued. "Let me know if I can do anything for you, okay? I'll let my dad know what happened. He'll probably call Arthur."

"Yeah. That'd be good."

After she left, Sierra asked, "Do you have to write up a report or something?"

"Technically, no, since we weren't called to the scene," Quinn said. "Practically? That incident on the airport grounds has now resulted in a death. I'm sure someone will ask for one, so I might as well get it out of the way now."

"This whole thing sucks all the way around." Sierra zipped her parka. The best way to avoid thinking about what had happened was to focus on something else, like work. "Do you need anything more from me? I should get back to the gate."

"You're not going back to work, are you?" Quinn came around the desk and pulled her into an embrace. "Honey, take the rest of the day. Call your dad."

Sierra held onto him, eyes closed tight against the emotions struggling to escape. "I need the distraction of work. If it's too … If I can't keep it together, I'll take the rest of the day."

Quinn tightened his embrace, then released her. "Are you sure? I can take you back to the hangar."

She pulled a tissue from a pocket and wiped tears from her eyes. "No, I'll be fine." Part of her wasn't so sure. "See you at home."

*　　*　　*

Quinn arrived home to the spicy scent of Sierra's homemade tomato and roasted pepper soup, her go-to comfort food along with grilled cheese sandwiches. His stomach reminded him he hadn't eaten for far too long. He unloaded his service weapon, locked it in the gun safe, and hung up his parka before he ventured into the kitchen. The pot of soup was simmering unattended on the stove.

"Sorry, Dad. Quinn's home; I gotta go. Say 'hi' to Mom." Sierra appeared from the direction of the living room, eyes and nose red. She ended the call on her cell phone and greeted him with a weak smile and a kiss. "Dad says 'hi.'"

"How are your folks?"

"They're fine. I told Dad about Alice. He'll let Mom know—she's out of town for work—and call Arthur."

There was an air of reticence about her. Not what he expected. "How are you?" Quinn asked.

"Fine." She started toward the stove.

Something was off. Quinn caught her wrist and pulled her close, searching her eyes for answers. He found none. "Talk to me."

Sierra hesitated, as if mulling a decision. "I can't stop thinking about what happened. I feel like I should have done more."

He brushed her ice-white lock of hair back against the dark chestnut of the rest and kissed her forehead. "You tried. That's all anyone can expect."

"I know, but I keep thinking about what Olivia said about how Alice had a checkup last week and she was fine." Sierra pulled away and went to the stove to stir the soup. "It doesn't make sense."

"What did your dad say?" A benefit of having a father who was a nurse practitioner: insider information on medical subjects.

"He said ICDs—implantable cardioverter defibrillators—are used to treat more serious arrhythmias, when the heart beats faster than it should or irregularly. He also said if Alice just had a checkup and the doctor didn't see anything concerning in the data from the device, then there's no reason for the device to stop working unless she had something catastrophic happen."

"Like what?"

"Aneurysm, major car accident, drowning."

"So, something else that would cause her death, not her heart."

"Pretty much. He also said if there was any sort of problem with a device like that, the FDA would be all over it. And, if that was the case, there would be a recall and whoever had an affected implant would have it replaced ASAP."

"Sounds like that would be a major issue for a manufacturer. Did you ask him if he knew of any recalls?"

Sierra set silverware on the dining table. "He said there haven't been any, but he'll let me know if he hears anything."

Quinn caught her again as she brushed past him. "I get it. You're a mechanic. In your world, stuff works, and if it doesn't, you fix it. And you can't fix something like that, even if it was broken."

She smiled. "You need to stop having those long conversations with my dad. He said the same thing."

*　　　*　　　*

A week later, Sierra and Quinn were enjoying a lunch date at an Irish pub. It was the start of her weekend; she should have slept more, but they hadn't gone out for lunch in weeks. She'd picked this new place, with traditional Irish fare and traditional music. They sat at a table with a view of the Irish band and drank in the music. Quinn seemed to be enjoying himself as well; he even knew the words to one of the lively drinking songs.

He stopped singing and pulled his phone from his pocket, checked the display, and excused himself. *Rats.* Sierra caught their server's attention and had paid the bill by the time Quinn returned. He grabbed his coat from the back of his chair and led the way out of the pub.

Sierra asked, "Work?"

"No. Olivia Holmgren. She wants to talk about her mother's case."

"Case? It wasn't really a case, just an unexpected death. And why call you? She's got my number."

"Because of the medical examiner's report."

Sierra slid into the passenger seat of Quinn's unmarked Airport Police Department SUV. "What did it say that inspired her to contact you?"

"According to Olivia, it basically said that Alice's ICD stopped regulating her arrhythmia correctly."

"So it malfunctioned? That makes no sense," Sierra said. "Olivia said her mother had just gotten the thing checked and updated. Even if it was a malfunctioning ICD that caused it, that's something the FDA should investigate, not you."

Quinn frowned. "Olivia doesn't think it was a simple malfunction."

"What else would it be? It's not like someone could have made the ICD malfunction. I'm not sure that's even possible," Sierra said. "Dad said those devices are tested to make sure stuff like interference or hacking doesn't affect them."

"You and I both know that, and I'm sure she does as well. She said she just learned of another person with that same model ICD who showed up in the ER yesterday. Their device malfunctioned, but their condition wasn't as severe as Alice's."

"Meaning they lived," Sierra said. "Two malfunctions of the same type of device in what, about a week? Weird."

"She asked if I could stop by VCS."

"Voyageur Cardiac Systems? That's the manufacturer of Alice's ICD. Why would she be there?"

"She works there."

*   *   *

They met Olivia Holmgren at the entrance of the VCS main building, where she led them to the security desk and waited while they signed in and received visitor badges. They followed her to a skyway that stretched to another building and through a maze of corridors.

"Thank you both for coming. I didn't know who else to call."

"I know you probably want more of an explanation of your mother's death," Quinn said, "but there really wasn't a case. I wrote up a report, but your mother … it was an unexpected death. I'm not sure I can do anything."

Olivia swiped her badge at a closed door, then opened it and ushered them through. "The ME's report mentioned her VT—ventricular tachycardia—and lesions. Mom's ICD kept her heart from beating too fast, but the lesions don't make sense. I showed it to Dad; it didn't make sense to him, either. Dad's been a cardiothoracic surgeon for thirty years. He's implanted hundreds of devices in that time, and he's seen how the technology has changed. He did a ton of research and consulted with Mom's doctor and her surgeon before they decided which device to use."

"Olivia, I should know this, and I'm sorry we haven't kept in touch, but how long have you worked here?" Sierra asked.

"A little more than two years. Why?"

"If your mom had a VCS device, and you worked here, and your father recommended this brand, that would look a little like buying your own product."

"Mom got her device a year or so before I started here. Besides, I'm in the Neurological Research department." Olivia turned down another hallway, descended a couple flights of stairs, and then swiped through another door. "When Mom started having heart problems, Dad couldn't be her direct physician—that would be unethical. He made sure her surgeon was someone he respected."

"You said someone else with the same device as your mother's showed up in an ER with problems. How do you know it was because of the ICD?" Quinn asked.

"Dad called me. It was one of his surgical patients. He's the one who installed the device."

"Isn't something like that the FDA's concern?" asked Sierra. "That'd be like asking Quinn to look into a problem with an airplane. That would be the FAA's jurisdiction, not Quinn's."

Olivia stopped and turned. "Look, Dad couldn't tell me who it was because of HIPAA, but I suspect it was Tricia Dolan. She works here at VCS. She asked me about Dad when she started having heart issues last year. I know she called in sick that day because I had to reschedule a meeting with her." Olivia stopped and turned. "Rumor has it Tricia's involved with the CEO."

Quinn said, "I'm sorry, Olivia. I'm not sure I can be of any help."

Olivia checked the hallway in both directions. They were alone. "Look," she said, her voice lowered to a whisper, "I filled out a report to the FDA about this after talking to Dad, and normally stuff like that gets reviewed by the CYA department before it's sent to the FDA."

"CYA?" Sierra asked. "Let me guess. The 'cover your asses' department."

Olivia offered a wry smile. "Yes. I asked about the report yesterday, but no one knows what happened to it. I talked to the CYA department, and they said they sent it to the CEO—that's the procedure before they send it to the FDA. They never got it back. When they checked, no one knew about it."

Sierra pursed her lips. "That doesn't sound right. You'd think voluntarily reporting an issue to the FDA would be good business sense, rather than the FDA coming in and shutting things down. Better optics."

"There's something weird going on, I know it. Just humor me. Please." Olivia led them into an office area divided up into cubicles, a drone of voices from across the office interrupting the silence. They wove their way to a cubicle in a far corner, where a woman with blue hair in a buzz cut and black-framed cat-eye glasses focused on two monitors. Quinn guessed her age at late thirties, early forties.

Olivia introduced the woman. "This is Indigo Germaine. She works on quality assurance testing of the software for the ICDs."

"It's 'Indy.'" The woman glanced up, gaze drifting to Quinn and Sierra, eyes wide, before settling on Olivia. She lowered her voice to a harsh whisper. "You brought a cop here? Are you crazy?"

Quinn wore his usual business casual, same as most of the people they'd seen on their way through the corridors. He whispered to Sierra, "Do I look like a cop?"

"I don't think so, but I'm biased."

Olivia bent toward Indy. "He can help."

"It was an anomaly."

Olivia glanced around the office space. "One of Dad's patients was in the ER. Her device seemed to have malfunctioned. She thought she was having a heart attack."

Indy raised a brow. "Not possible. Liv, you know the code is solid when I sign off on it."

Olivia slipped into Indy's cubicle and motioned for Quinn and Sierra to follow. "Show them what you showed me."

"I'm not supposed to …"

"Please?"

Indy sighed. "Okay."

While Indy typed, Olivia explained in hushed tones. "The ICDs can report information about the patient's cardiac activity, like an EKG."

"How would that work?" Sierra asked. "They're not big enough to transmit very far."

"Patients are given stations," Indy said, "kinda like wi-fi routers, which they're supposed to set up at home so we can monitor them. Except most people don't bother to set them up, which is why the device retains the data until the patient's next checkup." She pointed to the monitor. "This is the information, completely anonymous. It's tied only to the serial number of the device."

"What do these numbers mean?" Sierra traced a column on the screen. "Beats per minute?"

"That's one of the numbers. Other numbers tell us how often the device activates, the amount of energy it sends into the heart muscle, the heart's response, the deviation from average—"

Olivia interrupted. "Indy, just show them the important stuff."

"Fine." The numbers on the screen whizzed by as Indy scrolled. "Liv gave me the serial number of Alice's ICD." She indicated the screen. "This is when her device was updated, just a few weeks ago. It took three tries to complete the update of the firmware. That doesn't happen. I mean, like, ever."

"Do you have anything from the day it failed?" Quinn asked.

"No. I don't have the equipment to read the device even if I had the device."

Olivia leaned in. "It should be in the database."

Indy sighed. "I could get in trouble for this, Liv."

"Please?"

Numbers flowed on the screen, then stopped. Indy leaned toward the screen. "This is weird." She scrolled up and down. "This can't be right."

"Hey, Liv." A stout man leaned on the cubicle wall near Olivia. "Been seeing a lot of you lately. I'm starting to think you're looking to move down here where the real work gets done."

Olivia shifted away from him. "Justin."

"Who're your friends?" he asked, leering at Sierra. "Nice stripe. How much did that cost?"

"What? This?" Sierra teased out the ice-white tress from her chestnut hair. "It's hereditary. Sure beats letting Magneto use me to mutate New York City."

Justin's brow arched. "Marvel fan? Give me DC Comics anytime."

Indy waved a hand. "Anyway, this is Justin. He's one of the senior software engineers. What do you want, Justin?"

"Just wondering if you need help with anything. Sounded like you found a problem with the code. Not my code, but. . ."

Indy rolled her eyes. "Yes, Justin, your code is always perfect, except for that one time. And that other time. And—"

Sierra interrupted. "Hey, I've got a question, just out of curiosity. Can these devices be hacked?"

Justin chortled. "They're electronic, they have code, of course they can be hacked. It'd be tricky, since they're not connected to the internet—you'd need to be up close and personal with them. Hell, it'd be easier to hack into a bank, but I could hack them." He hesitated. "Not that I would, but I could."

"Okay. So why would a device malfunction? I mean, if it's got battery power and the code isn't a problem."

"Let's see." Justin ticked off each suggestion on a finger. "Lightning strike, screwdriver in a wall socket, stopping a bullet, doomsday code—"

Sierra held up a hand. "Okay, got it. A big enough electric jolt, which would overload the body's electrical system anyway, or physical damage."

"Anything that would interrupt the device reading the code," Justin affirmed. "Without the code, it's just a mess of silicon, wires, and transistors."

"Thank you, Professor Proton," Indy said. "Don't you have a bug to squash in the latest revision?" When Justin didn't move, she waved her hand. "Go. Away. Let me work."

Justin narrowed his eyes. "You know why you're in a corner all alone? Because you're a bi—"

Indy cut him off. "Smile when you say that." She pointed across the office space. "Your desk is over there."

"I bet you never treated Ralph like this," he grumbled as he left.

"Ralph wasn't an egomaniac." Indy leaned back in her chair.

"Is he *that* Justin?" Olivia asked.

"Yes. And I keep waiting for karma to bitch-slap him." Indy turned toward Quinn and Sierra. "Sorry about that. I always wonder how he can fit that big head through the door. Anything else?"

Quinn answered before Sierra could ask any more questions. "I don't think so. I've got to get back to the office."

Olivia nodded. "Still on for pickleball tomorrow?" she asked Indy.

"I've got a new paddle to break in. Catch you then."

Olivia led them a different way out of the software development area, taking a route through what looked like an extensive break room, complete with an espresso machine. Olivia detoured to the machine. "The developers have the good stuff. Either of you want one?"

"No, thanks." Quinn scanned the room while they waited. Four microwaves. Two vending machines, one stocked with fruit and sandwiches. Nice amenities. Sierra wandered to the area where small tables were arranged. Framed photos filled a wall, with "Community Superstars" painted in an arc above the collection.

Quinn joined Sierra admiring the wall of photos. "Looks like they do a lot of community service stuff." He pointed to a group photo. "They even have a snow shovel crew."

Sierra peered at the picture. "Hey, Olivia, do you know who this is?"

Olivia blew across her mug before taking a cautious sip. "Who?"

Sierra pointed to the man in the picture wearing a fluorescent-green-and-blue Seattle Seahawks stocking cap and scarf. "Do you know who this is?"

Olivia peered at the photo. "That's Ralph Calder. Used to work here. Top-tier software engineer. He was lead developer for the firmware—the core code we use—for several of our cardiac devices. They let him go after I started. He was one of the first engineers here. After his wife died, he wasn't the same. I think he had a breakdown or something."

"What happened to his wife?" asked Quinn.

Olivia continued to the main corridor. "I heard she was in a bad car accident or something. Enough force that her device failed."

"She had an ICD?" Quinn asked.

Olivia nodded. "That's one of the risks of the device. Leads are implanted in the heart muscle. If something happens, like a car accident, the leads could shift in such a way that the shocks are directed to the wrong part of the muscle, or they get dislodged or even break."

"Would she have lived if her ICD hadn't failed?" Sierra asked.

"Hard to say. There's nothing we can do to mitigate something like that. But, to be clear, that's not what happened to Mom's device; the leads were fine."

They reached the lobby of the building, where Quinn and Sierra surrendered their visitor passes. Olivia said, "I don't know what more to tell you. I know something happened with Mom's ICD."

"I understand," Quinn said. "You want to find an explanation for her device's malfunction, but it's not my jurisdiction. I'm sorry I can't be of more help."

As they headed back to the airport, Quinn asked, "What's with the guy, Ralph? Why did you pick him out?"

"When I was working on Alice, I saw a guy with the same Seahawks hat right up against the window with the crowd of onlookers. Couldn't miss him."

"Why did you notice him in particular? I mean, aside from the fan gear."

Sierra thought. "Mostly the glowing green, but he also left the window as soon as he saw me looking at him."

"Maybe he had a flight that just called for boarding."

"Maybe, but there was something else. He carried a duffel bag."

"Him and who knows how many other passengers."

"True. But he held it in front of him. Like a shield. It was weird." Sierra stared blindly out the windshield. Most people were curious, some to the point of being obnoxious about it. With the activity on the tarmac, unless a plane had been boarding at that exact time, people by their nature would have stayed glued to the window. "It probably wasn't the same guy anyway."

That wasn't all that was bothering her. *Olivia said the device leads weren't the problem with Alice's device. So what happened?*

Quinn glanced at her. "I know that look." He sighed. "You know what I'm going to say."

"I know, I know. Leave it alone."

"And how often do you listen?"

Chapter 2

Gina

A blizzard in Denver caused the cancellation of Gina Apate's connecting flight, leaving her stuck in Minneapolis/St. Paul overnight. She rebooked for the next day and reclaimed her overnight bag from luggage. A nearby hotel had an available room and a shuttle. Perhaps, she thought, it was serendipity.

She limped out of the terminal onto the icy sidewalk and stopped, leaning on her walking stick, looking for the shuttle. Even though there was no immediate need to do so, she stayed in character: a limp, a walking stick, tinted glasses, a black wig, and a Middle Eastern accent.

Disguise was a form of artistry she had perfected while serving as a field operative in the EYP, the national intelligence agency of her native country, Greece. Fluency in six languages aided her ability to modify her persona, as did the makeup skills learned from her involvement in theater at university. Operating behind a façade had become a valuable tool in her current profession. Neither her clientele nor national law enforcement knew her true identity, having seen only a continually mutating portrayal of her public image.

*   *   *

Over a late breakfast, Gina skimmed the local newspaper. There was a story on page 2 of the local section about the death of a college professor at the airport. There was a sidebar story, quoting an EMT who had responded to the call at the airport, about the anomaly of death by heart attack of someone with a heart implant device. The story went on to talk about the further irony of the deceased's husband being a cardiac surgeon, and her daughter working at Voyageur Cardiac Systems, the company that had manufactured the implanted device.

Gina quickly finished her breakfast, then went to the hotel's business center, where an internet search divulged a chat site where there was chatter about malfunctioning heart implants. Voyageur was mentioned. She looked up Voyageur's 10-Q and 10-K filings. Not surprisingly, there was no mention of any problems, nor was there anything hinting of a recent device recall.

Further search showed that the company's stock had been in a slow but steady decline for the past four months. *If the death at the airport goes viral, the worry-mongers and conspiracy theorists will go berserk,* Gina thought. *Voyageur's stock will drop like a rock.*

Using an alias, she added the story of the airport death to the chat room, leaving the innuendo that the death was caused by the failure of a Voyageur implant. Then she dialed the 24-7 office of her New York broker.

"Esme, this is Gina Apate. I want to make a trade for my trust. I want you to short 10,000 shares of Voyageur Cardiac Systems, ticker symbol VCSI."

"Short sale?" Esme asked, a tone of mild concern in her voice.

"Yes, you heard correctly. Short 10,000 shares of VCSI."

"You do understand the risks."

"Of course."

"Do you want me to put a stop loss on the trade?" Esme asked.

"Five percent above the entry price," Gina answered.

Five percent risk against a potential 100% gain? Gina mused. *If I'm right, the stock will drop ten to twenty dollars per share when the news hits.* It would be a no-risk way to pick up a couple hundred thousand dollars. She paused, pleased with herself, happy to be using her wits to make money for her own account rather than for her Russian and Middle Eastern clients.

Making money for other people was Gina's business. It hadn't started that way. She had been the black sheep of the family, entering government service after graduating from university rather than joining the family business. To complicate matters further, she had learned after joining the EYP that her family was under investigation for international money laundering.

Torn between loyalty to her family and her oath to uphold the law, Gina struggled, but her inner conflict ended suddenly when her father and mother were murdered, gangland style. Local law enforcement made a cursory investigation of the killings, and EYP showed no interest at all.

Enraged, and suspecting that her own employer may have been complicit in the executions, Gina quit EYP. Sustained by a trust fund established by her parents, she tried to track down the killers on her own, only to find every path blocked by people whom law enforcement could not, or would not, prosecute.

With both leads and money running out, and with growing contempt for law enforcement, Gina made a decision: if you can't beat them, join them. Using her parents' connections, what she had learned at EYP, and her own charm and guile, she planted herself squarely between the seamy underbelly of European commerce and the legitimate business world, providing services and putting together deals. She often used conduits, surrogates, buffers, and straw men to insulate herself, always tiptoeing around the edges of the law.

Or flat-out breaking it, in the service of her sketchy clientele.

A clientele, she suspected, that included those responsible for her parents' deaths.

*   *   *

Gina was at the airport by early afternoon, only to find that her flight had been further delayed because of the continuing storm in the Rockies. Sitting in the Delta Airlines club, she checked the New York Stock Exchange listings. Voyageur was off 2.4. By the time trading closed, it was down 6.5. It would likely drop further in overnight trading.

Maybe, Gina thought, *it's time to find out what's really going on at Voyageur.*

She dialed the number from the Voyageur website and asked to speak to Stephen Hartsburg, CEO of the company, saying she was a personal friend passing through town, just wanting to say "Hi."

Her call was transferred, and a woman with a frazzled voice answered: "Office of Stephen Hartsburg."

"Is he in?"

"No. He's out of town."

"When will he be back?"

"I don't know. Who is this?" the woman snapped.

"To whom am I speaking?" Gina responded, the tone in her voice conveying authority.

"Marilyn Applewhite, Mr. Hartsburg's executive assistant, and you're about to make me miss a plane."

"I apologize. I hope you're not going to Denver. The airport is closed."

"Detroit." Applewhite snapped. "Now, unless you have something really important, I need to end this call."

Gina thought for a minute after the call ended. *The CEO is gone, apparently with an unknown timetable for his return. His executive assistant is leaving, and from her tone, it sounds like she can't get out of town fast enough. Their stock is dropping rapidly. What is going on?*

She located the closest board showing departing flights. There were three going to Detroit within the next three hours. Two were leaving within forty-five minutes, making it unlikely that Applewhite could get from her office to the airport and through security in time.

Using one of her many pseudonyms, Layla Armijani, Gina bought a ticket on Delta 1476 and got the ticketing agent to assign her a seat next to "her good friend," Marilyn Applewhite.

*   *   *

Applewhite looked both exhausted and relieved as she dropped into the seat beside Gina. She loudly exhaled, then ordered a gin and tonic from the passing flight attendant.

"Tough day?" Gina offered, affecting a Turkish accent to differentiate her voice from their earlier phone conversation.

"You have no idea."

When Applewhite's gin and tonic came, Gina offered to pay for it, along with her own glass of white wine: a "goodwill gesture" to help Applewhite's day get better.

As they sat on the tarmac, waiting for the flight to leave, Gina made small talk. Applewhite ordered a second drink. By the time the plane was over Lake Michigan, the two women were trading life stories: Layla Armijani, an aging jazz singer on her way to New York to do a gig, and Marilyn Applewhite, an executive assistant of a publicly traded medical device company that was in deep shit, on her way to visit her sister.

As more information was divulged by her now-inebriated seat mate, Gina's interest in Voyageur accelerated. When Applewhite dropped the name Justin Biggs as "the asshole in the IT department" who was probably responsible for "the company's implant device problems," Gina, her opportunity meter in the red zone, filed the name away for future use.

Voyageur might be ripe for a liquidation. There might be millions to be made, not just a few hundred thousand from short sales.

But first, Gina needed to do some clandestine snooping.

Chapter 3

Hartsburg

Stephen Hartsburg sat in his office, adrift in an alien world, a place where nothing made sense, where nothing worked as it should. To be sure, the familiar physical trappings still surrounded him—the spacious corner office; the massive CEO's desk; the pictures with celebrities and politicians; the works of art that cost more than most of his employees made in a year. He had occupied this place, as CEO of Voyageur Cardiac Systems, a Fortune 500 corporation, for four years. He was still on the job, still drawing a huge paycheck, still functioning. But this was no longer his place, no longer his world.

He glanced at the small clock on his desk. Twelve minutes left.

In the universe Hartsburg knew, problems could be managed. Unpleasant projects could be delegated. Troublesome employees could be fired. Litigants and protestors could be defeated, worn down, or bought off. Bad earnings figures could be massaged and spun. People like Hartsburg, who were equipped with wealth, power, and aggression, prevailed over those who were not. Cause and effect.

He looked at the clock again. Eight minutes.

Who the *hell* did this person think he was, making threats to him and his company?

He looked down again at the printout of the email:

Mr. Hartsburg:

For over a year, you have ignored my communications concerning the known defect in the firmware for model VC-25-4750 family of cardiac devices, which caused the death of someone very dear to me, and of countless others. You are guilty of murder, as are all of your subordinates who have covered up the problem . . .

He slammed his fist on the desk. Where was his team? Where were his managers who were supposed to prevent things like this, to silence malcontents? Until this anonymous troublemaker had come along, they'd been able to keep the lid on concerns about the 4750. His anger gave way to fear, to thoughts of FDA investigations, manufacturing shutdowns, massive lawsuits, Wall Street hysteria, and Chapter 11. He would be kicked out of his job, disgraced.

He forced himself to calm down. There was simply *no proof* that he knew about the defect. If people did their jobs, there would be no evidence of the defect, period.

He looked back at the email:

Your negligence and subsequent cover-up will be overtaken by karma. If you doubt this, ask the family of Alice Holmgren.

Alice Holmgren? He'd checked her out. He had never met her, although he'd heard of her husband, a cardiologist, and their daughter, Olivia, who was employed by Voyageur. Alice had died of a cardiac incident at the airport. And she'd had a Voyageur ICD.

So what? Everybody died eventually, even people with Voyageur ICDs. How was Holmgren's death karma? He was supposed to feel threatened by that? When the dust settled, he would track down this anonymous asshole and make him wish he'd never been born.

He glanced at the clock. Four minutes.

His breathing grew shallow as he turned back to the email:

You need to come clean, Mr. Hartsburg. Go public with the defect. Admit your culpability. If you don't, what happened to Mrs. Holmgren will certainly happen again, and next time will hit closer to home.

Closer to home—what did that mean? Based on this vague prediction, he was supposed to simply chuck his career and tank his company? Sweat dripped from Hartsburg's brow onto his lap, dampening the pants of his expensive suit.

If you don't take this step by Wednesday at 7:30 p.m. CST, karma will be inevitable.

Another involuntary look at the clock: 7:28 p.m.

This jackass was bluffing, Hartsburg was sure. What could he do, release his rant on some conspiracy-theory website or social media? Without proof? What could he *do*?

Closer to home.

7:30.

His phone buzzed. His mother, Thea. *Good timing, Mom.* He ignored the call.

He risked a look at his computer screen. Nothing.

And then, after half a minute, a new email notification.

He clicked on the icon, reminding himself that he got dozens of emails every day, and many dozens more since his assistant, Marilyn, had been out of the office and was no longer screening them. He risked a look.

He exhaled. The new message was not from the anonymous sender. But then he looked more closely. Like the phone message, it was from his mother. He opened it.

And nearly fainted.

He read over the message again, his mouth open in horror. Then he stood up, turning around, breathing rapidly, hands on top of his head, before sinking back into his chair.

My God.

Chapter 4

Matt

The sold-out crowd in the Ted Mann Concert Hall erupted in applause and stood in unison when Dr. Magnus Danilson emerged from stage left and strode toward the conductor's podium. The beloved University of Minnesota professor was retiring after forty years at the helm of the university's School of Music. He was going to conduct an alumni orchestra in one final joyous farewell concert of his orchestral favorites.

Upon reaching the podium, Danilson bowed to the audience. He had the classic look of an orchestral conductor: long white hair combed back and touching his collar, tall, still fit for his age, with leonine features and intense eyes, dignified in his black tuxedo, white shirt and cummerbund, and perfectly knotted white bow-tie.

As he mounted the single step and raised his arms to prepare the musicians for his downbeat, the crowd fell silent. But instead of hearing the opening notes of Leonard Bernstein's *Overture to Candide*, the crowd heard Danilson groan as he clutched his chest and collapsed to the stage floor.

Gasps of surprise followed two seconds of stunned silence. Matt Lanier sprang from his stool in the bass section and rushed to aid his former professor. "Doctor Dan! What's wrong?"

"My heart," Danilson said, barely above a whisper. His face was contorted in pain. His breaths were rapid and shallow. Then his eyes went vacant. After exhaling a ragged breath, he went limp.

Confusion racked Matt's brain as he crouched over his mentor, his pulse pounding. A pit of helpless despair formed deep in his gut. How could this be happening? During rehearsals before the concert, Danilson had seemed in perfect health for a septuagenarian.

A man and woman from the audience rushed to the stage. "We're doctors," said the woman as they elbowed Matt aside.

The man kneeled next to Danilson and checked him for responsiveness and breathing. "He's not responsive. Not breathing. Call 911!"

The woman dialed 911 on her cell phone as the man began CPR. During the two seconds she waited for the call to go through, she noticed Matt and said, "Get an AED, stat!"

Matt bolted from the stage and ran to the wings, where he remembered seeing an AED near the green room after that afternoon's dress rehearsal. Rounding a corner, he almost ran into a man but sidestepped him at the last second. After yanking the AED from its box on the wall, Matt turned to go back and noticed the same man heading for the rear exit. He wore a navy suit, white shirt, and a navy, green, and gray tie. *Seattle Seahawks colors,* Matt thought. *Unusual in the land of Vikings purple and gold.* Strange that he wasn't heading toward the stage to gawk at the emergency. Stranger still that he carried a small case that resembled a clarinet case. Matt dashed to the podium to deliver the AED to the woman who'd asked for it.

She grabbed the device and hooked it to Danilson's now-bare chest. She and the man double-checked the protocol and gave Danilson two separate shocks to his heart. Getting no response, they resumed CPR.

By the time paramedics reached the scene, Matt was certain that Danilson was dead. The look on his face as he took his last breath soon after collapsing was unmistakable—the look of someone who had just seen the bright white light and surrendered to its magnetism.

*   *   *

The mood at Magnus Danilson's funeral service and interment, predictably somber, was made even more so by the shocking abruptness of his death. Matt stood in the bitter January cold at the gravesite, which added to the bleak mood of those who braved the elements.

Back at the church, when Matt's turn came in the receiving line, he shook hands with Danilson's son, Karl, hugged Danilson's widow, Thea, and said, "Good to see you both again. I'm so sorry for your loss. And I apologize for not getting to your place for dinner recently."

Thea waved dismissively. "We read the papers and heard about the conspiracy you stopped. I think you were a little too busy in the last year to worry about dinner with us old folks."

"True." Matt's smile was tinged with sadness. Thea was a strong woman to think of others in her time of grief. "Still, we should have gotten together before the retirement concert."

"Magnus would have loved that. He was thrilled you agreed to join the alumni orchestra." Thea's smile waned. She dabbed at her eyes with a tissue. "You were one of his favorite students. He gushed over you, said you had that extra special something that's so rare in musicians. He loved talking music with you."

"I didn't know I had anything special until he coaxed it out of me." Matt's voice nearly broke, overcome with sorrow that he hadn't been able to perform with Dr. Dan one final time. The maestro brought music to life with his energy and passion every time he performed. Because of Danilson, the U of M's string program was recognized as one of the best in the nation. Dozens of his protégés, including Matt, had gone on to illustrious music careers. The world had lost a brilliant musician and an inspirational teacher.

After one of those awkward moments typical of a funeral reception line, Matt said, "I couldn't help noticing the massive flower bouquet behind his coffin during the visitation. Who sent it?"

Karl scoffed and huffed. "My jerk of a stepbrother, Steve Hartsburg."

Matt arched his eyebrows. "Stepbrother?"

Thea said, "Stephen is my son from my first marriage, before I met Magnus."

"Oh, right," Matt said to Karl. "I'd forgotten you had a stepbrother. Magnus didn't mention him often. Last time must have been years ago."

Karl said, "The guy adored Dad, has boatloads of money, a private jet, but couldn't find time to attend the funeral? What a crock of—"

"Karl, please," Thea said, giving him an annoyed glare. "Not here."

Karl put up his hands in a halfhearted *sorry* gesture. "The sympathy card said he was out of the country on business and couldn't return in time. Yeah, right."

"Hartsburg," Matt said, connecting some dots in his brain. "The name sounds familiar."

"He's a bigwig CEO," replied Karl. "Voyageur Cardiac System. They make pacemakers, other sorts of medical devices that are implantable. A Fortune 500 company."

"Ah, I see," Matt said with a comprehending nod.

Karl said, "I'll bet Stevie H. was too embarrassed to come here because it was his company's device that failed. That was the official cause of Dad's death, according to the death certificate."

"If that's true," Thea said, "Karl believes I should sue Voyageur."

"You should," Karl interjected.

Thea shook her head. "Not with Stephen running the company. I'm sure he'll take care of the problem."

Karl looked doubtful but said nothing.

"Magnus had just been to the doctor for a checkup and an ICD adjustment," Thea continued. "His doctor said he aced all the tests and was good to go for another year." She lowered her head and pressed the tissue to her eyes again. "He didn't even make it a month."

Knowing how it felt to lose a spouse—or an ex-wife, in Matt's case—Matt's heart ached for Thea. No doubt the primary question circling through her mind was *Why?* The line behind him was growing, so Matt said, "I'd better go. If there's anything I can do, Thea, please contact me."

As Matt headed toward the church dining room for refreshments, that familiar feeling of powerlessness welled up inside. The same futility he'd experienced after his mother died of cancer when he was twelve.

Many other former orchestral students who revered Danilson had attended his funeral and were now gathered at one end of the dining hall. As they sipped coffee and lemonade and ate standard Minnesota church-lady, funeral-luncheon food, the stories about Dr. Dan flowed back and forth. Most recalled the demanding auditions they had endured to get into the elite Chamber Ensemble, their favorite touring moments, and the fast-paced rehearsals that never seemed long enough but always resulted in superior performances.

Matt was sitting next to one of his Chamber Ensemble friends from college, Cathy Judd, when she mentioned an incident Matt had never heard about. "Remember that whack job violinist who auditioned for the CE, didn't get in, then went ballistic on Dr. Dan?"

"Whack job?" Matt asked. "Who?"

"Oh, you probably weren't there because you play bass, and this was during the violin auditions."

"So, what about him . . . or her?"

"Well," Cathy said with a conspiratorial glint in her eyes, "three of us were waiting to audition when this guy, Justin somebody, Bragg? Briggs? Biggs? Anyway, he stormed out of the audition room, red-faced, muttering under his breath, looking ready to break his violin over his knee. That was weird enough, but then he stormed back into the audition room and reamed out Dr. Dan for a full minute. Called him every dirty word in the book, talentless, unfit to direct a third-grade flutophone class, and vowed to get revenge someday."

Matt recoiled in surprise. "You're kidding. I never heard that story."

"Danilson came out of the audition room with Biggs on his tail, still ranting. We offered to call the police, but Danilson said not to." Cathy shook her head. "Justin ranted for another minute before storming out. Dr. Dan told us the guy had a history of outbursts at teachers on campus but was harmless. You know. All talk, no action."

"Wow. Must've been something to see."

"I'll say," Cathy said.

As Matt drove home after finishing lunch and saying his goodbyes, he kept thinking that if he'd been in that audition room, Justin Biggs would have left it doubled over in agony, with at least one black eye and two bruised and swollen testicles.

*   *   *

Several days later, Matt got a call from Karl Danilson. "We need your help, Matt. It's about my father." Karl's voice sounded strained.

Matt's pulse quickened. "Name it."

"I was examining my father's laptop, looking for anything related to money, his will, or other obligations he had. Typical stuff."

"How can I help?"

"I'm calling because I found several threatening emails from an anonymous source. All were within the past month. The sender said he or she intended to quote, get you, unquote, and he'd never see it coming."

"Sounds serious. Shouldn't you call the police instead of me?"

"I did. They were nice about it, but they basically blew me off because the autopsy said Dad died from heart failure. Said to come back when I had evidence of foul play."

"That makes sense, I guess. But don't dismiss the possibility that a lot of crazies inhabit the internet. Could simply be a troll harassing an old man for laughs."

"I'm pretty sure it's not a troll."

"Why's that?"

"Because Mom got an anonymous email today from someone who said, and I quote, 'I'm glad the old SOB is dead. He had it coming.'"

Matt's heart thumped faster. Threatening someone was one thing, but reveling in their demise crossed a worse line. "I can't imagine anyone stooping that low. How can I help?"

"You knew most of Dad's former students at the funeral. You taught a lot of the bass players in the past decade at the U and worked with Dad occasionally."

That was true. When he was an assistant professor at the U of M, Matt had kept in touch with Danilson. They met for lunch occasionally. Over the years, Matt attended many of the University Orchestra concerts and often went backstage to chat with his old professor. A few times, Danilson brought Matt in to work with the string bass section when they needed extra rehearsal before a big concert. In the small world of string players in the Twin Cities and the University of Minnesota, Matt was a minor celebrity.

"Could you pass the word about this?" Karl asked. "See if anyone recalls a pissed-off student from their school days."

The switch flipped on in Matt's memory. "As a matter of fact, we were talking about one pissed-off guy at the luncheon."

"Who?" Karl demanded. "I'll beat the shit out of him if I get a chance."

"Easy, Karl." Matt forced calmness into his voice, hoping it would transmit to the grieving son. "There's a *slight* possibility that a violinist who failed his audition and vowed to get revenge might have sent the emails, although it's hard to see how he could have actually had anything to do with your dad's death. It was twenty years ago. Who would hold a grudge that long over a silly audition?"

"Please find him, Matt. At a minimum, I want to press charges against the asshole. Emailing death threats is a crime, isn't it?"

"I don't know for sure," Matt said. "Tell you what: Forward those threatening emails to me. I know someone who might be able to trace them to the sender. In the meantime, I'll do some digging. If I find something, I'll get back to you."

They exchanged email addresses, and Karl promised to send the emails that day. "Thanks, Matt. Mom will appreciate it."

"Give her my best, Karl. I'll be in touch."

Matt clicked off his cell phone and exhaled long and slow. It was ludicrous to think that a musician could get angry enough to harbor a longstanding grudge and then send threatening emails twenty years later. Yet, the mere thought of violent, intentional death stirred horrid memories of his recent past. On cue, he felt one of his PTSD headaches developing. His emotional outbursts, although few, were unpredictable and came with little warning.

*   *   *

The next day, Matt used what remained of his leverage at the university to smooth talk a file clerk into letting him check the Music School records and verify that Justin Briggs, Bragg, or Biggs was a student when Matt and Cathy Judd were in the Chamber Ensemble. Smooth talk plus the promise to the student employee of a pair of seventh-row center seats at Orchestra Hall for the Minnesota Orchestra's upcoming all-Beethoven concert had done the trick.

Since Danilson had selected all Chamber Ensemble members from the University Orchestra, it was easy to find the rosters for the orchestra during that time period. Sure enough, Justin Biggs had been a member of the University Orchestra back then, but not a member of the Chamber Ensemble.

Matt returned home, fired up his laptop, and typed *Justin Biggs* into the search box. After scrolling through several pages of entries and links, he found a blog Biggs had started as a college freshman. He described it as "a chronicle of college life in the twenty-first century."

The posts started out with common freshman topics: dorm life, roommates, fraternities, cafeteria food, and the difficulty of college classes compared to high school. But the tone changed in the middle of Justin's sophomore year from happy and eager to morose and angry. Matt skimmed ahead, checking an occasional post, absorbing the downward-spiraling vibe. Biggs's grades declined sharply. He broke up with his girlfriend, wasn't sleeping well, and dabbled in marijuana, ecstasy, and amphetamines.

Matt struck pay dirt in an early September post from Biggs's senior year. Justin maintained a seat in the University Orchestra for three years and had often written it was his sanctuary from the daily stress of college life. He was a talented violinist who figured it was time to audition for the elite Chamber Ensemble. Although Biggs hadn't mentioned going ballistic on Dr. Dan, he admitted in that post that it pissed him off about failing the audition. He "knew" he was more than qualified for that "over-hyped" ensemble and quit the orchestra altogether because Danilson was such a "second-rate judge of talent."

Before digging further, Matt emailed Cathy Judd for confirmation that they were referring to the same person. He attached a blog photo of Biggs and the incriminating blog post. "Is this the Justin who went ballistic on Dr. Dan?"

Cathy replied within minutes. "YES!"

*   *   *

Because Biggs is an uncommon surname, Matt easily found more details about *his* Justin Biggs. Born and raised in Mankato, Minnesota. Graduated from Mankato West High School. National Merit Scholar. Class valedictorian. Concertmaster in the high school orchestra. At the University of Minnesota, he studied pre-med for two years, then earned a bachelor's degree in computer science followed by a master's degree in software engineering. Biggs was also divorced, had no kids, and lived in Burnsville, a suburb of the Twin Cities.

Someone with his brains could have attended far more prestigious tech schools—MIT, Carnegie Mellon, Cal Tech—yet he stuck with the U of M. Biggs's staying home implied either a strong attachment to place and people or some sort of insecurity: social, mental, or emotional.

Maybe Biggs had been accustomed to being the biggest brain and talent in his world. Not making the Chamber Ensemble could have been such a shock that he let off years of accumulated steam in one viral tirade. Or maybe he had some other social issues that prevented him from handling failure the way most people do.

Matt could identify. He'd been a superstar throughout high school too: academically, socially, and physically, albeit in smaller Straight River, Minnesota. He knew that the pressure to maintain excellence was palpable. He was just glad his emotional makeup allowed him to accept occasional failures without going berserk.

Biggs's LinkedIn profile and Facebook page revealed that he currently worked at Voyageur Cardiac Systems. Stephen Hartsburg's company. Matt flushed with apprehension. Interesting coincidence.

Either way, Matt would track down Biggs and have a chat with him. At minimum, he needed to know if Biggs had sent the nasty emails to the Danilson family. He trusted his sight-reading instincts enough to determine that much about the man. But now, he wondered if Biggs was an evil genius who needed some serious counseling and therapy. Matt shook his head at the absurdity of the whole situation. *This makes no sense at all. But the Danilsons are part of my musical family. The least I can do is dig a little more.*

*   *   *

He called Zach Perez, a young friend fresh out of college and a computer whiz who now worked for the FBI. "Got a job for you, kid."

The silence on Zach's end was deafening.

"You there, Zach?"

"Yeah, yeah, I'm here."

"What's wrong?"

"Duuude, the last time you had a job for me, I almost died twice, then worried my ass off about you for two years until

Smythe got convicted." He was referring to their misguided but well-intentioned and ultimately successful quest to take down the Millennium Four conspiracy, led by the more-than-detestable real estate tycoon Leland Smythe.

"This one's much safer," Matt said. "I promise."

Zach exhaled into the phone. "What, then?"

Matt outlined the circumstances of Magnus Danilson's death and then explained Biggs's rant. "This jerk might be the person who sent threatening emails to Danilson shortly before he died and then emailed his widow, saying he was glad he died."

"Man, that's brutal," Zach said.

"Could you track those emails down, see if he's the one who sent them, and also find out as much as you can about the guy? He works at Voyageur Cardiac Systems in Eagan."

"Officially, I can't do it," Zach said. "Unofficially . . ."

"Riiight," Matt said. "Please? It's important."

Another long pause. "Oh, all right. I'll do this for you, but nothing more, okay? Just promise you'll keep my name out of it."

"Agreed."

"And if the cops come calling, we've never met. *Comprendes*?"

"*Te comprendo*. Thanks, kid. I owe you one."

"Yeah, I heard that just before the second time Smythe tried to kill me."

*   *   *

Restless, Matt drove to Voyageur Cardiac Systems that afternoon, intending to set up surveillance of Biggs, then "accidentally" run into him at a bar or restaurant and strike up a conversation. He figured Biggs, being single, would eat dinner in a restaurant most days, so catching him in a public situation should be easy. Armed with a copy of Biggs's LinkedIn photo, Matt backed his car into a space that gave him a clear view of the main employee exit and waited.

Sure enough, Biggs exited Voyageur headquarters at 5:45, well after most of the nine-to-fivers had left. He chatted with a colleague as they walked to their cars. Biggs got into a red Mustang, which he'd bragged on Facebook about purchasing last year. As he drove away, Matt followed at a safe distance, keeping the Mustang in sight. Biggs eventually turned onto I-35E southbound. Minutes later, he exited the freeway and headed west toward Burnsville Center, a regional shopping mall. But he drove a block past the mall and parked in the lot to the Porter Creek Hardwood Grill, a popular place for upscale American fare with a daily happy hour and comfortable atmosphere.

Matt parked a row over and followed Biggs inside, keeping well back while Biggs made his way to the bar and sat. He'd wait for him to have a sip or two of his drink first, then play the part of a fellow lone wolf on the prowl for attractive women while looking to unwind after a rough day at their jobs.

After Biggs had taken a sip of his beer, Matt walked over and said, "Mind if I sit here?"

Biggs eyed him, then nodded toward the adjacent bar stool. "Free country." He turned away and sipped his beer, a dark lager.

Matt ordered a similarly dark beer and sized up Biggs as he took the first frosty sip from his pint. He was average height, with a well-trimmed beard of dark brown that balanced his full head of hair. Blue eyes; a large, hooked nose; dark complexion for a white guy—tanning booth color? Fit but pudgy, like a weekend jogger who wants to lose ten pounds but hasn't yet.

Biggs's eyes constantly darted back and forth, and he gave off a nervous aura of finger tapping, head bobs and nods, sniffs, lip licks, and a leg that started bouncing up and down on the bar stool rung as soon as he'd sat down. As a musician, Matt was also guilty of foot and finger tapping, but those taps always accompanied the music that regularly coursed through his brain.

Matt switched into full improvisation mode. "You come here a lot?"

Biggs looked at him sideways, recoiled, and frowned. "What the hell? You trying to pick me up? Because if you are, I'm not into guys."

Matt immediately realized his gaffe and flushed, momentarily speechless. "No, no, I didn't mean it that way." He spoke apologetically and lowered his voice for a more masculine effect. "Sorry to mislead you. I'm just a single working stiff, new to the area, looking for a decent neighborhood hangout."

Biggs appraised him—a quick, up-and-down scan, and smiled. "No harm, no foul. But if that's what you use on women these days, pal, you'll be sitting here alone a lotta nights. Twenty-first century and all."

"What kind of work do you do?"

"Med tech. Computer stuff. Most people's eyes glaze over if I say more."

And Matt was in. Using the alias Mike Larson, he pretended to be a public-school music teacher with an interest in technology as it related to electronic music. A clever way to get Biggs to open up about his work. Eventually, Matt guided the conversation away from music technology and toward cybersecurity. It was tough because Biggs appeared to be uncomfortable the entire time. His nervous tics kept up their pace. His responses to Matt's questions sounded more like annoyed interrogation answers than friendly replies.

As Matt cautiously steered the conversation toward computer hacking, Biggs gradually relaxed enough for Matt to ask leading questions that could help him determine if this guy could send anonymous death threats via email. After two beers and an hour of pretending to be fascinated by Biggs's work, Matt had all he needed.

Biggs exhibited traces of underlying anger about everything —bosses, politics, the economy, the winter weather, his ex-wife. He certainly seemed capable of sending anonymous emails and reveling in someone's misfortune by releasing his anger through his taunting messages. As he left the bar, Matt wondered what other type of mischief could be perpetrated by a guy with Biggs's apparently impressive ability, and with anger issues.

*   *   *

Found something on your guy. Let's discuss privately.
The text from Zach Perez weighed on Matt's mind as he drove to Robbinsdale, an inner-ring Minneapolis suburb. He pulled up in front of Zach Perez's apartment, an older three-story building with a row of garages in the back, a wraparound yard, and a few mature trees and well-trimmed shrubs, half-buried in the snow.

Zach buzzed him in, then met him in the hallway upstairs. "Hey, Matt. Great to see you in person for a change. What has it been, a year?" They shook hands and did a quick man hug.

They'd become strong friends in the short time they had known each other, even though they were an unlikely pair. The musical genius and the technological genius. Different generations. Matt: white guy, medium brown hair, wearing khakis, button-down shirt, and a crew-neck sweater. Zach: half-Mexican, two inches shorter than Matt's five foot eleven and maybe thirty pounds lighter, with a mop of wavy black hair, black horned-rim glasses, a two-day growth of hair on his face, wearing jeans and a gray hoodie. Despite showing more poise and confidence than when they'd first met, Zach still looked too young and full of energy to be an FBI bureaucrat.

"Show me what you found, kid," Matt said after taking a chair next to Zach at the oversized desk that held two desktop computers—both with dual monitors—two pairs of desktop speakers, a circular light on a long arm used for video chats, a charging station, and a laptop in a carrying case. Thrift-store living room furniture filled the other side of the room.

"Just remember," Zach said, "you didn't get this from me."

"Once I have your data, this meeting never happened."

"Good, because what I did was technically illegal."

"Hey, you trusted me with your life. Trust me when I say I'll take this new secret to my grave. Besides, you're an expert at covering your tracks."

Zach gave him a dubious glance before speaking. "We have to break it down. First, there were the threatening emails sent to Danilson before his death."

"Right."

"I can't tell who sent them, and if I can't, it's hard to imagine who could. The sender was really good at concealing the source. Virtual private networks, anonymizing browsers, you name it. We're dealing with a pro."

Thoroughly unsettled, Matt said, "Go on."

"Then there's the taunting email sent after Danilson's death."

"Did you trace that?"

"Yep. It came from Biggs."

"Holy—"

"I should have said Biggs *apparently* sent them. Theoretically, somebody could have set him up. Borrowed his IP address, sent the emails, then deleted them from the Sent folder."

"I'll see if he denies it, the bastard."

"But what the hell?" Zach said. "We've got two different people sending nasty emails to your professor?"

"It makes sense when you think about it," Matt replied. "The ones sent before Dr. Dan's death—those were death threats. That's illegal. Somebody who does that is going to make damn sure they've covered their tracks. Gloating about Danilson's death after the fact—that's ugly, but not illegal. Biggs probably figured he had nothing to worry about."

Zach smiled. "He didn't know about you."

Matt nodded and chuckled.

"There's something else," Zach said. "I, well, took a look inside Voyageur Cardiac's system and—well, let's say I accidentally stumbled across the HR record of our friend."

"And?"

"Biggs's performance reviews show pretty much what you'd expect. Brilliant programmer, but he can't get along with anybody. They sent him to a shrink."

"Really?"

"Yep. Seems he was arrested in a road rage incident. The charges were dropped; seeing the shrink may have been part of the deal."

"Did you see the file of his conversations with the psychologist?"

"Nope. Therapist-patient confidentiality, I suppose."

Matt stood up and straightened his back. He'd been leaning over, looking at Zach's monitor. "So," he said. "Back to the threatening emails. If Biggs didn't send them, are you sure there's no way to find out who did?"

"If this was more serious than threatening emails, like if a crime occurred that fell under FBI jurisdiction, I might be able to officially dig deeper and use Bureau resources to try. But I'm not authorized to do that. I'm still on probation and don't have access to the good stuff. And besides . . ."

"Yes?"

"I don't think you'd ever find it."

As they walked out, Matt turned and paused by the door. "I don't know, Zach. Call it my heightened sense of conspiracy. Looking for something that's not there. But something about Dr. Dan's death doesn't feel right, not after those emails. Somebody threatens him, then he dies. They said it was natural causes, but . . ."

"I hear you," Zach said. "Those messages spooked me, too. And I've noticed my mind jumping to drastic conclusions about silly shit. Unrelated stuff."

"Smythe?"

Zach nodded. "Like if someone's looking at me funny, or I notice a car following me for more than a mile, I get nervous, edgy, wondering if it's one of Smythe's thugs who didn't get the memo to stand down."

"Same here," Matt said. "Probably worse for me, of course." They exchanged sympathetic looks. Two recent members of an informal club of victims that will forever be looking over their shoulders.

Matt pursed his lips and smiled grimly. "I'll mull this over, see if something else comes to mind. But I don't think I'll sleep well tonight."

*   *   *

At 5:30 p.m. the next day, Matt was waiting in his car in the parking lot of Biggs's condo complex, running the engine to stay warm and hoping that Biggs wasn't eating out. At 6:00, Biggs's red Mustang turned into the lot and parked. As Biggs walked toward the main entrance, Matt followed ten yards behind.

When Biggs had punched in the security code and passed halfway through the door, Matt shouted, "Hold the door," and hustled forward.

Biggs held it without looking behind him, apparently used to being on both sides of the request many times.

Matt grabbed the door. "Thanks."

Biggs waved a hand and muttered, "No problem," before continuing toward his unit on the second floor.

Matt waited for him to take the stairs, then raced up behind him to the hallway. He spotted Biggs standing at the third door from the end, pulling out his keys. Taking rapid but stealthy strides, Matt reached Biggs just as he was pushing the door open. "Hi, Justin. Remember me?"

Biggs jumped at the sudden noise, then turned to see who was talking. Matt shoved him inside, then closed and locked the door.

"What the hell?" Biggs exclaimed before a flash of recognition showed in his eyes. "You? Um, Mike Larson, is it?" His face reddened as he backed away to get out of arm's reach of his uninvited guest.

"Awww, you remembered me," Matt said with a phony smile. He moved forward, intent on controlling the situation from the outset.

"How'd you find me?" Biggs said. "Why'd you barge in?"

Matt steered him to the living room and told him to sit on the sofa. He drew himself up to his full height, trying to appear as intimidating as possible. "I won't hurt you unless you start something. If you do, I promise I'll put you in the hospital."

"Hurt me?" Biggs exclaimed. "I'd like to see you try. And what did I do? What the hell do you want?"

"Answers."

"To what questions?"

Matt set his jaw into a hard line and spat out the words. "Did you send death threats to Dr. Magnus Danilson?"

Biggs gave himself away. His eyes shifted away immediately, and he crossed his arms in a defensive posture. "Dr. Dan from the U of M? Why the hell do you care?"

Matt nodded, still glaring at Biggs. "So you remember him?"

"Of course. I was in orchestra for three years before I bailed."

"You bailed because you failed the CE recital," Matt asserted. "And so you sent him death threats."

"Twenty years later? Are you crazy?"

"We've got you cold, Biggs. I had the emails traced to you."

Biggs's expression fell. "It wasn't a death threat . . . Okay, I wasn't sorry when the old guy bought it, and I let his family know. He was overrated by a factor of ten. That's not a death threat, and I sure as hell don't know about any messages except the one I sent."

Matt studied the programmer. This time, he saw no deception. It looked as though Zach was right—the death threats and the gloating after-the-fact email had been sent by different people.

"You're telling me," Matt said, "that you didn't know Danilson had received threatening emails before he died?"

"Before? Hell, no. For God's sake, Larson. You think I'm holding some sort of grudge against the guy almost twenty years later? Enough to send him death threats? Why would I do that? I didn't even know he'd died until a couple of days later."

"It was in all the papers, some TV news too."

"Yeah, but I was incommunicado, at a retreat up north."

"What kind of retreat?"

Biggs looked away. "Anger management," he mumbled.

Matt stifled a laugh.

"All right, I did some things I wasn't proud of when I was young," Biggs said.

"No kidding. It's all in your blog. Drug use, depression, anger issues."

Biggs groaned. "I don't think three people read that blog."

"Make that four now," Matt snapped.

"All right. The company sent me to an anger management retreat. I did my duty, even though I'm working for a bunch of clowns. I keep my nose clean, but anybody messes with me, I'll kick their ass."

"You sent a grieving family a message gloating about their loved one's death. And in this case, the deceased happened to be not only my mentor, but a truly great man. How sick is that?"

"Go to hell."

Matt paused. "And then he dies from a heart attack, wearing an ICD made by your company."

Biggs, looking genuinely surprised, threw his hands up. "So I'm supposed to be the service rep? The warranty guy? I don't do hardware; what does it have to do with me?"

"I don't know. But somebody sent those death threats. I have a feeling you might know who it is."

"How the hell would I know?"

"All roads seem to lead to VCS somehow."

Biggs rolled his eyes.

"What about some sort of cover-up?"

"As in, there's a defect and no one's admitting it?"

"Something like that. Danilson's death needs to be explained somehow." Matt's frustration grew at continually digging for something most likely not there. But he'd gone this far . . .

Biggs gave him a conspiratorial shrug. "If . . . and it's a *huge* if . . . there's a cover-up at VCS, it's got nothing to do with me. But it's a big company. Lots of players higher up than me. The law of averages says there's at least one or two spineless weasels on the payroll who don't want to jeopardize their five-figure bonuses by admitting they or someone else in the company screwed up."

"A name would help."

Biggs moved his gaze up and out and frowned. "There was a guy in IT whose wife died. She had a VCS device that failed. The company said it was due to a car accident that knocked the leads loose."

"Is that account true?"

Biggs shrugged. "It's probably bullshit, but who can know for sure? Anyway, this programmer said the firmware was faulty."

"Firmware? What's that?"

Biggs rolled his eyes. "It's the basic, low-level software that controls the device. It's baked into the ASIC." Before Matt could pose his question, Biggs added, "That stands for Application Specific Integrated Circuit. That's the device's brain and controller. Anyway, this guy claimed the company knew the firmware was flawed but still put it on the market."

"So who is this guy?"

Biggs leaned forward. "Even if I had a name—and I don't—I wouldn't give it to you, you pinheaded prick."

Matt's sight-reading ability felt off because of the growing pain in his head. Biggs sounded sincere, but Matt knew not to underestimate a psychopath's acting ability. Biggs himself might be one of those "spineless weasels" who was high enough on the pay grade to know something.

"I don't know why everyone's messing with me about this, anyway," Biggs said. "I'm a superstar at VCS, even though no one's figured that out yet."

"Who's 'everyone'? Others are investigating?"

"Well, one other person. Some annoying bitch in a wheelchair. Wilkinson. A lawyer with VCS."

"You talk to her?"

"Hell no. Blew her off." Biggs pulled another business card from his wallet, tossed it to Matt, then crossed his arms over his chest. "Here. You deal with her if you don't believe me."

Matt caught the card with one hand and read it: *D.P. Wilkinson, Attorney*. He put it in his pocket.

Biggs stood up and stepped forward. "Are we done here? I got things to do."

"I guess so."

"Good. Now get the hell out of my house, Larson. Take your conspiracy theories and stick 'em up your ass." Biggs shoved Matt in the shoulder.

Big mistake! Bottled-up anger from the past week, fueled by his PTSD instability, surged through Matt. He pivoted, then wound up and walloped Biggs in the eye with his fist. Biggs recoiled, shouting in pain, and bounced off the wall. Matt ripped off a kick to Biggs's groin that would have impressed an NFL punter. Biggs doubled over, then crumpled to the floor, moaning and whimpering. "You . . . son of a bitch," he hissed through clenched teeth. "Who needs anger management now?"

Matt knelt next to Biggs, massaging his sore hand. "That's for going ballistic on a man who had ten times the musical ability you ever had, you tone-deaf piece of shit. And I still think you know something. I want that name."

"Fuck you."

"I'm not letting this go. I'll be back."

"Go for it. Come back and get your ass kicked. And I'm calling the cops."

Good luck arresting Mike Larson, dumbass. Matt stood up, feeling ashamed. He'd lost control. Biggs may have had it coming, but . . .

He stormed out of the apartment, slamming the door behind him.

Chapter 5

Hartsburg

*D*anilson's death was karma. Do we need Tricia to supply more?

Stephen Hartsburg set aside the printout of the second email he had received from his anonymous tormentor and glanced out the window of his log-paneled study at the snowy expanse of Gull Lake. A week ago, he'd been at the top of his game, powerful and confident, a brilliantly successful engineer and CEO. His future, with the company and with Tricia, had seemed assured. Now he had lost all power and control.

He took deep breaths, trying to center himself.

What was his place, who was he, in a world he couldn't control? For a fleeting moment, he thought about the revolver in his desk drawer. A way out?

Not yet.

He had people to deal with problems, but they had failed him. In particular, the one person he could always count on, his assistant, Marilyn, had ghosted him, calling in sick and ignoring his urgent messages. When the going got rough, she had walked. And now, there was no one he could rely on, no one to make the problems go away.

Hartsburg's breathing slowed, and he wiped his forehead. He looked back at the email. Who the hell *was* this person?

It didn't matter. They knew. They had him, cold. They knew about the defect in the 4750. They knew he'd received reports of the defect to submit to the FDA but hadn't submitted them. Worse, they knew about Tricia. What this person claimed to be able to do — to deliberately create or utilize a defect somehow — was impossible. Yet he or she had apparently done it. And what they wanted . . .

> *The price has gone up, Mr. Hartsburg. Public disclosure is no longer enough. You are to make a charitable contribution of $30 million, roughly your compensation for the past year. The money must come from your personal resources, not from company funds. You have ten days, at which time you will receive instructions on where to wire the money. At that time, you will receive the text of a statement resigning your position and accepting responsibility for the deaths, which you will issue publicly.*

A *charitable contribution*? Really? And a public *mea culpa*? The gun was preferable.

What his tormentor didn't know was that Hartsburg couldn't meet the demands. Even if he was willing to go public with the defect, taking his company down; even if he was willing to assume responsibility and go to prison, ending his career, ending his life as he knew it—he couldn't raise $30 million. True, his net worth was well north of $100 million. But nearly all his wealth was tied up in Voyageur stock, in restricted grants and options that couldn't be sold or pledged for loans. He couldn't sell it now, anyway. Next quarter's earnings would be down, and he'd be guilty of insider trading. He kept only three or four million in his personal portfolio. His home and vacation properties were worth about $10 million but carried mortgages and couldn't be further mortgaged in a week's time. Presumably, the extortionist didn't know about the $15 million Hartsburg had stashed in offshore accounts, away from the prying eyes of the attorneys his wife was sure to hire when he finally divorced her to marry Tricia. But there was no way to access those funds; the process would require financial finesse and a lot of time. Bottom line: He couldn't raise the money.

And he'd be unable to stop the threat to Tricia, whatever it was.

As he had been unable to save Magnus. Magnus, his stepfather, the only real father he had ever known. A wise, gentle man, a much better man than Hartsburg would ever be and a better father than he had deserved. And who knew? There could be others.

"Stephen?"

Tricia.

"Stephen, where are you?"

He exhaled and turned to look at her. Tricia was beautiful, a slender blonde in her late thirties with amazing wide eyes. He watched her, thought about her dying at the hands of a self-righteous madman. His mouth went dry.

She walked into the study, looking concerned. "What are you doing in here? You were going to take the evening off."

"I know, I know."

She walked over behind him and put her hands on his shoulders. "I know you're still upset about Magnus. I understand."

He nodded.

"And it seemed like a good idea to come up here for a few days, to get away. But I sense that something more is going on."

He forced a smile, took one of her hands. Was he really that transparent? "It's not that big a deal."

"Tell me about it."

"No, no. As you said, we came up here to relax."

She leaned down beside him. "Stephen, we can't have secrets. You need to share whatever is bothering you."

He stood up and put his arm around her. "It's nothing I can't handle."

"Are you sure about that?"

He exhaled and motioned her toward the leather sofa, then went over and sat next to her.

She waited expectantly.

Starting slowly, hesitantly, he ended up telling her everything, beginning to end. It made him feel weak and pathetic. Even then, he couldn't bring himself to tell her the real reason for the extortion attempt, instead spinning it as merely a threat to expose a defect.

"So, there's no risk to me?"

He didn't answer. In fact, there was plenty of risk. The extortionist could apparently sabotage Voyageur ICDs. He could try to have Tricia's device replaced, but what if the saboteur found out about the attempt and killed Tricia first? He couldn't risk it.

"It's being managed, Tricia."

She gave him a puzzled look. "But that attack I had that sent me to the ER—how did that happen if there's no problem with my ICD?"

"It was just a hiccup. That kind of thing can occur. That doesn't mean there's anything fundamentally wrong."

"But what about Olivia Holmgren's mother? And of course, there was your stepfather."

"It would be reckless to draw conclusions. All kinds of things could have caused their deaths. Magnus—well, he was old."

Tricia thought about it. "If there's no actual defect, then how is this person able to threaten you?"

Hartsburg gave her a weary shrug. "It's easy to exploit deaths and injuries, whether they're caused by a real defect or not. Just the appearance of a problem is enough to cause public outcry. Investigations, our stock price cratering. This creep obviously intends to use these incidents to ruin me."

For Hartsburg, the lie came so easily—so convincingly—that he was almost tempted to believe it himself. But something more, something a lot worse, was going on. He couldn't deny that, and he couldn't tell Tricia.

He started to choke up, and Tricia took his hand. "It's okay. You'll think of a way out."

He forced a smile. "Of course I will."

"You keep saying that. Don't you have an actual plan?"

"I'll think of something."

Tricia let go of his hand and sat up abruptly. "Stephen, you need to get hold of yourself. Sitting here, engaging in wishful thinking, won't cut it. The Stephen Hartsburg I know would be fighting back. You'd have a plan. You'd go after them."

"But how—"

"You say you have ten days, right? Use them. If they take you down, they take you down. But man up, for God's sake. Go down fighting."

He took a deep breath. "What do you think I should do?"

"It seems like you need to find out who this person is. Don't you have anybody who could help you do that?"

An image flashed through his consciousness, a face. Nancy Nguyen, Voyageur's general counsel. Extremely smart, but he didn't know her well. And she was painfully honest. But he wouldn't have to tell her everything, would he? She could find someone reliable to investigate, find the extortionist.

"I guess there's somebody I can try," he said.

"Good. Now, I don't know who this blackmailer is, but it seems to me he must have some kind of inside information. He apparently knew that Olivia's mother and your stepfather had VCS devices. Could it be that somebody got into our database? And aren't there people who could trace that?"

She was, Hartsburg knew, a hundred percent correct.

Another mental image appeared: his old friend Bill Gersohn at MIT, a man who commanded plenty of serious IT talent. The

Voyageur hack could well be an inside job; Hartsburg needed somebody from the outside to investigate.

"There's a guy I can call," he told Tricia.

"Great. That's the Stephen I know." She embraced him.

Hartsburg returned the embrace. But his mind was on a third person he could consult, about the $30 million demand. He would do so only as a last resort. But what the hell was this situation? He could call the man who had set up the offshore bank accounts for him, a man he had never met, but who appeared to have a lot of skill in solving sticky financial problems. And this predicament was as sticky as they came. His name was Henri Hawke, and if he agreed to help, the price would undoubtedly be exorbitant. But what choice did he have?

Bottom line, he had ten days to throw a Hail Mary. To try to find out who was extorting him, and then to eliminate the threat or negotiate. He had a plan, but it relied on the help of people he didn't know, didn't trust, or both, and he would be putting Tricia's life in their hands. But it was all he had.

And if it failed, there was always the gun.

Chapter 6

Weezy

Louise Napolitani hunched forward, concentrating on the hacker who was mounting a denial-of-service attack on one of the big cloud storage providers. MIT's Computer Science and Artificial Intelligence Laboratory (CSAIL) was quiet, most people at lunch. White noise from the ventilation system dampened the sound of comings and goings and other keyboards. A hint of some Middle Eastern spice issued from the sandwich being consumed by the burly, bearded guy who always gave her a friendly nod when they passed in the corridor.

She noticed Bill Gersohn threading his way through the workstations. He meandered toward her, no doubt having forgotten where she sat.

"Uhh, Napolitani?"

"Dr. Gersohn?"

"It's Bill. You're not a student anymore." Gersohn always tried to be just an ordinary guy. Nearly impossible for a person who had won the Fields Medal at 28 and was a Rhodes Scholar before that.

Weezy turned away from the problem of the hacker. "Yes, boss."

That got a grin.

"Umm. I have a situation that might turn into a job, at least for a short while. It'd pay more than the assistantship, and they'd put you up and pay expenses, and, well, it might be up your alley."

His hand was on the back of her chair, partly on her neck, just a little, tentative. She sighed inwardly. She really liked him. Brilliant, exciting conversations, good-natured joking. But she wasn't ready for more. Yet.

"My alley?"

"A problem with a large company's database, possibly caused by hackers. I know you are. . . uhh. . . familiar with the dark web, so I thought this might pique your interest."

Gersohn pulled out a chair from the next station over, leaned forward, and said, "I got a call from a friend of mine. Cal Poly engineer. Brilliant guy. Went to work for a small company that got acquired, and so on. Now he's CEO of the big company that swallowed the little one. Medical devices. The backbone of the company is their database—patient identity, history, and so on—and it may have been hacked."

"May have been?"

"Probably was."

"Probably?" This was getting irritating.

"Uhh . . . was. You interested?" Gersohn looked expectantly at her.

"So, this really smart guy in a big company which must have a secure database protected by a team of data security people wants outside advice? My advice?" Weezy gave Gersohn her Are-You-Shitting-Me look. "Who is this guy?"

"Louise, the whole issue of data security is extremely sensitive for a company that puts hardware in people's bodies. He doesn't want to divulge the company name until he interviews you. I don't know the full story. My friend probably suspects the breach came from inside, but he hasn't told me that. Having it made public would be a disaster for the company. Besides the clear message from the IdeoPulse situation—"

"He knows about me?"

"I think he saw the *Wired* article, among others."

"Got it. So, I'm that notorious person who he wants to work on his super-secret project. Bill, this doesn't make any sense. There are plenty of people in the bullpen who can do plain vanilla cybersecurity and remain anonymous. It's probably a simple hack. He doesn't need me."

"You saw the flaw in—what'd Grant Purves call it, his 'Big Freakin' Idea'?—when his pool of brilliant people didn't. My friend thinks you're the ideal person to look beyond the obvious and help find the hack and maybe the hacker."

"Got it. What happens when someone recognizes me?"

"I . . . uhh . . . I don't think it's a matter of physical danger."

"Don't think, but don't know, right?"

Gershon did that slant-eyed, look-anywhere-but-at-you thing he did when he was nervous.

"You didn't discuss that part, did you?"

Still, the "pay more" part registered heavily. Maybe more, the possibility of being alone in a quiet space to work on her Rev14.2 software when she wasn't on the job. She hoped the program was her ticket to fame and fortune. Or at least a car and a place of her own.

"How much is he paying?"

"Oh, I'm sure it would be more than a hundred per hour."

"Bill, tell him that I'll give a 20% discount because of my inexperience. Four hundred an hour."

*   *   *

"Ms. Napolitani," the man on the monitor said. Weezy sat cross-legged on her bed in her room at home, facing her laptop on the bedside table.

"I am. And you are?"

"Your temporary employer, I hope." He sat in an armchair in a homey room with honey-colored pine paneling, a fish mounted above a doorway, and a stone fireplace. He looked to be in his 50s, fit, sandy hair going to gray, blue eyes. He wore a red-and-black plaid wool shirt in keeping with the hunting lodge aspect of the place. She had positioned her laptop such that the backdrop to her camera was the periodic table she'd had on her bedroom wall since fifth grade. More professional than the sailboat curtains her mother refused to change and the stuffed animals that still occupied a shelf above her desk.

"You will not meet me in person," the man said. "I am away from my office, but this secure address is always available. If you agree to do the work I am proposing, I will use this channel to send you material related to the project and payment. Because our patient database has no connection to the internet, you will have to do the work on site in Minneapolis. The project may take a couple of weeks."

Weezy nodded. "I'll consider it, but I have to know who I'm working for."

"And I need your word that you will not discuss this project and my identity with anyone, whether you agree to do it or not. Bill says I can trust a promise from you."

"I will mention it to no one."

The tension around the man's eyes seemed to relax. "I am Stephen Hartsburg. I'm CEO of Voyageur Medical. We are a Fortune 500 company with operations in six states and four countries, and of course, sales worldwide. Our headquarters and R&D are in the Twin Cities. We make several medical devices, all of which are implantable—pacemakers, defibrillators, insulin pumps, cortical stimulators, several others. The ability to implant, monitor and control our devices is our core technology."

Weezy nodded.

"The problem is, someone has apparently breached—hacked, I guess you'd say—our database and stolen information about a handful of customers. That's all I know right now, and that's why I called Bill for advice. We're not sure what the person will do with the data. Chances are good—"

"How would a data breach lead to trouble for someone wearing a device? Aren't the devices themselves super secure?"

Hartsburg looked mildly irritated. Maybe Fortune 500 CEOs weren't used to being interrupted. "Yes," he said. "And I see you're a quick study. The devices themselves are very secure, so we think the hacker can't do much to hurt anyone. Doesn't matter, though. We can't tolerate a data breach."

"Which you would have to report—"

This time, Hartsburg didn't look irritated. He grinned and nodded. "You're right. We have to report any significant risk to the FDA, which regulates all medical devices. And I can see by your expression you're wondering why that hasn't happened."

"Uhhh . . . yes."

"It's complicated. If there is a significant problem—and that's defined in voluminous detail by the FDA—we need to go through a complex process with them. But this may be a one-off. Right now, FDA guidance doesn't require us to file, but we need to solve the problem quickly, before we pass into FDA's 'Required Action.'"

Hartsburg leaned forward. "I need you to find out how the breach happened and, if possible, who did it. That's the job. Even if a breach hurts no one, we have to plug it."

The project could be exactly what Hartsburg said it was. On the other hand . . . She shifted, uncomfortable in her cross-legged position. Bill Gersohn would never support an illegal data activity, but Bill was an academic and a bit naive. The varnish covering the illegal schemes she'd seen on the net was always bright and shiny. She already had to worry about IdeoPulse's lawyers; if she was implicated in some questionable legal enterprise, she and her precious Rev 14.2 software would go down the black hole that swallows good technology when it collides with the industry's cutthroat business practice and its lawyers. To put off that thought, she asked Hartsburg to tell her about Voyageur's cybersecurity. After fifteen minutes, Weezy had a good feel for it. He was a smart guy, an engineer, and it turned out he knew the details of Voyageur's protection better than she would have expected of a CEO, not that she knew that many CEOs.

"Based on what you've told me, your security is top-notch," she said. "You have the best commercial software and a crew of smart analysts keeping watch. I know a couple of hackers who could probably get through your defenses, one being me, so I'll try. Call it a stress test of your firewall."

Hartsburg's brow furrowed.

"Another possibility," Weezy continued, "is someone has been able to put a back door in your system without your people knowing it. Based on what you've told me about your security staff, that seems unlikely . . . and if it happened, chances are it was done by an insider. If no one can get in from the outside, and there's no back door, then it's likely an employee has somehow gotten around the physical security you described and is taking the info out. That would be your bad guy—or the employee the bad guy paid."

Hartsburg shrugged.

"Yeah," Weezy said. "Obvious, I know. But in most situations like this, it's the obvious that gets ignored in favor of the exotic. When do you want me to start?"

"Now. As soon as you can get to the Twin Cities."

Weezy thought through what she had to do at CSAIL. Actually, it wasn't much. "I can be there three days from now."

Hartsburg looked disappointed. "Three days?" he said. "Can you make it in two?"

She hesitated long enough to save face. "Yes. And you agree to my hourly fee?"

He chuckled. "Clever to introduce the idea of a substantial fee as if it included a discount for inexperience. Seems a bit steep, but—"

"Uhh, Mr. Hartsburg, I'm a couple of years out of school, paying for my education, living at home, and—"

"And also fresh out of a 200K salary," Hartsburg said. "But the fee's okay if you're as good as Bill says you are. And it's Stephen, Ms. Napolitani. Is Weezy okay?" He grinned, the seriousness gone for a moment.

"Weezy's okay between you and me, but I have a bit of notoriety—"

"A bit?" Hartsburg chuckled again. "You mean the *Wired* article featuring 'the brilliant analyst who stuffed Grant Purves's Big Freakin' Idea'? Or Purves's interview describing 'the crazy . . . I think there was a B-word, an F-word and possibly a C-word in there . . . who never understood the genius of his idea'? Yes, I believe you need to work under an assumed identity. You'll be LeeAnn Nardelli while you're with us."

"Okay. I'm game."

"Glad to have you working on this, Weezy," Hartsburg said. "I will send you a package of information later today. It will include background on the cover story for the job, which is to update part of our system and some material about our products."

"I must report to someone, and that someone's going to want actual work done, right? How am I going to figure out how to do the cover work and find the system weakness?"

Hartsburg cocked his head and grinned. "Ms. Napolitani, would it be possible for you to act as if you are a normally intelligent person? Conjure up a few problems that delay you in the conversion project you'll be officially assigned to. Convince your supervisor that you're a regular sort of coding person who's never worked on the problem you've been hired for."

She was starting to like the guy.

*   *   *

Later that day, a flag popped up on Weezy's phone indicating the package Hartsburg had promised was waiting to be downloaded. As much as she wanted to read it, CSAIL wasn't the place. She left a little early, took the T home, and shouted "Home" as she trotted through the living room and up a flight to her room and her computer.

The package that came through the secure link had plane tickets, the name of the hotel where Weezy would be lodged, pictures of the outside and inside of Voyageur headquarters and the data systems annex, specs for the company's products, and a chit for the central cafeteria. There was contact information for Nancy Nguyen, the general counsel, and Annette Freivald, a manager in Human Resources, whom Weezy was to contact when she arrived. Hartsburg had attached a note: "Freivald has been told you're an employee of our accounting firm and you'll be doing a procedural audit of the Systems and Programming division. Systems and Programming requested a contractor to update part of our system, so your arrival should surprise no one. If anyone starts prying, play dumb and let me know."

*   *   *

Weezy told herself it would be best to stay away from the Voyageur database until she was on site, but her curiosity convinced her to take a peek. She dropped through the company website to a very good standard firewall. Good for them. When she got through that, she saw the business stuff: accounting, sales and marketing (purchased software), personnel (also purchased). No connection to the ICD database. Again, good for them. She thought she should probably stop, but there was plenty of communication to people who must have access to the database. She began searching the computer of a person who must be a programmer and who hadn't turned off their computer. Maybe, like a hungry mouse, she could sneak through a crack and . . . she hit a digital tripwire. She cut off the attack before they traced her, but she was sure she could get in with some time and patience. She reported this to Stephen Hartsburg, who did not seem suitably worried. Odd, given his earlier concern about data security. She wondered what she wasn't being told.

Running under her research was a thread of concern about her father. A few months ago, Louis Napolitani had passed out in the seafood store he had built to a successful business. He was taken to Mass General and stabilized. The ER doctor diagnosed ventricular tachycardia, and tests disclosed an 80% blocked artery. A stent opened the artery, and his doctor suggested a cutting-edge implantable cardioverter-defibrillator that could function as both a pacemaker and a defibrillator. An ICD was implanted — Boston Scientific, if Weezy remembered correctly. Gersohn and Hartsburg had claimed that the person who stole Voyageur's patient data probably wouldn't be able to do any harm with it, which didn't allay her concern at all. Why did they have to keep mentioning it if it wasn't a damn problem?

In fact, the several odd things Weezy had noted were starting to paint a simple picture: someone had gotten into Voyageur's database and copied a few names with their data. Hartsburg said the hacker probably couldn't do anything with it. But a hacker wouldn't go to the effort of taking a few names for the fun of it. The names would have to be worth something. How would knowing a person had a pacemaker be an advantage to, say, an enemy? Maybe it would hurt job prospects of, say, a stunt person or a high-stress CEO. Or maybe someone suspected a malfunction in a certain patient's device. Or a person might have a weapon that targeted pacemakers . . . in a sci-fi story, but unlikely in real life. Maybe there was something she'd missed in the data chain, and her dad's pacemaker might help her see it.

Her dad had a small device next to his bed that he said sent data to his doctor. She remembered him saying, "You gotta be within ten feet of the thing for it to pick up, though." *Okay*, she thought, *very low power radio frequency*. He added, "Doc says they monitor the signal and tell me when to come in. Sometimes they gotta upgrade the software in the ICD."

Over a nearly sleepless night, Weezy put together how the system worked, based on her dad's experience and a deep internet search: When an ICD was implanted, it was programmed based on an analysis of the patient's heart rhythms. At home, the device passed data to a bedside device, which sent it to a secure website. The doc's office had a machine called the "programmer," which pulled in the data from the website. The patient went into the doctor's office for adjustments, usually once a year, and the office computer would apply version updates, if applicable. The ICD must include at minimum a battery, a management chip, and an antenna of some sort. The chip or chips would be application specific—ASICs—which would read the heart's data, report it, and deliver a steadying pulse or a shock if necessary.

If Hartsburg was worried about a product malfunction, he'd have a team of engineers on it. But instead, he was making a special effort to have a data scientist involved. Was he really that worried about a small data breach? Or did he suspect a hacker had figured some way to manipulate the device and was trying to identify a target or targets?

She sent a note to Hartsburg:

What variables were taken in the hack? Also, how often does new software go out to the doctors' offices? When was the last time?

He sent back:

I don't think the data reported are relevant to your job, but there's a list attached. Software is updated rarely and passed into the device at a normal office visit.

*   *   *

The Delta flight prepared for landing. The plane dropped through a thin cloud layer, made orange by the setting sun. It was dusk below as they passed over snow-covered fields with an occasional farmhouse. Then, in short order, more houses, snow cover, and trees, lots of trees. Quickly over a river, a busy highway, and a bump as the plane landed.

Weezy usually carried a backpack with a couple of changes of clothes when she traveled, but this assignment was more of an unknown. Gersohn, never a fashion hound, had looked her up and down the day before she left, noticed the T-shirt (crimson with "Harvard Sucks" in white), the cargo pants, the lime green socks and white Nikes. He reminded her that she was going to be working in a large corporation which probably had at least an informal dress code. He took in her expression and said, "Napolitani, remember that you're supposed to be invisible, doing scut work no one else wants to do. Your looks will no doubt get attention"—did his cheek color slightly?—"but otherwise, you need to blend in."

The night before her departure, she was in her room, sorting clothes. She had the California casuals in one pile, the small pile of nice tops and skirts in another. Pretty small piles. She had borrowed her dad's big shell suitcase and knew she would have space left over. Her brother Petey knocked on the door frame and entered. He sat on the end of the bed, sucking his lower lip the way he did when he had something to say but couldn't figure out exactly how.

"You flyin' Delta, huh?"

"Yup. Direct flight."

"Y'know, you really oughta have some personal protection with you." He hurried on. "I was thinking we used to give female Marines pepper spray when they were going off base. Not a bad idea for you to have some, too. So I . . . uhh . . . had some sent to the hotel you're staying at."

Weezy squinted at her brother. "We talking overkill here, big bro?"

Petey shrugged. "Yeah, maybe a little, but can't hurt, y'know."

Warmth spread through her at his tough-guy way of caring for her.

She wrapped him in a hug. "Gonna miss you, big guy."

* * *

She'd been assigned a middle seat, which she didn't mind. At 5'8' and slender, she had to worry a little about space for knees, but the seat was more than wide enough. The elderly woman on her right assumed that Weezy would want to know the details of her trip to Worcester for her grandchild's birthday party. The guy on the aisle suggested they meet for a beer because they were, after all, Bostonians traveling to a strange land.

The jetway to the terminal was bone-chilling cold. It was 23 degrees below zero outside, colder by a dozen degrees than she'd experienced in Boston, and it felt that cold in the jetway. The woman behind her said, "A bit nippy today."

There was a guy with a sign that said "Nardelli" when she emerged from the concourse. He took her to a car parked at the cab stand. He was a Somali man named Warsame, and he explained that the service was expecting to pick her up and drop her off at Voyageur tomorrow. For now, he'd deliver her to the hotel.

Minneapolis was more spread out than Boston, and fresh snow gave the utilitarian buildings along the interstate a frosted look. The hotel was comfortable and had high-speed internet. She retrieved the pepper spray Petey had sent, unpacked, fired up her laptop, and entered the secure portal Hartsburg had set up. No new messages.

She ordered out for Chinese. By ten o'clock, she was in bed, tired from the trip and the last two nights spent in research rather than sleep. But it was so quiet, and the unanswered question restated itself: if stealing personal data from Voyageur's database wasn't going to lead to much, why did Hartsburg need her? Why the secrecy?

*   *   *

The next morning, Weezy showered, dressed in conservative slacks (the one pair she had), a nice long-sleeved blouse (ditto), and black flats. Feeling uncomfortable but corporate, she went to what passed for breakfast at the hotel. Her phone said eighteen minutes to Voyageur, and her instruction package said for her to arrive at 9:30, so she called the car service to pick her up at 9:00.

Voyageur's campus was impressive in an understated sort of way. Practical construction in sand-colored panels, lots of windows. A central building rose several stories, fronted by a circular drive. A lower building to her right was connected to the main by a walkway at the second level.

Weezy entered a spacious foyer, a three-story open space rising to skylights. Several free-form sculptures graced the open space. Tasteful, not gaudy.

At the guard station, Weezy presented the LeeAnn Nardelli offer letter. The guard made a call and had Weezy take a seat. Shortly, a woman dressed in an upscale business casual blouse, slacks, and low-heeled pumps emerged from the elevator behind the guard station. Her dark brown hair was shot through with gray, and she had the physique of a person who, as Weezy's mom would say approvingly, took care of herself.

"Ms. Nardelli?"

Weezy hitched for a moment, cursed herself for inattention and answered, "Yes, and you must be Annette Freivald."

The woman smiled and extended a hand. "Welcome to Voyageur."

They shook hands.

"We need to do some paperwork—minimal because you will be what we call a contingent worker—in my office. Since we're on the ground floor, though, I'll show you around here first."

Freivald gave Weezy a quick, efficient walk through the building. They passed through the employee lounge "where computer staff usually take breaks to use their phones, since your phone will go in a locker outside the programming area. We had a lot of pushback on that at first, but people adjusted quickly, and I think most now enjoy not being interrupted" and a nice, airy cafeteria where Weezy would eat meals "which are available from seven o'clock through three-thirty, so if you don't like the hotel breakfast . . ." Then it was up to the third floor and Freivald's office. She motioned for Weezy to sit, closed the door, and said, "I understand you are part of our operational audit. I was puzzled at first, because the auditor is not undercover for most departments. And I hear from your accent you're from out East, so this must be a special case."

"Extending the audit to security protocols is a recent development," Weezy said, improvising. "There aren't many auditors with my training, so we're spread thin. And yes, I was brought up near Boston."

The paperwork went quickly and was all online. Finished, Freivald handed Weezy a badge with a lanyard. "Do not lose or forget this pass," she said. "Without it, you won't be able to get into the programming section." She led Weezy down a spiral stair to the second floor and across the walkway to the lower building.

Freivald and Weezy passed through a door that required a swipe of each badge into an anteroom. Two walls were filled with what looked like safe deposit boxes. "The ones with green lights are available," Freivald said. "Swipe your pass to open, and stash your phone. The system will know which one you used and get you back to it at the end of the day." Freivald turned to a steel-framed door, swiped, and they stood on the floor of the largest programming space Weezy had ever seen, probably 40,000 square feet of high-end cubicles. Glassed-in offices occupied the back wall.

"Phew," she said. "Big."

"We do all the programming here," Freivald said as she led Weezy toward an office. "Database management, programming for calibrating the devices in the doc's offices, and firmware that goes into the devices in manufacturing. Those glassed-in spaces at the far end are support for the US and South America. We have other centers abroad." She leaned into an office. "Samira, your contractor's here." Then she turned to Weezy. "Samira Choudhary will be your supervisor for the project."

The woman behind the desk raised a finger in recognition but kept writing on an old-fashioned steno pad. After a few seconds, she inspected her work, said, "Good, about time," and stood from her desk. She was short and broad, with soft brown skin, dark eyes, and black hair. Her face wore a frown. "Nardelli, right?" She held out her hand. Weezy stepped forward, preparing to shake, then realized Choudhary's hand was palm up and she was looking at Annette Freivald. "Drive?"

Freivald looked disconcerted and produced a thumb drive. She hesitated, not handing it over. "Umm, just tell me where to set her up. I know you're busy."

So, they're not telling Choudhary about this project, Weezy thought. *That'll make life interesting.*

Choudhary cocked her head, then gave a little shrug and said, "Put her in 87B." She finally glanced at Weezy and looked her up and down, maybe with a trace of disgust. "When you get settled, come see me and I'll tell you what to do."

Ten minutes later, Freivald had shown Weezy where the bathroom was, located 87B, inserted the thumb drive in the computer at the side of the desk and clicked through a series of setup questions, assigned Weezy a password, given her an impersonal smile, and disappeared through the entry.

Weezy was tempted to cruise the system, get an overall idea of design, but realized she had no formal assignment yet. She threaded her way back to Choudhary's office.

"So, you're familiar with the Carson EXV v2 interface?"

"I'm familiar with a number of interfaces. I've not worked with the EXV v2, but—"

Weezy considered what a volcano about to blow might look like as she watched Choudhary's jowls redden and tremble. "I gave the personnel service a detailed description of what I wanted, and 'worked with something maybe a little like the EXV v2' was not part of it. Goddamnit, Nardelli or whoever you are, I—" Choudhary stopped, hung her head and chuckled. "So Freivald inserted the thumb drive and then carried it away, didn't she?"

"Yes. She used it to set up my station."

"Well, isn't she the cagey one? She was just helping out, huh?" Choudhary cracked a grin. "So, what are you really supposed to be doing?"

Weezy froze, then stuttered, "M-migrating an old interface over to a new one."

"Bullshit." Choudhary's jaw muscles twitched.

"Pardon?"

"The ivory tower across the bridge is doing something squirrelly here. I really don't care what it is, but I need that v2 migrated to v4. So, before you do whatever nosing around they told you to do, migrate that software. If you can't do it, tell me by the end of the day, and I'll get someone who can."

Choudhary stared at Weezy for several long seconds, then dropped her gaze to the work she had been doing.

"Go," she said.

*   *   *

Weezy spent the next hour reading the specifications for both versions of the software she was assigned to migrate. At 11:30, she noticed people moving past her station toward the door that led to the main building. Must be lunchtime here in the Midwest. She jumped into the code. Probably keep it simple, in keeping with her profile as a competent, but not brilliant, programmer.

"Can't write C++, huh?"

A hand rested on the edge of her desk, supporting the red-sleeved arm of a man with garlic breath. Weezy stifled a tart reply.

She turned to contemplate the guy. Pudgy, with the requisite programmer-geek pallor. Red western-style shirt with the mother-of-pearl snaps. *Really?*

"Y'know, you're doing it the hard way. I could help out." He smiled, closer to a leer, and seemed unembarrassed as he inventoried her attributes. The physical ones.

Weezy's mind was rolling through the ways she could humiliate him. Not counting closely, because there were so many.

"It's a pretty straightforward job, but you know the system better than I do, uhh"—she squinted at his badge, which said *Justin Biggs—Lead Programmer*—"Justin. Shouldn't Ms. Choudary assign you to do the job?"

He chuckled. "Choudhary doesn't assign me squat. I'm the firm's lead programmer; I only deal with the complex stuff . . . Attribute management, firmware coordination, safety protocols. The hard stuff."

"Oh, well, thanks for the offer. I'll knock you up if I need help."

"Knock me up?" He looked at her strangely.

"Sherlock Holmes said that to Watson all the time, and when we were kids, we used to love using it. We had no idea what it meant, but it made the teachers blush," she said.

That apparently had the weird-shield effect Weezy was going for. The guy backed off a couple of steps.

"Ask anyone to find me if you need help," he said and made his way toward the bridge to the main building.

The next time Weezy looked at the time, it was 2:00 and her stomach was telling her it was past time to eat.

She followed Freivald's instructions, freed up her phone, and walked across to the cafeteria feeling much better about the assignment. The migration wasn't going to be difficult, and she would have plenty of time to work on the breach project.

*   *   *

The cafeteria was nearly deserted in late afternoon. The main lunch line was closed, but there was a salad bar that included a pot of chili and the other makings of a taco salad. Perfect. Weezy put a salad together, took a cup of chili, paid, and scanned the cafeteria. She picked a table near the windows overlooking a snowy field. She took a seat, opened the secure portal on her phone, and began tapping out a message to Hartsburg.

Day one, and I'm busted. My supervisor (Samira Choudhary) figured out that I'm undercover. I can handle it.

She was preparing to explain when she realized someone was across from her.

"May I join you?"

Weezy looked up from her phone, prepared to be irritated. The woman was in a wheelchair. She was blonde, older than Weezy, but not old-old. She wore a sand-colored jacket and matching slacks that looked expensive. Probably an exec of some sort. She extended her hand to Weezy. "Pen Wilkinson."

Chapter 7

"James warned me that you can be a bull in search of a china shop," Nancy Nguyen said, giving Pen a lawyerly appraisal from behind her large desk. "We need discretion."

Pen Wilkinson stared right back at the general counsel of Voyageur Cardiac Systems, Inc., a short, elegant woman in her mid-forties, her dark hair pulled up in a bun. Nancy was an old friend of Pen's boyfriend, James Carter, and had asked her to come to company headquarters in Minnesota for a temporary job. Pen was a lawyer, but this job sounded more like an investigation. "It's all a matter of perspective," Pen said. "How badly do you want to know the truth?"

"It's imperative that we find who sent that email to our CEO, and fast. But the whole idea of bringing in an outside investigator is to get a good objective look while preventing panic or overreaction."

Or lawsuits or bad publicity, Pen thought. "I'll do my best and keep you informed," Pen said. "But obviously, if there's anything criminal, I'll have to report it."

"Of course. Now, the situation is problematic in several ways. First of all, we don't have an actual copy of the email sent anonymously to our CEO, Stephen Hartsburg. Second, there was an implied threat, but nothing explicit."

"Which is why you haven't brought in the police."

"Correct. Third, Stephen will not be available to help us. He's out of town."

"Isn't this important? Doesn't he want to help us?"

"Of course. He's just juggling a lot of things right now. And he's having a rough time since the death of his stepfather, Magnus Danilson, a couple of days ago. They were very close."

"So, what do we know?" Pen asked.

"The email deleted itself after about a minute," she said. "We weren't able to recover it. Stephen remembers that it referred to a known defect in the model VC-25-4750 family of cardiac devices, which caused the death of 'someone dear to' the sender. This person blames Voyageur and says that Magnus Danilson's death was karma."

"How did Danilson die?"

"Natural causes, but I don't know specifically. The sender of the email is demanding that Stephen resign and publicly take responsibility for the defect by next Wednesday."

"Or what?"

"There's no overt threat. Exposing the defect, I suppose, but there's no mention of violence or extortion."

"And I can't question Mr. Hartsburg?"

"Unfortunately not. And his longtime assistant, Marilyn, went out sick and isn't available, either."

"Not a lot to work with," Pen commented.

"I know. Sorry. At least I can give you this." She slid a sheet of paper across the desk. It was a letter from Nguyen, directing all Voyageur employees to give Pen their complete cooperation. She handed over a second item, an identity badge. "This will give access to all company facilities," Nguyen said. "For your office, you can use a conference room down the hall. I'll show you."

"Nancy, I understand that this project is need-to-know. But there's something I need to know: Who else is working on this?"

"I never said—"

"I know. But I can't be the only investigator you've hired. This looks like an inside job."

Nguyen didn't respond.

"You need a computer geek, somebody from the outside, to track down this defect and, more to the point, track down who has gotten into the VCS system."

She swallowed. "I can't get into that."

Pen took that as confirmation. "Nancy, if you want me to take this job, you can't have me working in the dark, potentially at cross-purposes. That's a dealbreaker."

Nguyen bit her lip. "I promised Stephen I wouldn't tell a soul."

Pen waited.

Nguyen exhaled, then pulled out her phone, scrolling through it. Pen nodded and produced her own phone.

"There," Nancy said, clicking on her screen. "Stephen brought in a young computer whiz to check our databases, to see if somebody has been collecting information about the VC-25-4750 devices. You've got her name, number, and picture."

Pen read the contact information. "LeeAnn Nardelli."

"That's her undercover name. Her real name is Louise Napolitani. Talk to her if you have to, but for God's sake, keep it on the sly. I could get fired if Stephen found out."

Pen nodded and tucked her phone and Nguyen's letter into her purse, which she then stashed on the little shelf underneath the seat of her wheelchair.

"I'm counting on you," Nguyen said. "We need the truth, and we need discretion. Both."

"Right."

Pen left Nguyen's office and rolled down a corridor, passing a series of executive offices, including the one belonging to Stephen Hartsburg. The doorway to the inner office, presumably used by Marilyn Applewhite, was dark. Pen found the conference room that would serve as her makeshift office but didn't go in right away. She continued past the room, and two doors down saw what she was looking for: the break room.

Pen returned to the conference room, set up her laptop and phone, and called James Carter, who remained at home in California.

"Hey, honey. How did it go with Nancy?"

"There's a lot going on here that I don't know about. I hope Nancy doesn't know, either."

"She doesn't. She's a straight shooter. In fact, she's chronically on the outs with Hartsburg for telling him stuff he doesn't want to hear or telling him not to do things he wants to do."

"How about Hartsburg?" Pen asked.

"Smart, but he's an asshole. He'll cut you off at the knees without a second thought."

"Can you make some calls for me? I need you to check your sources in the industry about the VC-25-4750 family of ICDs. They may have some kind of defect." Carter's venture capital business was concentrated in the medical device industry, and many of his clients were based in Minnesota, a center for med tech startups.

"I'll see what I can find out," he said. "It would just be scuttlebutt—nobody can talk specifics."

"Fine." She paused. "James, did you really tell Nancy I was a bull in search of a china shop?"

He just laughed.

Pen's next call was to Marilyn Applewhite, Stephen Hartsburg's assistant. She may have called in sick, but she seemed like a crucial person to talk to. Pen got voicemail and left her a message.

A few minutes later, Pen saw what she had been waiting for: a woman headed for the break room. She gave it a minute, then followed. The woman was thickset, fiftyish, with a helmet of iron gray hair and blue glasses. "Hi," Pen said.

The woman looked up, curious.

"I'm Pen. I'm an attorney, working on a project for Nancy Nguyen. I just started work today."

"Oh, hi. I'm Liz." Underwhelmed. They shook, and Liz filled her mug at the coffeemaker on the counter before sitting down.

Pen reached underneath her chair and produced the box of bagels and donuts she had bought on the way to VCS. "I came prepared," she said, putting the box on the table. "Help yourself."

"Thanks," Liz said, taking a powdered donut. As she chewed, she asked Pen about her project.

"Routine stuff," Pen said, improvising. "An insurance audit to assess the legal exposure of top execs."

"Then you'll probably need to talk to Jack Cornish, the CFO. I'm his assistant."

"Yes, I'll probably need to do that," Pen agreed. "Actually, I'd hoped to talk to Mr. Hartsburg today, but I guess he's out of town and Marilyn is out sick."

Liz shrugged. "I guess. She didn't look sick yesterday. And she seemed to spend a lot of time on the phone, yakking with her sister in Detroit."

"I know it sounds unusual," Pen said, "but I may need to interview the immediate families of some of the top people."

"That may be tough for Mr. Cornish. He's divorced, and his kids live on the coasts."

"How about Mr. Hartsburg?"

"His wife, Claire, is a really nice lady. They live over in Sunfish Lake. But . . ." She lowered her voice. "I don't think they've been doing too well. They're not close, according to Marilyn."

They were interrupted by the arrival of a second woman, named Carla, who proved to be the assistant to a vice-chairman. After introductions, Carla eagerly took a bagel, sat down, and joined the discussion. It didn't take long to establish that Hartsburg had a girlfriend named Tricia who worked for VCS, somewhere in IT. When pressed, both Liz and Carla admitted that several top execs had seemed nervous about potential problems with the VC-25-4750 ICDs. But they seemed much more nervous about next quarter's earnings.

And then break time was over. Both women thanked Pen for the treats and returned to their offices.

Back in the conference room, Pen's phone rang: James.

"There are rumors of a defect with the VC-25-4750 products," he said. "Apparently, something serious that could cause fatalities. If that's true, the FDA will learn about it sooner rather than later; they should be notified by the company, but patients' physicians could report it directly."

"What if the rumors are true?" Pen asked.

"The company would take a huge hit, financially and PR-wise. Shutdowns of production; lawsuits; investigations; recalls. Concerns about their other products. The biggest concern would be if the company covered it up. Then they're in deep trouble."

"Is it possible that Hartsburg may not have known about the defect?"

"Could be. Nancy says he's notorious for not wanting to hear bad news. He regularly shoots the messenger."

Pen described what she had learned in the break room.

"You use the donut trick again?" James asked.

"It always works. I've branched out into bagels."

He laughed.

"Thanks, James. Talk to you tonight."

Pen pulled out her laptop and made notes of what she had learned from the assistants in the break room. Then she went back over her notes of her meeting with Nguyen, wondering what she hadn't been told.

She realized that Nguyen's premise was flawed. Supposedly, no threat of violence or demand for payment had been included in the vanished email – just a vague reference to "karma." There had to be another threat, one that Hartsburg hadn't disclosed. What, then, would be a threat significant enough to make Hartsburg quit and issue a *mea culpa*? Nguyen thought the sender was threatening public exposure of the devices' defect, but that couldn't be right, since public exposure was the entire point of the threat—the goal, not the leverage. Pen had to assume a more serious threat had been made and withheld from Nguyen by Hartsburg, one that presumably was personal to the CEO. But what was it?

A threat to the personal safety of Hartsburg or his family was possible; the CEO had, after all, left town. She'd have to check on his family. The other obvious possibility was a demand for money, in exchange for the emailer's silence. It was a big leap; she'd heard nothing to support that theory. But it was time to find out. She picked up the phone and called Claire Hartsburg.

*   *   *

Pen stopped in the main lobby and bundled up, struggling into her heavy coat and wrapping a scarf around herself. Then she rolled out of the headquarters building, a six-story structure. Next door was a large, two-story building housing IT and research and development. The buildings were situated on a sprawling wooded campus in suburban Eagan, south of Minneapolis and St. Paul, graced by acres of lawns, ponds, and walking trails. Or so she guessed—everything was now snow-covered. Both the parking lot and the buildings themselves seemed sparsely occupied; according to James, large numbers of employees had switched to working from home. Pen, shivering, got into her hand-controlled wheelchair van and drove toward Sunfish Lake, a wealthy suburb not far from the Voyageur campus.

Stephen Hartsburg wasn't talking, but maybe something useful could be learned from his wife. Pen pulled up at the gate in front of a sprawling half-timbered house and announced herself through an intercom. The gate slid open.

Claire Hartsburg, a trim, smiling figure with honey-blonde hair, opened the door for her, and Pen had to wheelie up a short step into the house. They shook. "Pen Wilkinson. Thanks for seeing me, Mrs. Hartsburg."

"No trouble at all," Claire assured her. "Come on in." Pen had told her on the phone that she was doing routine background research for the liability insurance covering Voyageur's officers and directors. Now she displayed her attorney ID and Nancy Nguyen's letter, which wasn't directed to family members, but which she hoped would suffice.

Claire read the letter. "Stephen isn't available."

"I know, but we have just a few questions for immediate family members, too."

"Come in and sit down," Claire said, before realizing her gaffe. "Forgive me—"

Pen smiled. "No problem at all."

Claire led her down a hallway to a family room off the kitchen with a large picture window overlooking the lake. Pen took off her coat, declining refreshments.

"What can I do for you?" Claire asked. She was being accommodating, Pen realized, but not without an undercurrent of suspicion.

"First of all, let me offer my condolences on the death of your father-in-law," Pen said.

"Thank you. It's been hard, for both Stephen and me. Magnus was a brilliant man, an amazingly talented musician.

But so kind and generous—the only father Stephen remembers."

Claire Hartsburg looked wired, unnaturally energetic, perhaps stressed and barely holding it together. Even so, Pen couldn't see any evidence of a physical threat to her or her family.

"I heard that Dr. Danilson's death was sudden."

She nodded. "Yes. He had a bad heart, of course. That's why he had an ICD. Ironic, isn't it?"

Ding, ding, ding. Pen was suddenly on full alert.

"We were told it was a 'cardiac event,'" Claire continued. "But I haven't heard any details."

"I'm so sorry." Pen dearly wanted to ask more questions but decided not to press her luck. She took out a notebook and asked a series of innocuous questions about possible claims against the company and the Hartsburgs personally. Claire answered all at greater length than necessary, apparently just needing to talk. She also glanced over occasionally, warily, at Pen.

Finally, Pen closed her notebook and thanked her host, and they headed to the door. "You have a lovely home, Claire," Pen said.

"Thank you. You know, just a couple of days ago, Stephen asked me what I thought it was worth. I had no idea. And then he asked what he thought our Aspen home could sell for. I asked why he wanted to know, and he just shrugged it off. We also have a place up on Gull Lake. I imagine that's where he is now; he said he needed a few days off."

Curious and more curious, Pen thought. He was thinking about selling their homes? Or mortgaging them?

Pen was zipping up her coat when she felt Claire's hand on her arm. She looked up. Claire hesitated, then said, "I've answered all your questions. And you seem like a nice person. But I need to know why you're really here."

"I told you—"

"Do you know something about Stephen? Something is going on."

Pen took a breath, trying to take in the sudden change of tone and subject. "Yes, something is going on," she said. "But we don't know what. And unfortunately, Mr. Hartsburg is not communicating with us." Pen didn't think Claire was in danger, but there wasn't much she could say to reassure her.

Meanwhile, Claire's façade had collapsed. Tears had formed, and her mascara was running. "He's up there, at Gull Lake," she whispered. "With *her*."

Pen waited.

"With Tricia."

*   *   *

Pen drove on side streets out of Sunfish Lake and noticed a white Mercedes SUV behind her. She got onto Highway 62. So did the Mercedes. After a few miles she took the exit onto Interstate 35E. The Mercedes followed. She slowed down and sped up. The SUV matched her speed. But when she took the exit for Voyageur's headquarters, it sped past, staying on the freeway. Sighing with relief, she pulled into a spot in the Voyageur visitor lot.

Pen sat for a few minutes in the van with the engine and heater running, trying to sort out the things she had learned from Claire. She gave no sign of either her or her husband being under physical threat. But their meeting had left plenty of other unresolved questions. If Magnus Danilson had died from an ICD defect, what did that mean? And how did the sender of the email to Hartsburg know it? And what to make of Hartsburg valuing his homes? He made tens of millions every year, and if Voyageur was being extorted for money, the ransom would presumably come from the company, not the CEO personally. Finally, Claire had confirmed that Hartsburg had a girlfriend named Tricia; what significance could that have for, well, anything?

Still parked in the van, she pulled out her phone and called her nephew, Kenny, barely nineteen, but a serious hacker. After some scrapes with both law enforcement and criminals, he now worked for the good guys, which fortunately included Pen. In his spare time, he was a student at the University of Minnesota. "Hey, Aunt Pen. Are you in town?"

"I am. We'll have to have dinner before I go back. In the meantime, can you do me a favor?"

"Of course." She always hesitated to ask, knowing that Kenny's mother, her sister Marsha, would be furious if she got him into any trouble.

She gave him a brief rundown on Stephen Hartsburg, asking him if he could find the CEO's girlfriend.

"Okay. What's her name?"

"Tricia somebody-or-other. She might be at a residence or resort on Gull Lake, which I presume is in northern Minnesota." *Nothing like nailing the specifics*, she thought.

"I'll give it a shot."

"Thanks."

Pen clicked off. It was time, she thought, to shift her focus inside the company. She pulled up the contact information for Louise Napolitani.

*   *   *

It wasn't hard for Pen to spot Louise Napolitani, or LeeAnn Nardelli, in the Voyageur company cafeteria. Pen glanced once more at the picture Nancy Nguyen had provided as part of Napolitani's contact information, matching it to the young woman

91

at a table near the entrance. Napolitani looked to be in her early twenties, fifteen years younger than Pen. She was a slender five-foot-eight, well short of Pen's six feet, with frizzy brown hair that contrasted with Pen's shoulder-length blonde locks. Studying her more closely, Pen could tell that she was actually very attractive, with an angular face and full lips. She just needed to sharpen her wardrobe a bit, put on a little makeup, and get a decent haircut.

Pen rolled up beside her. "May I join you?"

The woman looked up.

Pen held out her hand. "Pen Wilkinson."

Napolitani looked startled. "I—I'm LeeAnn." She gestured toward the table. "Go ahead."

Pen placed a sandwich and a can of Diet Coke on the table. "Thanks." She clasped her hands in front of her on the table. "We don't have a lot of time, Louise. I know who you are and why you're here. I'm here for the same reason." She held up her phone, showing her the contact information and picture, then handed her Nancy Nguyen's letter.

Napolitani carefully read the letter and looked up. "I don't know. I'm not supposed to talk—"

"Neither am I," Pen said. "But we just don't have time to work at cross-purposes. Let's take it as a given that no one will know we're cooperating. No one. I'd be in as much trouble as you."

Napolitani's features tightened. She looked away, then back at Pen, still uncertain.

"I'm an attorney. Privilege applies," Pen added, knowing her assertion was questionable.

Napolitani seemed to relax a bit. She sipped an energy drink through a straw, then squinted at Pen. "How'd you end up in that wheelchair, anyway?"

Pen felt one of her usual flashes of annoyance. Weezy was like a lot of smart people, she supposed, sometimes oblivious to social niceties. "Car accident."

Napolitani nodded.

"I'll start," Pen said, and then filled her in on her meetings with Nguyen and Claire Hartsburg.

Napolitani returned to her energy drink, then sat for a long moment, seeming to come to a decision. "We really, really have to keep this on the QT. And . . ."

"And?"

"Call me Weezy."

Pen smiled. "Sure, Weezy."

"So, let's talk about this threat to the company. You're saying you can't trust what you heard from Hartsburg? Your own client?"

"My client is the company, not Hartsburg personally." It was a distinction that was growing in importance. "But no," Pen continued, "I don't believe him."

"So, he's a lying dumbass."

"Um, yes."

Weezy, who had been playing with the straw, carefully set it on the table. "Hartsburg asked me to find out whether Voyageur's cardiac device database had been hacked, but he wouldn't say why."

"Well, has it been hacked?" Pen asked.

"Oh, yeah. I could tell that within about ten minutes. All you had to do is look at the biometrics, which didn't match up with the—never mind, you wouldn't understand it."

Pen felt annoyed again. Weezy was probably right—she wouldn't understand it. But still . . .

Weezy continued, "Figuring out who did it will be a lot harder. I suspect an inside job, an employee with a certain level of company access, but not to the cardiac patient DB. But who-ever got in knew what they were doing."

"Can you tell what they were looking for?"

"Still working on that. By the way, I looked up Magnus Danilson, Hartsburg's stepfather. He had a Voyageur ICD, a VC-25-4750."

"Any indication of a malfunction in his device?"

"No way to tell—the doctor's report hasn't been filed yet. You could call up his doctor and ask."

"We'd need a court order and a good reason," Pen said. "Doctor-patient confidentiality survives even if the patient doesn't. But never mind—you wouldn't understand."

Weezy's look went from annoyed to amused to eye-rolling in about a two-second span. She shrugged, fidgeted, looked around the cafeteria.

Pen tried to process the news about Danilson. He'd had a Voyageur ICD, and he'd died from a cardiac incident. Due to a device malfunction? Maybe. But even if it wasn't, his death could be seen by the sender as "karma." At the very least, it would be a hell of a coincidence.

Pen's cell phone buzzed. She glanced at the screen; she'd gotten a text from Kenny. "Just a minute," she said.

Patricia Doran, currently at a dwelling on Gull Lake, near Brainerd. So is Hartsburg.

The text included a Minneapolis address and a phone number.

She glanced at the screen in disbelief. How on earth did Kenny find out this stuff?

She didn't want to know.

Pen replaced her phone and reported the text's news to Weezy.

"Hartsburg has a girlfriend," Weezy said. "So what?"

"I don't know. But it seems important somehow. Wait—can you check to see if this woman has a Voyageur device?"

Weezy shrugged. "I suppose. Seems like a hell of a long shot, though."

"Yes."

"And I'm not sure what it would mean if she did."

"I'm not, either."

Weezy stood up. "Forward me the text with her identifying information. I'll let you know."

"Thanks—stay in touch." Weezy started to walk away when a horrifying thought gripped Pen's brain.

"Weezy?"

She turned back.

"I'm just thinking out loud here," Pen said, "and I know how it sounds, but . . ."

Weezy waited.

"We know the patient database was hacked, right? That could mean somebody is researching defects in the VC-25-4750 devices on the sly. Or . . ."

She waited.

"These ICDs are connected to the internet, right?"

"Sort of indirectly," Weezy said.

"And they have software."

"Obviously."

"Could somebody intentionally hack into these devices and tamper with them? Shut them down, or give the patient a shock?"

Weezy's expression gave her away. She'd thought about it, too. "Have you seen any evidence of that?"

"No," Pen replied.

Weezy sat down again. "It would be a really long shot—heck, probably impossible. Science fiction, when you think about it. But I could think of a couple of ways to try it."

An icy sensation made its way hesitantly down Pen's damaged spine. "You'd need access to the patient database to pull it off, right? Or at least to target individual patients?"

Weezy nodded slowly. "And we know at least one unauthorized person has gotten access recently."

They looked at each other for a long moment.

"Are we worried yet?" Pen said.

*   *   *

As Pen left the Voyageur campus, she called Kenny to thank him for the information on Tricia. "So, Hartsburg is up at the lake," she said.

"His phone is, for sure."

"You mean you can't confirm his actual presence with enhanced satellite imagery and facial recognition?"

"Well . . ."

"I'm just kidding, Kenny." But she wondered if he could do it. "You'd be interested in the person I just met with," Pen said. "She's from MIT and does computer forensics, among other things. She has an unusual name: Weezy."

"Holy crap," Kenny said. "*That* Weezy? Who took down IdeoPulse?"

"I didn't know she was famous."

"Not famous," Kenny said. "Legendary. Wow."

"Stay handy," Pen said.

Pen spent the night at the condo owned by James Carter in downtown Minneapolis. They used the place frequently, on business trips or visits to Kenny or James's teenage daughter, who lived with her stepfather in a Minneapolis suburb. Increasingly, she also came here just to see friends; Minnesota had become a second home for her. Now she lay in bed, tossing and turning,

96

combining and recombining all the mental puzzle pieces constituting the Voyageur Cardiac case, knowing that some of the pieces were missing altogether. And knowing that she needed answers, fast.

*   *   *

Pen's phone woke her up the next morning. She didn't recognize the number.

"Hello, this is Pen."

"Good morning," said Weezy. "Do you have a minute?"

"Sure." She tried to clear her head.

"There's a guy here at VCS that I think we need to look into. He's one of the best programmers in the company—maybe in the industry. But he's a serious creep, and he's showing a lot of interest in my work."

"So, he might be able to hijack an ICD and to exploit that in an extortion scheme."

"Definitely."

"What's the name?"

"Justin Biggs. B-I-G-G-S."

"Okay. I'll see what I can find out."

"In the meantime, I'll see if I can find time to look through the patient database some more."

"Go for it."

*   *   *

At 9:00 a.m., Pen returned to her makeshift office at VCS, carrying a latte she had bought at a nearby Caribou coffee shop, and pulled out her laptop. She Googled Justin Biggs, narrowed down her search to Minnesota, and found his LinkedIn page and a possible home address, but not much more. She found his internal phone number and gave him a call.

"Biggs."

"Justin? My name is Pen Wilkinson. I'm working for Legal."

"What, did I do something wrong?"

"Not that I know of. I just have a few questions."

"About what?"

"About your work on the 4750."

"You have a problem, talk to my boss about it."

"I have a letter which grants me—"

"You hard of hearing? I said talk to my boss. Is that a really hard concept to understand?"

Pen paused, took a breath. "All right. Who's your boss?"

"You're a really smart lawyer. Look it up." He disconnected.

Pen took a few more deep breaths, thinking about her next move. She wasn't going to talk to Biggs's boss; her inquiries had to be targeted and discreet.

Her phone chirped: a text from Weezy.

Tricia Doran has a VC-25-4750.

Pen's stomach gave a lurch.

Somebody was messing with VCS, its patients, and maybe even its CEO, big-time. The need to talk to Biggs was urgent.

*   *   *

At 6:00 p.m., Pen stationed herself in the parking lot of a condo complex in Burnsville, a suburb adjacent to Eagan, armed with the picture of Justin Biggs she had found on his LinkedIn page. She'd found his address on Google. As she watched the entrance, she found her mind wandering to the subject of implanted cardiac devices, a subject to which she had never before given the slightest thought. Could they really be used as weapons? It was a scenario that had never come up in her dealings with Nguyen, but Weezy thought it might be possible. For a company and a group of employees who were committed to saving lives, it was the ultimate nightmare.

Her phone rang. "Pen, it's Weezy. I checked out that Justin guy I told you about. In fact, I actually walked over to his desk and talked to him."

"And?"

"I'd say he's definitely a person of interest for your extortionist. He's an asshole, for sure, but he's got a lot of knowledge about the 4750. I'd be interested in your take on him."

"He blew me off when I called him. But I'm ready to take another shot in person. I may be able to do that momentarily."

"Watch out. I'm told he has an ugly temper. In the meantime, I'll keep looking. Talk later."

A red Mustang pulled into the parking lot. A man got out and headed for the entrance. *Who the hell drives a flashy sports car in Minnesota in winter?* Pen wondered. She quickly opened the van's door, lowered its profile, and extended the ramp. By the time she made it to the steps, the man, wearing a parka and watch cap, was already at the door, his keys out.

"Justin!" Pen called.

He turned around.

"Could we talk, please?" she asked.

He came slowly down the steps; she could see now it was the man from the LinkedIn page, a nondescript guy, average height, stocky, with a short beard and dark complexion.

"Who are you?" he demanded.

"My name is Pen Wilkinson. We talked this afternoon. I'm an attorney for Voyageur Cardiac Systems."

"Oh, you again. VCS can go to hell."

"They sign your paychecks."

He snorted. "A bunch of clowns."

She handed him her card. "We need to talk about deaths resulting from Voyageur device malfunctions."

He glanced at the card, pocketed it, and squinted at her. "Did Larson send you?"

"Who's Larson?"

"I had nothing to do with any deaths. I've had a guy named Larson on my ass, claiming I knew something about the death of somebody."

"Who was it? And how—"

"You can pound sand." He turned on his heel and went up the steps and into the building, slamming the door behind him.

Pen stared at the closed door. *That went well.* What did she do now? If Biggs was guilty of something, she didn't know how to prove it. If he was, in fact, innocent, she was nowhere.

She returned to the van, pulled out of the lot, and spotted a white Mercedes SUV parked on the other side of the street. The driver wasn't visible. When Pen started to turn onto the street, the SUV pulled out of its parking spot and sped off before she could read its license number

Pen made a U-turn and followed but soon lost the vehicle in the late rush-hour traffic. *Damn.* Who the hell was messing with her? And what to do about it?

*   *   *

She drove back to VCS headquarters and returned to the executive floor, where she found Liz, one of the administrators who had enjoyed her donuts.

"Hi," Pen said. "Just wondering if Marilyn is back in the office yet."

"She left," Liz replied.

"You mean she was back in the office?"

"Long enough to do a few hours' work and then retire."

"Wait a minute," Pen said. "She returns from being sick, then comes back long enough to retire?"

"Effective immediately."

"Isn't that strange?"

Liz studied Pen, giving her a disappointed look. No more donuts. "Sure. She talked about retiring every once in a while, but to just pull the plug like that—it was weird, especially with Mr. Hartsburg being gone, too."

"What are her plans?"

"I don't know, but she got out of Dodge fast. I don't think she's in Minnesota."

Back in her conference room office, Pen pulled out her phone, called Kenny, and asked him to find Marilyn Applewhite.

"Any idea where she might be?"

"If she's not at home, she has a sister in the Detroit area. Look there."

"Got it."

Chapter 8

Hawke

In Henri Hawke's line of work, desperation begets opportunity, and Stephen Hartsburg, the man at the other end of the telephone line, was desperate.

Alternating between anger and whining, Hartsburg railed about the difficulty of running a multi-billion-dollar medical company, about the impossibility of knowing every flaw or problem, and the sheer underhandedness of the blackmail he was facing. Somewhere in his diatribe, he asked Hawke's help in raising $30 million for ransom, but nowhere was there a hint of remorse or a speck of accountability.

Hawke listened, bemused. He could raise the money, even in the short time that Hartsburg's extortionist had dictated, but he wasn't ready to offer his services to the self-righteous CEO. Not yet.

"I truly regret that I am unable to provide assistance," Hawke cooed into the mouthpiece of his headset.

"I . . . I . . . I'll pay you twice your usual fee," Hartsburg sputtered.

"It is not the size of my fee that is the issue," he responded. "It is the repayment of the thirty million you wish to borrow. The people with whom I do business do not make loans where the prospect of repayment is so bleak, and a default is not something you should even consider. The consequences would be, shall we say, quite unpleasant."

"But I have assets I can pledge!" screeched the panicky CEO.

"Remember," Hawke responded in his silky voice, thick with an accent that hinted of both French and Spanish, with a frosting of Catalan. "I know of your assets. I moved them offshore for you. The sender of this annoying email has promised to eviscerate both you *and* your company. If there is substance behind this threat, a safe assumption since you are calling me, it's likely that you will be imprisoned and your company will be only a tragic memory. Your offshore assets are less than half of what you will owe, and the rest will be worthless."

"My house, and my ski lodge . . ." Hartsburg started, but Hawke interrupted.

"My people are not in the business of real estate foreclosures. They deal only in liquid assets."

Hartsburg had no response.

Hawke waited, counting slowly to ten, before breaking the silence. "Perhaps you would do better to hire me to locate your blackmailer. For that it will cost you only my usual one-hundred-thousand-dollar fee."

Hartsburg grudgingly agreed.

"I will come to Minnesota on Tuesday," Hawke said. "Be at the Mall of America at four p.m. your local time. I will call and tell you where to meet me. Bring my fee in euros, please."

*   *   *

Hawke strolled through the massive shopping mall, glancing at the huge indoor amusement park at its center, glad for the respite from the below-zero temperature outside. He took the escalator to the second level, where an anxious Hartsburg waited for him at a gelato shop. Hawke nodded to his client, then ordered *cioccolato all'arancia,* which he savored while listening to a second helping of Hartsburg's whining.

By the time Hawke took his last spoonful of the chocolate-orange delight and had inspected the briefcase filled with euros to confirm that his fee had been paid in full, he had learned that Hartsburg's personal administrative assistant, Marilyn Applewhite, had taken sick leave on the day the email arrived and had not returned to work.

Hawke picked up the briefcase, nodded to Hartsburg, and left.

*   *   *

It took him less than twenty-four hours to find Applewhite, hiding out at her sister's home in Grosse Pointe, Michigan, a toney suburb of Detroit that boasted miles of Lake St. Clair shoreline and quiet neighborhoods.

It was not the sort of place where you would expect to find a short, rotund man, smelling of pomade and dressed in an expensive suit and a fedora, sitting at your kitchen table when you get up in the morning.

Applewhite, her bottle-blonde hair in disarray, dressed in a pink robe and fuzzy slippers, froze as she walked around the corner into the kitchen. "Who the hell are you?" she blurted in a gravelly voice born of too many cigarettes.

"Do not be alarmed, madam," Hawke answered. "I am a humble messenger, here to urge you to return to Voyageur Cardiac . . . for a day . . . or two."

"What? Why . . .?"

Hawke interrupted, his voice more authoritative: "Please sit down, madam, and I will explain the very good reasons for you to do as I ask." His glance downward drew Applewhite's attention to his hand resting on the kitchen table, which he slid aside, revealing a Ruger LCP II mini-pistol.

104

"You threatening me with that little peashooter?" she flared. "It's gonna take more than that. Get your ass out of my house before I call the cops."

"First of all, it is not your house," Hawke said with a small laugh, impressed by the woman's *chutzpah*. "And do not let the size fool you," he added, cocking his head and swinging his feet back and forth. "Neither in the man nor in the gun."

Applewhite snorted, a scowl still on her face. "I've thrown bigger assholes than you out of my office, and that gun doesn't scare me."

"It was not my intent to scare you nor to do you harm, but I do need your undivided attention," Hawke purred, patting the five-inch-long pistol lying on the table. He nodded toward the chairs.

Reluctantly, she slid into one of them on the opposite side of the kitchen table, her eyes darting back and forth, looking for an escape route or, perhaps, a kitchen knife.

"You work for the CEO of Voyageur Cardiac, Stephen Hartsburg . . ."

Applewhite started to say something, but Hawke held up his hand to stop her.

". . . as his executive assistant. You, and you alone, are responsible for who communicates with him, and who does not. Now, Mr. Hartsburg, and in fact all of Voyageur, is facing a dilemma. There is a person trying to extort money from Mr. Hartsburg because of a flaw in a device, a flaw that has been kept secret by the company. This person claims that he, or she, sent communications to Mr. Hartsburg many times but never received acknowledgement or reply. Now, you have . . . shall we say . . . taken an unplanned vacation, coincidentally at the same time that Mr. Hartsburg received a demand for payment of thirty million dollars from this person. But you know this, of course, because you saw all those communications, including the one demanding thirty million."

"I . . ."

"This does not at all look good, Ms. Applewhite, or may I call you Marilyn?"

Applewhite glared at him. "What do you want?

"If you stay on vacation, Marilyn, who do you think is going to become the scapegoat for this corporate *peccadillo*?" Hawke fixed the woman with a pitying look. "Surely, you are familiar with situations where the guilty CEO goes scot-free, while the hard-working assistant molders away in prison."

She straightened in her chair, composing herself. "I did not . . ."

"There is no need to plead your case to me," Hawke said, again interrupting. "I am simply a messenger. A messenger who comes to you with an opportunity to be a hero in this drama, rather than the victim."

"How? What opportunity?" The tone in Applewhite's voice indicated interest.

"I am attempting to find the person who is threatening Mr. Hartsburg. If I can find that person, we may be able to avoid the nastiness that is being threatened. But I need your help to do this. I need access to your emails, your calendar, and any other records you may have kept about attempted communications with Mr. Hartsburg over the past year or two. I also may need access to company personnel files. If you come back to work for a day or two, you can provide me with access to all that material."

"That may help you and Voyageur, but it won't make me a hero," she snapped. "I will just go back to running interference for that pompous featherweight. I'd rather face you and your pea shooter than do that."

Hawke observed her for a moment, impressed by Marilyn as he always was by fearless women. He could see why Hartsburg had chosen her as his gatekeeper.

"Your assistance in locating this person will be greatly appreciated by Mr. Hartsburg and his board of directors," he replied. "It will allow you to properly submit your resignation, and in turn, receive appropriate severance for your years of loyal service.

"More importantly, it will enable you to discreetly place an appropriately-worded memo in your personnel file, with a copy in a safe place, of course, absolving you of any wrongdoing with respect to this faulty medical device. And, of course, including anything else you wish . . . to set the record straight."

Applewhite nodded. For the first time, her expression softened.

"The only thing I require is your absolute discretion with respect to the information you provide me. Only you and I are to know this."

"Why?" Applewhite sat back. "Aren't you employed by Voyageur?"

"Part of my obligation is to provide management with plausible deniability when it comes to whomever the extortionist may be, in the event we need to deal with him . . . or her . . . outside normal channels."

"Or give you leverage to squeeze a little more juice out of the orange?" Applewhite offered.

"I am hurt that you would think that of me," Hawke said in mock indignation. "As I said, I am just a messenger."

"A messenger with a gun."

Hawke shrugged, his eyes twinkling. "And perhaps a bit more. Did I mention that there is a bonus for your cooperation and discretion?" He slid an envelope across the kitchen table. "In expectation that a woman of your intelligence would see the merit of what I have requested, I brought this for you."

Applewhite opened the envelope and riffled through an inch-thick stack of $100 bills. An airline ticket to Minneapolis was the last item in the envelope. She nodded. "Now you're speaking my language. But you should know you're not the only one digging around in Voyageur's shit."

Hawke cocked his head. An unspoken question.

"It's a damn free-for-all," Applewhite continued. "A few days ago, Hartsburg hired some whiz kid to find out who hacked Voyageur's database, and there's also an attorney nosing around inside the company looking for God knows what."

"What's his name? The attorney."

"It's a her, and her name is Doris Wilkinson. She goes by 'Pen.'"

"Exactly what is she doing?"

"Not really sure, but it has something to do with the black-mail attempt," Applewhite answered. "According to my source, she's smart as a whip and has solved some major crimes, and she's easy to recognize. She's in a wheelchair. In her mid to late thirties."

"Tell me about the hacker."

"I think Hartsburg hired her to find out who hacked our database. She came in trying to keep everything a secret. Said her name was LeeAnn Nardelli, but her real name is Louise Napoli-tani. Goes by Weezy."

"Perhaps when you return to Voyageur you could locate both of these ladies for me. I would like to talk to them."

Applewhite looked down at the envelope and riffled through the currency.

"Is that a yes?" Hawke prodded.

"Yes," she replied, nearly in a whisper.

"By the way, have you been contacted by either the young hacker or the attorney in the wheelchair?"

Applewhite looked him in the eye. "No."

Hawke studied her for a long moment, then stood up. "Very well."

"I'll see you in Minneapolis," she said. "But only for two days. No more."

"Beyond two days," Hawke responded in an evocative tone, "there might be a place in my organization for someone with your talent."

*   *   *

The next morning Applewhite was back in her office at Voyageur, welcomed with open arms by management and co-workers. Hartsburg was notably absent.

By mid-afternoon, she had provided Hawke with a list of thirty-one people that she had prevented from communicating with Hartsburg in the previous twenty-four months. Eight of them were underlings at Voyageur, employees with whom Hartsburg could not be bothered.

Hawke spent the evening flipping through the personnel files of the eight, then doing research on them via the internet. He also took the time to do research on Pen Wilkinson and Louise Napolitani.

Three of the eight Voyageur employees were IT savvy: two senior programmers and an electrical engineer. He focused on them first, looking through their social media, then returning to their personnel files to confirm that the wife of one of the three, a senior programmer named Ralph Calder, had died two years ago.

He found the late Mrs. Calder's full name in her husband's personnel file, then found her now-defunct Facebook page on his computer. It confirmed she had a heart condition. A deep dive into Calder's Facebook and Twitter accounts confirmed that the death was sudden and unexpected. Soon after his wife's death, he'd disappeared from social media.

Hawke's review of Calder's personnel file provided one further piece of vital information. Calder had been a key figure in the early development of ICD model VC-25-4750.

*   *   *

Small, dirty windows effectively prevented the mid-afternoon winter sun from adding warmth to the room. Only red, blue and green neon signs touting this beer and that liquor, and yellowish ceiling lights, lit the dingy bar that smelled of yesterday's beer. Decades of cigarette smoke oozed from every surface.

At the bar, an empty shot glass and a half-filled beer bottle kept company with several empty longnecks sitting in front of a lone man, lost in his own thoughts.

A sheet of paper suddenly appeared on the bar before him, causing him to jerk, startled. He turned, unsteadily, to see who had put it there.

Hawke stood, looking up at the man on the stool. "We need to talk. We have mutual interests," Hawke said.

"What?" Calder asked, looking down at the short, rotund man whose clothes and perfumed fragrance were clearly out of place. "Who the fuck are you?" The words were slurred.

"It is not so important who I am. It is you who are important," Hawke said, hoisting himself onto the bar stool next to Calder. "I believe this is your handiwork." He pointed at the piece of paper in front of Calder.

Calder glanced at the sheet containing his email to Hartsburg and momentarily recoiled. "I don't know what you're talking about. I've never . . ."

"Oh, but you do!" Hawke interjected. "You are Ralph Calder, whose beloved wife died suddenly as a result of her Voyageur ICD's failure. You do not believe the company's explanation for that death, that the leads were knocked loose in an auto accident. You believe the device's software, on which you worked, was faulty. Management refused to listen to your complaint. And you seek vengeance."

Calder stared at him, mouth open.

"I, on the other hand, am the person who has been asked to provide you with thirty million dollars."

Calder rose from the stool, a deer in the headlights. A tall, gaunt man pushing fifty, he towered somewhat unsteadily over Hawke. "How'd you know about all that?" he slurred.

"Sit down, Mr. Calder," Hawke ordered in a whisper, the brittle smile on his face emphasizing the warning in his voice. "I am about to make you a very rich man. It would be most impolite for you to leave."

"Fuck you, I don't…"

The bartender, aware of the impending altercation, side-stepped quickly down the bar. "Everything okay here? Can I get you something?"

"Is fine," Calder mumbled, sitting back on his stool and un-clenching his fists. "I'm good," he said, eyeing his half-full beer bottle.

"Perhaps we should move to a booth, away from prying eyes and ears," Hawke suggested.

"I'm not going anywhere with you. Get the hell away from me."

"Very well," Hawke said, "but when I leave, your thirty million goes with me." He slid off the barstool and started for the door.

"Wait a minute," Calder slurred, panic showing in his gray eyes. "I guess we can talk." Hawke altered his direction toward the booths in the back of the bar. Calder followed.

Once settled, Hawke stared coldly across the booth. "We will not just *talk*," he said. "You will tell me everything I want to know.

If you don't, or I don't like your answers, you will never collect the thirty million dollars. And you will be counting your life expectancy in days, not years. Do you understand?"

Calder looked frozen. He tried to speak, but when nothing came out, he nodded, his unruly brown hair flopping back and forth.

"Your email refers to a charitable contribution," Hawke said, his tone moving from threatening to friendly in a heartbeat. "To whom is this contribution to be made?"

"I . . . I . . . I . . . haven't got it in place yet," Calder stuttered.

"So, it's really not a charitable contribution at all. You are trying to make yourself look like a hero."

"I don't care about the money, 'cept to take that asshole, Hartsburg, down!"

"Who is to be the benefactor of this sizable sum, if not you?" Hawke asked. "This is a fortune many would kill for."

Calder looked at him, his eyes fighting to focus. "Anybody that got killed because that asshole, Hartsburg, wouldn' listen . . . wouldn' even talk to me. He killed my wife. If he had listened to me, Lois would still be alive. His minions put out a cover story that it wasn't the firmware, that her leads got knocked loose. Total bullshit. I should know—I helped develop the firmware. I had to stop Hartsburg before that fucking machine killed more people. He wouldn' take it off the market 'cause of the money they were making. Hundreds of millions."

"What about the wife of the doctor who implanted the device in your wife? Did Alice Holmgren die because of the defect?"

Calder blinked several times. "How'd you know 'bout her?"

"I know everything, Mr. Calder. I know when your wife, Lois, had her implant, and when she died. I know that you are a devout man of faith who has fallen on hard times and into the bottle since Lois passed away. I know your very soul, Mr. Calder.

So, what about Alice Holmgren? Did she die because of the defect in VC- 23-4750?"

Calder's head seemed to shrink into his shoulders as he shook it.

"That was an accident. I was just testing it out, and, well . . ."

"And what about Dr. Danilson? Was that an accident?"

Calder's jaw muscles tightened. "That was collateral damage. Sometimes in war there's collateral damage, and I'm at war with Hartsburg. He wouldn' fuckin' listen, so someone close to him had to die so he'd pull VC-25-4750 off the market."

For a fleeting moment, Hawke thought about demanding to know exactly how Calder had managed to use these devices for blackmail. But he rejected the idea. He probably wouldn't understand the technical details, he told himself. But the truth was, he was better off not knowing.

Calder, looking exhausted, sat back in the booth, his hands folded and his head bowed. After a minute he sat up, shrugged his shoulders and swiveled his head to loosen the muscles.

"Hey, Charlie," he called out. "How 'bout another beer and a bump. And somethin' for my friend." He looked at Hawke.

"Pernod?" Hawke asked the bartender. "No? Do you have ouzo?"

He turned to Calder, who now had a crooked smile on his face, as if he'd repented and been forgiven.

"I am still curious about the charitable contribution," Hawke said. "Curious as to who or what a principled man such as yourself would see as worthy of such a large sum."

"I wanna set up a watchdog organization so that companies like Voyageur can't get away with shit like this anymore."

Hawke sat back in the booth. "And you'd be the chief watchdog?" he asked after a pause.

"Me . . . and some other people who know this industry and know the kind of shit these companies pull."

An idealist without a clue, Hawke thought.

"You're brilliant; an IT guy," he said. "You know how to make electronic things that I can't even imagine, but that is a far cry from operating a multi-million-dollar organization like you're envisioning."

"I . . . I haven't figured that out yet," Calder stammered. The conversation paused as the bartender delivered the drinks.

"Perhaps I can help you with that," Hawke said after the bartender left. "I can help you set up a discreet, offshore operation that will solve those problems. You see, I am here not only to provide you with the thirty million dollars, but also to help you fulfill your dream and keep you out of prison."

At the word "prison" Calder sat up straight. "I'm not going to prison. What I did, I did to save lives. I'm a hero. They don't put heroes in prison."

Hawke nodded, seeing no benefit in debating with the delusional drunk. He handed Calder a business card. "I'll be in contact in the next day or two to set up the delivery of the funds," he said. "The business card is in case you need to reach me." He left without drinking the ouzo.

*   *   *

Back in his hotel room, Hawke put in a call to Hartsburg. "I have the attention of your blackmailer," he said.

"You found them? Who is it?"

"I have made contact through an intermediary, and we are setting up a meeting."

"Where is the meeting? I'm going to be there," Hartsburg declared.

"Unfortunately," Hawke responded in his best soothing tone, "a condition of the meeting is that you *not* be there. It will take place in the next day or two."

"But . . ."

"This meeting is the first step to save your company and your reputation," Hawke said. "It would be foolish to snuff out this opportunity before we've had the chance to explore it."

There was quiet on the other end of the line. "What about the money?" Hartsburg finally asked.

"It seems that they intend to set up a watchdog organization to assure that nothing like VC-25-4750 happens again, and they are going to use your thirty million dollars to fund it."

"But I don't *have* thirty million dollars," Hartsburg whined.

"If Voyageur can be saved, I may have someone who would be willing to provide the funds," Hawke answered.

After they hung up, Hawke switched burner phones and left messages with several of his international contacts: *Seeking $35 million. In transit 48 hours. 5% plus $350,000 finder's fee.*

*   *   *

The next morning a sober and hesitant Calder called Hawke. At Hawke's suggestion, they met at a French restaurant in St. Paul.

"I am truly sorry about yesterday," Calder apologized as he spread butter on a piece of French bread. "It had been a particularly bad day. I found your card this morning. About all I remember is that you said you have Hartsburg's money and would help me set up a company to monitor the cardiac implant industry. Can you do that?"

"I can, but it will not be easy." Hawke let the moment linger while he took a bite of his *croque monsieur*. The unintelligible voices of the early-afternoon patrons, punctuated with occasional laughter and the clinking of wine glasses, filled the void. Calder buttered the same piece of bread for the second time.

"Structuring your enterprise will not be the difficult part," Hawke said after taking a sip of Sancerre and patting his lips with the linen napkin. "The problem is, thirty million dollars is too little to fund an enterprise designed to monitor the cardiac device industry. You'll burn through that in the first year."

Calder took a bite of his now twice-buttered bread.

"We could start out smaller," Calder offered.

"There is no *smaller* in what you are contemplating," Hawke responded. "You uncover the flaw in the first version of VC-25-4750, and when you try to stop it, you'll be immediately buried in a lawsuit that will chew through your thirty million in a heartbeat."

"Then I want a hundred million."

"That would put Voyageur out of business, or at the least, force it to file bankruptcy. But you don't want to put companies out of business," Hawke reasoned. "If that's your goal, they'll fight you tooth and nail. Your watchdog will be short-lived, buried in paperwork and legal costs. What you really want is to make sure they do things the right way. You want the company's cooperation, not its hostility. You want Voyageur to fix VC-25-4750 so no one else suffers your wife's fate. Isn't that what Lois would want? Shouldn't that be her legacy?"

As Calder absorbed Hawke's words, their waiter appeared at the table.

"Can I get you anything else?"

"Another glass of wine for me, *s'il vous plait*, and another beer for my friend," Hawke answered. Calder shook his head.

"I've had enough."

After the waiter left, he looked at Hawke. "You're right. I want Lois's legacy to be that she improved health care, not that she destroyed it."

"In that case," Hawke said, "I suggest you modify your demand to require Voyageur to pull VC-25-4750 off the market with an acknowledgment that it has flaws, and with a pledge that it will bring out a new version without the flaws, one that has been approved by your watchdog company."

"I want a public admission of guilt from Hartsburg!" Calder said in a forced whisper, anger boiling back to the surface. "I want that son of a bitch to suffer like he's made me suffer. I want him behind bars."

Hawke stared at him for a long moment, then said in measured tones: "You should not be so eager to ascribe guilt to another." He paused, giving Calder's rage a chance to subside. "I understand your thirst for retribution. I have had that same thirst from time to time, but I have learned that how you seek it must be prudent, patient."

The rage faded from Calder's eyes.

"Let's call Hartsburg's confession an apology," Hawke suggested. "We'll word it so that he expresses his sorrow for Lois's death, while admitting he has become aware of the flaw in VC-25-4750 and is withdrawing it from the marketplace. He'll also express his hope that nothing like this ever happens again and will promise that Voyageur will vet all future medical devices through your organization.

"This apology *will not* be made public . . . *at this time*. If Hartsburg or Voyageur ever breaks that promise, or if you are ever charged with any crime related to this, we'll make the apology public, which will unleash a torrent of lawsuits and bring Voyageur to its knees . . . and send Hartsburg to prison."

Calder nodded. "That's smart," he said. "I can live with that, but what about the money?"

"You'll still get the thirty million. It will be enough to get your organization off the ground, build the infrastructure and start investigating, but it's not enough to take any action. That will have to wait until you have additional funding."

"I meant, when will I get the thirty million?"

"When you have established your charitable organization," Hawke replied, "unless you have established the organization since we talked yesterday."

"Yesterday I don't remember. Is that part of what you can help me with?"

"I will, but it will take a few days. Patience, Mr. Calder. It is a virtue that will bring a reward far beyond your most extravagant dreams."

He watched Calder walk away, feeling increasingly curious about the special leverage the man apparently had over Hartsburg and Voyageur Cardiac Systems. He apparently had some ability to predict device failures, or even, perhaps, to make them happen. The threat had been enough to make Stephen Hartsburg desperate to raise the entire amount demanded. Tremendous leverage, indeed.

*   *   *

In an Uber on the return to his hotel, Hawke checked messages on his international phone. There were several asking for elaboration on the $35 million request he had floated. One simply said, "I have someone" and left a phone number. The country and area codes indicated that the call had come from Ljubljana, Slovenia.

Hawke pursed his lips. He knew the area: castles and rivers, striking architecture, truly a beautiful place, but he couldn't think of anyone there with whom he had done business, nor of any clandestine financial sources in that location. Was the message legitimate? Or a setup? His thoughts drifted to Interpol.

On its face, there was nothing illegal about his request, but he had to assume that Interpol was, or would become, aware of it. He decided to wait before returning the call. Instead, he again called Hartsburg.

"Do you know who the blackmailer is?" was the CEO's first question.

"Not yet," Hawke lied. "They have taken very elaborate measures to protect their identity, but we should know soon. I had a productive negotiation with their proxy. I confirmed that their interest is, indeed, the establishment of a watchdog entity for the medical device industry. While there is no progress relative to reducing the amount of money being demanded, I was able to negotiate more favorable terms on several other matters.

"First, there will be no public statement or confession by you, or anyone associated with Voyageur. I have persuaded them that it is not in the best interest of this soon-to-be-minted watchdog enterprise to force Voyageur out of business."

Hawke could hear an audible sigh of relief from Hartsburg.

"Instead, there will be a private apology from you . . ."

"I *will not* . . ."

"Please, Monsieur, do not interrupt. Wait until you have heard the totality of what I have accomplished on your behalf. Then we will discuss it."

Hawke paused. There was only heavy breathing from the other end of the call.

"Very well, then," he continued. "As I said, there will be a carefully worded private apology, and there will also be mutual covenants binding all parties, eschewing any legal action, civil or criminal, and any form of disparagement. All of this will ensure that Voyageur survives, unscathed, as will you and your reputation. And, of course, you will have to remove the device from the market, or recall it, as soon as possible.

"In addition, there will be a contract between Voyageur and this new watchdog organization to do business in the future, *and* a public acknowledgment that you, personally, provided the funds that allowed the nonprofit to get started. So, you see, Mr. Hartsburg, what at first felt like extortion has now been turned into a magnanimous charitable contribution on your part . . . and to allow the oversight of your own industry, no less."

Hawke waited for Hartsburg's reaction. And waited.

"Great," Hartsburg finally said. "I'll be a big hero, but I'll be ruined financially. I'll have to liquidate everything I have to come up with thirty million dollars."

"Ah, but don't you see?" Hawke replied. "With Voyageur still in operation and you still the CEO, I can now raise the money for you."

"Maybe I don't need you," Hartsburg said. "I can probably go to my bank and borrow the money."

"Perhaps," Hawke answered. "If you can find a bank that will lend you what is essentially the equivalent of your real net worth . . . in less than a week. And there is the matter of disclosing in your personal financial statement the fifteen million dollars you have parked offshore. Disclosing it will likely raise dreadful tax issues. On the other hand, to fail to disclose it to your friendly banker is criminal fraud. And, oh, there is the 10Q disclosure that will be required in Voyageur's annual security filing. The public pledge of your Voyageur stock to a regulated banking institution for a thirty-million-dollar personal loan should make quite the splash in the stock market."

Again, there was silence.

Hawke broke it by saying: "You know my number. Call me if your banking endeavor doesn't work out."

"No! Wait! You're right," Hartsburg sighed. His voice had lost its edge. "Can you raise the money without it going public?"

"But of course," Hawke answered. "Discretion and secrecy are my stock in trade. But you already know that."

*   *   *

It was past noon when Hawke's call with Hartsburg wrapped up. He ordered room service, settled back in the only comfortable chair in his hotel room, and flipped through a magazine focused on local shopping, food, and entertainment. He looked for dance clubs but found none. *Too cold,* he thought. *One cannot dance when one's limbs are frozen. What do people do in this intemperate environment?*

His food came, and he pushed it around the plate, wishing he had braved the elements and gone to one of the French restaurants he had seen in the magazine. He made a vow to never do another deal in Minnesota in the winter. He finally pushed the plate away and looked at his watch: 1:00 p.m. That would be 8:00 p.m. in Slovenia. He dialed the number from the phone message.

"Aalo?"

"This is an international call for the on-duty commander of the Ljubljana Policija station. Please connect me," Hawke ordered, speaking through a handkerchief covering the phone.

"What?

"Is this the *policija* station in Ljubljana?" Hawke repeated.

"Uh. No." The party on the other end hung up.

Out of the night stand beside his bed Hawke took a new phone, one of four he had bought the previous day at a local Walmart. He dialed the number again. As expected, no one answered. He would call again at 2:00 a.m. using a third phone.

*   *   *

"Aalo?" It was the same voice from thirteen hours earlier.

"What time is it?" Hawke asked, this time not disguising his voice. "And how is the weather in Trieste?"

"I am in Ljubljana. Who is this?"

"You answered my inquiry. Thirty-five million dollars. You can call me Henri."

"Mr. Henri, I welcome your call." The voice was suddenly business-like. "I am Branko Horvat."

"So, you are Croatian," Hawke said.

"How do you know?"

"Your surname. Horvat. Half of Croatia is named Horvat."

"Not quite," he laughed, "but, yes, there are many of us. I've lived in Ljubljana for twenty years. Not so many Horvats here."

"Your message said you have a source," Hawke said, bringing the conversation back on point. "Are you the source, or is it someone you know?"

"An acquaintance . . . with a trust."

"With thirty-five million in available funds? Tell me more about your acquaintance."

"Tell me about the borrower," Horvat countered.

"The borrower is a major shareholder of a medical device manufacturer. The person's shares will be delivered as security for the loan. In addition to the five percent fee, your friend will receive a percentage of those shares."

"Your request said that the loan funds would only be at risk for forty-eight hours, for which she will receive one million seven hundred fifty thousand dollars *and* the shares of the company? How many shares?"

"That is something that needs to be discussed in person with your client. Might I suggest Barcelona in two days?"

*　　*　　*

They met at the Hotel Majestic in a small conference room overlooking Passeig De Gracia. Horvat was exactly as Hawke had expected: fiftyish, swarthy, brutish, and wearing a too-small three-piece suit that looked like it was made before he was born.

Gina Apate, Horvat's "acquaintance-with-a-trust," was quite the opposite. She wore an ensemble straight out of the best shops of Paris, complete with hat and veil that gave her a mysterious air and camouflaged her face. She spoke with a confident authority that quickly relegated Horvat to minion status.

"Ms. Apate," Hawke said after introductions, "to make sure we are all proceeding with the same understanding, let me review the terms of this transaction."

"There is no need for that," she interrupted. "I know your proposal, and I know that it involves Voyageur Cardiac Systems. I know that the company has significant issues with one of its implant devices. I know the company's management is in chaos because of those issues. Despite knowing all of that, I am still willing to make the loan if my terms are met."

"Very well." Hawke sat back in his chair, folding his hands over his midsection while his mind raced. That Ms. Apate knew more about his client than he did was most disconcerting.

"My up-front fee to make the loan will be ten percent of the loan amount, not five percent as you have proposed," Gina began. "I also will receive twenty-five percent of the stock owned by the borrower; immediately, not when the loan is repaid." She paused.

"Is that all?" Hawke asked.

"No. I want a seat on the Voyageur board of directors."

Hawke involuntarily lifted an eyebrow.

"And," she continued, "I need to know the reason, and the mechanism, by which the thirty-five million will be back in my trust account within forty-eight hours."

"As I was about to explain," Hawke responded, "thirty of the thirty-five million will be used to fund a non-profit organization established to monitor the cardiac implant industry. You, or your designee, will have full control over that organization, including all finances. So, in essence, you are taking thirty million dollars out of one of your pockets and putting it in another.

"In addition to your owning the watchdog organization, the thirty million will be repaid to you over five years, with interest. And you should not lose sight of the opportunities a medical watchdog of this nature could provide, such as significant fees in exchange for medical device approval; fees that could easily run in the millions.

"The other five million will be used to pay fees related to the loan, including your five percent fee for making the loan. The five million will be repaid in ninety days. The entire thirty-five million will be secured by the stock of Voyageur's CEO, Stephen Hartsburg."

Apate responded, demanding a bigger fee and additional shares. Hawke parried, and the pair's subsequent negotiations would have put a Moroccan rug merchant to shame.

Finally, Apate made her "last" demands: "A seat on the board of directors; repayment of six million, payable in thirty days, for the five million; and all of the borrower's stock, including any stock options, will be deposited in an escrow account with instructions to convey all of it to me if I do not receive the six million, or any payment installment of the thirty million, on time."

Hawke waited to be sure nothing more was forthcoming from behind the veil.

"Your terms are far beyond what I am authorized to offer," Hawke finally responded. "But I know that you are a shrewd negotiator and would not pass up the opportunity to generate revenue from the entire global medical device industry."

He held up his hand to stop an interruption.

"What I am prepared to offer is a fee of one-point-seven-five million, five percent of the shares owned by the borrower, and full control of the non-profit watchdog organization. I will need to discuss the seat on the board of directors and the timing of your receipt of the shares with my client. Perhaps we should reconvene tomorrow?"

"I will not accept anything less than what I have laid out," Apate shot back.

"Then there is no need to meet tomorrow," Hawke said, seemingly unconcerned. "I will respond to others who have expressed an interest." He began to rise, stopping part way. "I could inquire about ten percent of his stock."

Apate agreed to meet again.

*   *   *

Back in his small, cluttered office on Ronda de Sant Pau, Hawke thought of calling Hartsburg but discarded the idea, knowing that Hartsburg had no choice other than to accept whatever terms he negotiated. Instead, he spent the evening doing a deep dive into Gina Apate's life, tapping his sources throughout Europe.

There was ample information about her younger years. She was born into wealth and attended university, where she graduated with honors. She was a martial arts competitor, winning several awards, and was fluent in five languages, including both Russian and Farsi. She appeared to have been recruited directly out of university by the Greek National Intelligence Service, commonly known as EYP.

Once she was employed by EYP, information became scarce. But the death of her parents, allegedly a burglary turned deadly at their home, put her back in the spotlight. For two years after their deaths, Gina was a vocal critic on social media, railing against the ineptitude of Greek law enforcement. Then she went silent, as if she had dropped off the face of the earth.

At least she and Calder have that in common, Hawke thought.

It was Apate's two-decade-long disappearance that concerned Hawke. Neither the web nor inquiries of past associates provided much information on her current life, other than that she appeared to be an intelligent eccentric with a trust fund who did some loan brokering for some unsavory characters, a client list much like his own.

All of which made her a person neither predictable nor reliable.

*   *   *

The next morning broke bright and warm. They met at a sidewalk coffee shop.

"Is Mr. Horvat joining us?" Hawke asked as they sat down.

"He has returned to Ljubljana. His services are no longer needed."

Hawke nodded and made a mental note to check for homicides in Barcelona overnight.

"Very well," he said. "My client is willing to give up ten percent of his stock, which he will transfer immediately. He is not able to promise you a seat on the board of directors, but at the next election, if there is a vacancy on the board, he would be willing to support your candidacy."

"Thirty days," Apate said. "I don't care what he has to do. Without a seat in thirty days, no deal."

They bickered over espresso and interest rates, stock options and crullers. Having agreed upon every detail after two hours of haggling, Apate called a car and left the meeting.

Hawke stayed to finish his third espresso, with the feeling that the negotiations were not over. His intuition suggested that Apate knew about Ralph Calder's special leverage over Hartsburg and was maneuvering for a way to exploit it. With a seat on the board of directors, she would be privy to a wealth of inside information about the company's engineering, employees, and finances.

He took a final sip of espresso and stood up. It was not the first time he had paid off a blackmailer for a client. But he had never had a client double-crossed by either the blackmailer or a financier—that would be bad for business indeed. If Gina Apate knew what special hold Calder had over Hartsburg, Hawke would have to find out as well. That meant that special attention had to be paid to the young IT wizard and the attorney-investigator Hartsburg had retained. *This deal is going to be a wild ride*, he thought.

Chapter 9

Pen

It was close to noon the next day when Pen got off the plane at Detroit Metro Airport. It was an endless, dreary ritual, waiting for the entire plane to clear, then for an attendant to bring an aisle chair; transferring, leaving the plane; retrieving her wheelchair on the jetway; and then texting and meeting up with the guy who delivered the hand-controlled rental van she had reserved last night. It was nearly two hours before she began the drive to suburban Grosse Pointe, and another hour before she got there. At least, she thought, it was not as brutally cold here as in Minnesota.

Tracking down Marilyn Applewhite was a move that reeked of desperation. Something was seriously amiss at VCS. All signs pointed to the use of ICD defects as part of an extortion plot, but she was out of leads. With time, Pen was sure she and Weezy could nail the culprit. But how many people would die in the meantime?

She followed Kenny's directions through a quiet, affluent neighborhood lined with big trees. The house owned by Marilyn Applewhite's sister was a large, half-timbered place, not dissimilar to the one occupied by the Hartsburgs in Sunfish Lake, Minnesota.

Three steps blocked her access to the front door. She pulled a telescoping pointer from her purse and used it to press the doorbell. A disheveled-looking blonde woman in her forties answered. "Yeah?"

"Marilyn Applewhite?"

She gave Pen a suspicious nod.

"I'm Pen Wilkinson. I left you messages about the research I'm doing for Nancy Nguyen."

"How did you—aw, hell, everybody seems to know I'm here. I can't talk to you. I worked for Mr. Hartsburg, not Nguyen."

"Right now, you don't work for VCS at all," Pen pointed out. "It's me or the FBI."

"Right," she scoffed.

"Your future doesn't look good, Marilyn. As it stands now, I think criminal fraud, failure to report product defects, conspiracy to conceal product defects, and obstruction of justice would be a given. And when the entire scheme is uncovered, I can see a RICO indictment in your future."

"What the hell . . ."

"You can't hide forever, Marilyn. If you talk to me now, maybe we can figure a way out of this."

She bit her lip, looked away. "I just can't."

"Mr. Hartsburg can't protect you. He's in trouble himself—deep trouble. I'll be making my report directly to the board, not him."

Marilyn pondered this. Her likelihood of cooperating was about fifty-fifty, Pen thought. That was about the same ratio of truth to bullshit she'd just given Marilyn.

"You know I'm a lawyer," Pen added. "You probably don't know I'm a former federal prosecutor, with a lot of friends at the US attorney's office and the FBI."

"All right, all right!" she shrieked. "I thought I was done with Voyageur. Just come in and get it over with."

"Coming in" was tricky. Ultimately, Marilyn's teenage nephew was summoned to help pull Pen up the steps into the house. They ended up at the table in her sister's smallish kitchen. The nephew seemed to be hovering, and Marilyn told him to beat it.

Marilyn sat down. "I don't know what you want from me."

"Let's start with who else has been here to see you."

She looked up, startled.

"You said everybody seemed to know you were here."

Marilyn sighed. "A foreign lawyer named Henri Hawke. He's a slimy little creep, but . . ."

"But?"

She managed a small smile. "He's also charming as hell. Anyway, he was working for Stephen and knew he was being extorted."

"For how much?"

"Thirty million. But it's supposed to go to a charitable foundation."

"What the—"

She held up her hands. "I don't understand it, either. It sounded like a crock to me."

Pen made a mental note to find out who the hell this Hawke was and who he was working for. "What did Hawke want from you?" she demanded.

"To help him figure out who the extortionist was."

"And?"

She stared at Pen with a blank expression. "I went through the motions of looking, but I already knew. There's a brilliant programmer. His wife died because of a defect in the 4750."

"Justin Biggs?"

"No, although he's a wacko. It's a firmware glitch that causes the ICD to malfunction. This guy was a senior developer—smart as hell, and he knew about it. He told management about the glitch, but nothing got done. The official story was that her leads were knocked loose in a car accident. That would have absolved the company."

"Did Hartsburg know about the defect? And the cover story?"

"There's no record of his knowing."

"Did he know?"

She blew out a breath, exasperated, but didn't say anything.

"It will come out," Pen said.

"You're not recording this?"

"No. You have my word."

Finally, Marilyn leaned forward. "Several people seemed to have suspicion about the firmware. But it was radioactive. Everybody was afraid to dig into it, Stephen most of all."

"And you made sure nobody who wanted to talk about it got through to him."

"Yes," she whispered.

"How many lives do you think that cost?"

Marilyn sat up. "Don't get judgmental with me. I was doing my job."

"What about Danilson?"

"Mr. Hartsburg's stepfather? What about him?"

"The guy who wrote the extortion message said his death was karma. And whoever it was—they might have broken into the patient database."

Her hand rose slowly to her mouth as her eyes widened. She really hadn't known.

"And Tricia Doran has the same kind of device."

"My God. Magnus Danilson. And now Tricia."

"Tell me," Pen demanded. "Who the hell is this guy?"

"I can't tell you. I owe my career to Stephen. And Hawke—he's smooth, but he seemed dangerous. He threatened me with a gun."

"He'll go down. And Hartsburg is finished, too. It's reality time, Marilyn—do you want to go down with them?"

"Oh, God . . ."

"There might be a chance to save Tricia, but she is under serious threat. Do you want another death on your conscience?"

She stared into space for a long moment, then grabbed Pen's notebook and pen, scribbling a name onto it. Then she got up and left the room. The interview was over.

Pen took a deep breath and looked at the name.

Ralph Calder.

Pen returned to the van and texted Weezy. *Any luck identifying our extortionist?*

She held her breath, waiting for Weezy's reply, which came thirty seconds later.

Ralph Calder.

Chapter 10

Sierra/Quinn

Sierra crept into the church, Quinn at her back, and slid into one of the rear pews, making as little sound as possible while the pastor intoned the opening prayers. They would have gotten here on time for the memorial service for Alice Holmgren if they hadn't run into traffic issues.

If she'd saved Alice's life, they wouldn't be here at all.

Olivia had asked them to come. Sierra had planned to come anyway to show support for Olivia and her father, even though it'd been years since their families had spent time together. Sierra and Olivia had hung out together as kids at the lake, and Alice had been fun, kind, and always willing to teach. Sierra's grandmother had tried to teach her how to crochet, but it hadn't made sense until Alice showed her how.

Olivia had asked Sierra and Quinn to look into what happened to Alice, but there was nothing either of them could do. There were even limits to what Olivia's friend Indigo, working inside Voyageur Cardiac, could do to dig into the unfortunate failure of Alice's ICD.

And that didn't sit right with Sierra at all. She still couldn't figure out how a piece of technology like that, after being checked by a doctor, after having undergone numerous tests and updates, would just up and quit. Quinn was right; the mechanic in her wanted an explanation for the failure, because it was something that should be fixed.

After the service, Sierra nudged Quinn to escape the mass exodus from the church proper and head to the fellowship hall for the after-funeral luncheon. There was little worse, in her opinion, than lining up to offer condolences like a receiving line at a wedding. She caught Olivia's attention and motioned toward the hall. Olivia nodded, then resumed collecting condolences.

The gathering place held long tables arranged like a school cafeteria on either side, each table holding an insulated coffee carafe, a sweating pitcher of ice water, a stack of Styrofoam cups, and a bowl filled with packets of assorted sweeteners and powdered creamer. Additional tables on the far side were set up for a buffet-style luncheon, complete with covered steel pans and Sterno cans supplying heat. *A few steps up from the usual cold ham and cheese sandwiches with dollar buns and cole slaw*, Sierra thought. The ubiquitous plates of homemade bars, including many variations of Rice Krispies treats and lemon bars, commanded a table all their own.

Quinn tugged her to a table near the entrance and poured himself a cup of coffee, inhaling the fresh-brewed aroma. "You okay?"

"All except for knowing absolutely no one here except Olivia and her dad--sure, just peachy."

"Sierra?"

Sierra spun toward the voice, then closed her gaping mouth. "Dad, you made it. I thought …"

"I rearranged my schedule." Mark Bauer, in a dark navy suit with his graying blond hair pulled back into a ponytail, separated from the incoming crowd. He shook Quinn's hand in greeting and then reached out to Sierra. "I'm glad you came."

"Of course we came," Sierra said as she returned Mark's embrace. "Where's Mom?"

"Your mom's in Seattle this week for work." His expression reflected a deep sadness. "Wish she could've been here. I remember when I introduced Liza to Arthur, back when we started dating and he was my mentor in college. Arthur told me later he knew Liza was my person." Mark gave a quiet chuckle at the memory. "We keep in touch, even though we don't get together every year like we used to. I still go to his seminars."

"I wish I could have done more. I was there. I tried to save her. I did everything I could, but . . ."

"She died because her device failed." Mark grew solemn. "You tried." He pulled Sierra into another hug. "You tried, and that's all you could've done."

Sierra swallowed the knot of grief that rose in her throat. "I know. It's just . . ."

Mark offered a smile. "You're a mechanic, and you want to fix stuff. Just like your grandpa."

Olivia, accompanied by a lean man with gray hair and watery blue eyes Sierra recognized as an older Arthur Holmgren, stopped beside Mark. "Is that Sierra?" Arthur asked, a grin brightening his face. "You always looked so much like Liza."

"Hi, Arthur." Sierra gave him a gentle hug; he wasn't the robust man she remembered. "I'm so sorry for your loss."

Olivia accepted the hug Mark offered. "Mark Bauer, the star student Dad always talked about when I was going through college."

"Star student who should have gotten his MD," Arthur said.

"Nurse practitioner is enough for me," Mark said. "I see patients, and my student loan is paid off."

"Sorry we were late," Sierra said. "There was a car accident on the Crosstown. Arthur, this is Quinn Moore. Quinn, this is Dr. Arthur Holmgren."

Arthur shook Quinn's hand. "Just Arthur. Nice to meet you."

Olivia invited them to join her and Arthur at a table closer to the kitchen and the food. The pastor arrived and said the communal blessing before the buffet was opened. After they settled back at their table with lunch in hand, Arthur focused on Sierra.

"Olivia said you were there with Alice when . . ." Arthur's voice faded. He squeezed his eyes shut and breathed deep. "Tell me what happened."

A knot materialized in Sierra's throat. She'd gone through it in her head every day since it happened, and she still felt she'd somehow missed something. Quinn, sitting beside her, laid a hand on her leg. The weight comforted her.

"I was waiting for passengers to deplane—"

Arthur held up a hand, palm out. "Deplane?"

"I've told you she's an airplane mechanic," Mark said, pride filling his voice. "She was working on the ramp where the planes park."

Arthur's brows rose. "Is that so?"

"It is. I was right there when Alice got off the plane." Sierra continued to describe the events of that day, how she'd tried to help, the guilt rising up yet again like a stone balloon into her chest. "I'm so sorry, Arthur. I remember when we'd go to your cabin. Alice always taught us a new game or had us do crafts. I still remember her every time I crochet."

"That was the teacher in her," Arthur said. "She loved watching you kids." He dabbed at his eyes with a handkerchief he pulled from a pocket inside his suit coat. "You did everything you could. Her device failed. It shouldn't have happened, but it did."

That reminded Sierra of something that had been bothering her despite her father's reassurances. "You're a cardiothoracic surgeon. What's the failure rate for ICDs?"

"Less than one percent. If a device's failure rate rises to one and a half percent, there's a good chance they'll be recalled."

One percent--that'd be one out of every one hundred people with a device. Long odds. "Have you seen any issues lately with ICDs?"

"There have been a couple over the past month or so. That's why I told Olivia to file a report with the FDA."

"I did, Dad," Olivia said. "I sent it up the chain, and it disappeared. No one knows what happened to it."

Arthur winced. "You said it disappeared on the way to the C-suite for final approval. Doesn't take a genius to see that game. I've stopped recommending VCS devices to my patients."

Something in Arthur's tone sparked Sierra's interest. "Olivia and her friend Indigo found some weird stuff from recent device updates," she said. "Do you think the issues you've seen are related to that?"

Arthur and Olivia exchanged glances before he answered. "Anything is possible."

Mark held up a hand. "Sierra—"

"Dad, please." She plunged on before she thought better of it. "Do you know a man by the name of Ralph Calder?"

"Ralph Calder." Furrows lined Arthur's forehead. "He sent me some nasty letters blaming me for his wife's death. I was his wife's surgeon. She had an ICD that malfunctioned."

"I never heard about that. Did Mom know?" Olivia asked.

"She did. I asked her not to say anything." Before Olivia could protest, Arthur continued. "It appeared to be leads dislodged by impact, in a car accident, something no one could have prevented. I shared the letters with the hospital, and the legal team did whatever they do. I didn't hear from him after that. Why do you ask about Calder?"

"Because I'm pretty sure I saw him at the airport when I was trying to save Alice."

Arthur furrowed his brow. "Probably a coincidence that he happened to be there. How many people go through that airport every day?"

"You might be right." Sierra's gut didn't agree. She'd said as much to Quinn days ago. He had reminded her the case-that-wasn't-really-a-case was, in effect, closed, and even if her gut was right, there was nothing they could do.

The question Sierra couldn't answer: why would he be at the airport because of Alice? Although, if he'd sent nasty letters to his wife's surgeon blaming him for her death, he could have targeted Dr. Arthur Holmgren's wife in retaliation. Except he never touched Alice or got close to her. So why was he there?

"Liv," Arthur said, "can I give you the station to bring back to VCS? Maybe they can reprogram it for someone else. I don't need it taking up space, and if it can be reused, I want them to reuse it. If not, they can recycle it."

Wait. "Station?" Sierra asked. Indigo had mentioned a station. "What is that?"

Mark answered, "It picks up data from an implanted device and sends it to the hospital or clinic so they can keep an eye on the patient. They review that data when the patient comes in for a checkup and make any necessary adjustments."

"Except most patients don't bother to set them up," Arthur said. "We have to read the historical data from the device at the checkup instead of current data in real time. It's better if we can get that regular feedback, because if something is off, we can bring the patient in sooner to adjust it."

Sierra processed that. "That's what Indy mentioned, right?" At Olivia's nod, she continued. "The station would have to be wireless to get data from a device like an ICD."

Arthur nodded. "It is. Each station is matched with a device. Patients are supposed to set the station up in their bedroom near their bed or someplace near where they sit and watch TV so it can get the data from the device while they're not moving around. I set up Alice's."

"How big is this thing?"

Arthur held his hands up a short distance apart. "About the size of a cable box, I suppose. Maybe a little smaller."

"And what's the range?" Sierra asked. "How close does the station need to be to the patient in order to receive data?"

"Pretty close. Maybe ten or fifteen feet at the most."

Sierra caught Quinn looking at her, one brow arched high. He was signaling for her to stop before she said something she couldn't take back.

As if. The mechanic in her had to figure out how it worked. "Okay, so the station gets a wireless signal from the device, and the data gets to the hospital through the internet, right?"

Arthur nodded. "The data sent back to the hospital is encrypted. The station is keyed to the patient's device by the serial number and only communicates with that device."

"But data sent back to the hospital is not wireless, right?" Sierra was a mechanic, but she'd tinkered with her share of computer stuff. "It would be through a network cable because there's probably no way for a patient to access the station to connect it to a home wireless network."

"Yes."

That gut feeling that kept nagging at her grew stronger. "Theoretically, could the hospital send instructions back to the device? Like if the programming needed a tweak?"

Arthur shook his head. "The devices are programmed at the clinic or hospital. We have programming heads, like small flat pucks, we use to connect with devices for adjustments."

"I'm saying 'theoretically.' Could someone communicate with a device through the station?"

"I don't think so. The station just receives signals. It doesn't go the other way."

Sierra paused, dragging through all she'd learned about digital electronics and radios back in aircraft maintenance school. "It sends and receives signals, so it's a transmitter and a receiver—a transceiver. The station sends signals through the wired network. It wouldn't take much to do it wirelessly."

Olivia leaned forward. "What are you saying?"

Quinn tapped her shoulder and nudged her to her feet before she could answer. "Hey, I think we should get going. I have to get back to the office, and you have to work tonight. Arthur, it was nice meeting you, and again, so sorry for your loss. Mark, good to see you."

Quinn knew her. If he was steering her out of the conversation, she should probably stop while she was ahead. "Quinn's right. I should get some sleep before my shift. Arthur, take care. Dad, good to see you."

Olivia followed them out of the fellowship hall and pulled them to a stop. "Wait." Her eyes tracked back to the hall and her father. "What did you mean about the receiver?"

Quinn said, "I don't think—"

Sierra cut him off. "There isn't a whole lot of difference between a wireless receiver and a transceiver. I mean, technically speaking. What if someone actually did modify the station so it could talk to a device wirelessly?"

Skepticism filled Olivia's eyes. "The device has to listen."

"But it does. If the device is inside a person, there isn't an exposed socket or leads, at least with Alice. Your dad said they update the device's programming with something, so it has to be wireless."

"Sierra," Quinn said, "we need to go. Olivia, sorry for your loss."

*   *   *

"Really?" Sierra stared out the windshield. "We couldn't stay for another five minutes?"

"Sierra." Quinn had that tone, the one that meant he thought she was digging too deep into something she should leave alone. "You don't suggest a theoretical reason for someone's death to

140

their loved one at their funeral. Especially if that theory might change everything they know about the death."

Aha! "You knew where I was going with that. It would explain why Ralph Calder was at the airport. He had a duffel bag which, by the way, he was carrying in front of him. Add a decent power supply, and you could extend the range of that station. Hell, you can boost a radio signal with more power—why not a wireless network signal?"

"You forget, each station is keyed to a single device."

"Do you think those stations are manufactured already keyed to a device? Think about it; too much work to keep them together, especially if they're built in different places, which I can almost guarantee they are. Devices that are implanted into a person would need specialized manufacturing facilities, but the stations wouldn't. They probably make those stations in a plant that makes wireless routers. They'd have to be programmed when a device is implanted. If it can be keyed to one device, you can be sure it can be re-keyed to another."

"I know what you're doing." Quinn took the exit toward Apple Valley. "You're trying make this a situation where if you'd known something else, you could have saved her."

"No, I'm trying to find a reason that Calder guy was there. If he sent threatening letters to Arthur—"

"It's not a case. Even if you're right, that somehow Calder was able to take his wife's station and re-key it to Alice's device, and turn it into a transceiver or transmitter or whatever and boost the power, how does that change anything? Arthur said he's seen a few ICDs with issues in the past few months. Don't you think it's far more likely that her ICD had an issue, too? What do you like to say? Occam's Razor."

"The simplest explanation is the most likely one. That still doesn't explain—"

"Honey, take a breath."

It was their code for taking a break from whatever subject they were discussing. Sierra took a deep breath and let it out to a count of five. Quinn was right. Even if whatever theory she came up with was solid and maybe even real, Alice was still dead, and Sierra still couldn't save her.

She couldn't stop thinking about it. After they got home, Sierra waited until they'd both changed out of their funeral attire into their "at home" wardrobe. She threw on some sweats and followed Quinn, who stuck to jeans with a flannel shirt over a long-sleeved T-shirt, into the living room.

She dropped onto the couch beside him, figuring it'd been enough of a break from the topic. "Quinn, I've got an idea."

"Do I need to worry about this?"

"You don't even know what I was going to say."

"I do, and it's a bad idea."

He knew her better than she did herself sometimes, but he was wrong on occasion. "How do you know what I was going to say, and if it's a bad idea?"

He leaned back and laid an arm along the top of the couch behind her. "I know you. I know how tenacious and stubborn you are. You are going to ask Olivia if you can get Alice's station so you can tinker with it."

Not even close. Sierra grinned and tried to suppress a yip of triumph. "Ha! Nope, smart guy. I can make a computer work, but I'll leave the circuit boards and chip programming to the experts. I was going to suggest talking with Mr. Ralph Calder—" She pressed a hand on Quinn's chest to stop his protest. "Wait, listen to me. I just want to know if it's possible, what I explained about the station. I'm pretty sure it is—"

"No." Quinn took her hand and kissed it. "It was probably a coincidence he was at the airport at that time. He may or may not be involved at all. We don't know, and I'm not going to let you get yourself caught up with a harassment charge."

"Harassment? How could going to his house as an electrical engineering student and asking how those stations work be considered harassment?"

"You're not an electrical engineering student."

"He doesn't know that. It's my dissertation, and I found an article he wrote—"

"No, you didn't."

"Actually, I did when I did an internet search on him. Interesting article, too. It's a few years old, but still relevant."

Quinn stared at her for a long moment, his eyes searching hers. "Damn it, Sierra."

She fought a grin. "You want to know, too. Admit it."

He tried not to smile and failed. "I'm probably going to regret this. I'm going with you."

"You don't have to."

"Yes, I do. Someone's got to keep you out of trouble."

Chapter 11

Matt

Matt stewed all weekend about his encounter with Biggs. For starters, the man was an asshole and full of himself. But he also impressed Matt as being brilliant and cunning. And now, based on plenty of nonverbal clues, such as eye contact and the timbre in his voice, Matt concluded, based on long experience, that Biggs wasn't above lying when it suited him. The most notable instance: *"Even if I had a name, I wouldn't tell you . . ."*

Biggs had a name, all right, and Matt resolved to get it, even if he had to beat it the hell out of him.

He needed to talk to Biggs again, despite being loathe to do so. But he couldn't go at him in attack mode like their last meeting. He needed an edge, something more subtle. For that, he needed to do some serious research, starting with asking Zach Perez for help.

He called Zach and caught him at home. "I only need a *small* favor this time."

Zach laughed. "They're all small to you, *amigo*. You need to work on your definitions of relative size."

Matt returned the chuckle. "I guess you're right. But this one *is* small. When you hacked the Voyageur personnel database, did you happen to get a list of *all* the employees? Especially the top executives, including the C-suite folks."

"I *saw* the list of employees. It's SOP for most large companies to keep a master list. The FBI requests them quite often from companies when they investigate white-collar crimes. But if any-one downloaded or copied it, they'd be arrested in about five minutes. That's definitely *not* a small favor I'll do for you."

"*Wonderful,*" Matt said with exaggerated sarcasm, feeling in-stantly depressed. "Do those records include former employees like retirees, fired employees, ones who died while employed?"

"Of course. The IRS requires records going back four years. Their positions, salaries, hire and fire dates, retirement dates—"

"Good. That's what I need to see. Is there *any* way I can see those employee records?"

"I had a hunch you'd be asking me for more help sooner or later, so I made myself a backdoor entrance to the files."

"Meaning?"

"Meaning I'll need to have you here looking over my shoul-der when I go back in. Can't stay long or VCS security might de-tect a breach."

Matt pondered for a long moment. He was pushing the limit of their friendship. Zach would have every right to tell him to buzz off and give up his investigation. "If you help me with this, kid, I'll make it well worth your while."

Zach laughed, long and heartily. "Two dinners, minimum. And you promise to leave me alone for six months after you get this case figured out."

"Deal!" Matt exclaimed. "The best restaurants in town. Your choice."

"Come over tomorrow after work. I'll be home at six."

"Thank you, Zach. Seriously, I owe you big time. And my paranoid alter ego appreciates this more than I can express."

*   *   *

Matt brought takeout burgers and fries to Zach's apartment the next evening, and they settled into the risky business of hacking into the VCS system again.

Finishing his last French fry, Zach looked up at him. "You still sure you want to do this?"

"Yes."

"Then let's get at it." They sat down in front of one of the monitors on Zach's desk, and the young IT whiz began, deliberately and with several pauses, worming his way into VCS. After about five minutes, he looked up. "Here we are—the HR database. How do we find your guy?"

Matt consulted a sheet of notes he'd made. "First, eliminate all current employees."

"Done."

"Okay. Cross off all the women. We're looking for a 'guy,' according to Biggs."

Zach nodded, typed and looked up.

"Now let's look at employees who terminated between one and four years ago."

The young hacker typed, then nodded.

"Can you narrow it down to employees based in Minnesota?"

"Piece of cake." Zach manipulated the data fields on his screen and looked up. "Next?"

"IT employees."

Zach peered at the screen, did some scrolling, and frowned. "They've got a division called 'Technology and Information Services.'"

"That's it. Now, let's look at those TIS employees who worked in the Research and Development department."

"Got it."

"Now, is there any way to separate the software developers from the hardware people?"

This time, Zach's search involved more typing, more pauses, and more frowns. "I don't know, Matt. I don't see an easy way of doing it."

"Then let's just leave it for now. How many names do we have?"

"Sixty-one." He looked at the time display on his phone. "We've been in for a while."

"Almost done," Matt promised. "Can you eliminate all hourly employees?"

Zach typed, nodded.

"Last field. Biggs is a director-level manager. Can you narrow it down to everybody who's higher than that?"

"That's basically department heads and VPs."

"Okay. Next—"

"Whoa, you said that was the last one," Zach protested.

"Sorry, I lied. One more. Is there a field for dependents?"

"Sure."

"Can you find any employees whose spouse died before their termination?" Matt asked.

"I'll have to look at them one at a time, but there are only eleven names left."

Zach scrolled through the remaining employee records, finished typing, then pressed a key. Across the room, a printer began churning out a list.

Matt went over and collected the printout. "Just five names," he said, peering at the list. "I think I can work with this."

Zach pushed back from his desk. "Good."

"I'll get out of your hair now," Matt said. "Thanks again. Let me know when you want your gourmet dinner. Maybe next week?"

"Sure. I'll give you some time to track down the culprit. Good luck."

At home, Matt opened up his laptop and searched the internet for information about each of the five men on the list. Most had several social media profiles. LinkedIn was by far the most popular, along with Facebook, Instagram, and Reddit. He determined from LinkedIn profiles that two of the men were clearly hardware engineers. Biggs had said that the wife of his unnamed employee had suffered a device failure due to software issues. If the mystery employee had knowledge of the defect, he was likely to be a software specialist. Matt moved the two hardware guys to the bottom of the list.

Next came an employee who had apparently worked in both hardware and software. Matt put the name aside and moved on. The two remaining candidates were both software guys. But a search on one of them proved interesting indeed; he didn't have any recent internet presence.

Ralph Calder had been a department head, one level below a vice president. Based on his job title, it appeared he'd been at least a level or two above Biggs. He'd be a logical person to talk to, if he could be found. But Matt didn't want to waste his time checking out a man who, with no internet presence, might be hard to find. Calder could have moved to a different country and canceled his social media accounts just to eliminate the stress of dealing with them every day. He could even be dead.

After mulling his options for five minutes, Matt decided another chat with Biggs was in order. This time, he vowed, he'd keep his composure and not beat Biggs badly about the face and head.

Unless he had to.

*   *   *

Biggs saw Matt coming from across the VCS parking lot at six o'clock that evening as he walked toward his car. When Matt stopped in front of him, Biggs scowled and turned, squaring on him. "What the fuck do you want, Larson? Gonna take another swing at me for saying that the Twins are also overrated by a factor of ten?"

Matt held up his gloved hands in a surrender gesture. The icy wind and colder-than-average January day were the main reasons he'd come to VCS and waited for Biggs to leave work. It was a neutral, public site, and the frigid weather implied their conversation would be short. Nevertheless, what he had to say and how Biggs reacted to his words were vitally important.

"Relax, Biggs. I was wrong to punch you. But you're still a douchebag."

Biggs snorted. "You came here just to tell me that?"

"Not just that."

Biggs shivered and winced from a sudden gust of wind. "Then get to the point." He started walking toward his car, so Matt followed.

"I've got one question for you."

"Make it fast, before my mouth freezes shut."

Matt sped up, passed Biggs, stepped in front of him and turned around, blocking Biggs's path. Biggs stopped just before they bumped chests. With an exaggerated sigh and a look of contempt, he said, "What?"

Focusing on Biggs's beady eyes, Matt said, "Did Ralph Calder send the threatening emails to Danilson?"

The muscles around Biggs's eyes contracted ever so slightly. His expression was already angry but now shifted to one of slight surprise as well. "If I give you an answer, will you get out of my face permanently?"

Matt raised his gloved hand to mimic the "Scout's honor" salute. "I promise . . . unless you screw me over here. If that happens, we're gonna have us a big ol' problem."

As Biggs opened his mouth, his gaze dropped to Matt's raised hand. "No."

Biggs brushed past Matt to get to his car. Matt let him pass, watched him get into his car, and hurried to his own car. Once inside with the heater blasting out a stream of weak heat, he allowed himself a pleased smile. "Once a liar, always a liar."

This time Biggs had shown an even bigger tell than averted eyes or change in tone or pitch. "If I give you an answer . . ." stood in stark contrast to a more normal response, such as "If I tell you . . ." *An answer* implied Biggs would tell Matt anything to get him off his back.

Ralph Calder was now on Matt's suspicion list, but finding him might not solve anything. A serious forensic technician and law enforcement people would be required just to prove Calder had sent the threatening emails. Tough enough. But proving Calder had somehow caused Danilson's death might be next to impossible.

Matt walked to his car. *Why am I doing this?* The adrenaline rush from almost mixing it up with Biggs again was waning, and he suddenly felt tired and frustrated. Helping the family of a dead friend and mentor seemed quixotic now. But the thought of Danilson, dead, juxtaposed with the image of a smirking Justin Biggs, recharged his resolve.

Matt put his car into gear and headed home. He owed his career and so much else to Magnus Danilson. And now, with his career yet to restart after successful surgery on his hand, he was in a position to return the favor.

Chapter 12

Hartsburg

Stephen Hartsburg fairly bounced into the den of his lake home, going through a mental checklist that really amounted to a victory lap. He'd already completed item number one: telling Tricia she was safe, and they could soon both go back to VCS. The extortion threat had been neutralized, thanks to Henri Hawke.

Now Hartsburg could begin the cleanup.

He walked over to his desk, sat down, and swiveled around, idly looking through the large picture window at the swirling snowscape of Gull Lake. With the extortion threat under control, the main priority now was limiting the damage he had inflicted on himself by hiring investigators to find out who had been cracking the company database and extorting him. Their involvement had to be ended, pronto. He turned back to his desk, picked up the phone, and called general counsel Nancy Nguyen. She picked up on the first ring.

"Yes, Stephen?"

"Nancy, that, uh, situation we talked about—I've got it under control."

"Really? How did you—"

"The details aren't important. I'm just telling you we won't be needing those investigators. The cybersecurity lady and the attorney."

A brief silence. "Stephen, we can't just let this go. Serious crimes have been committed, and serious questions have been raised about the 4750."

"I told you, I've got this. There's no need for further investigation."

"We have a duty to investigate. *I* have a duty. And I also have a right to know what's going on."

"That's not going to happen. I want those investigators terminated, now."

"Look, we need to talk about this."

Typical Nguyen, he thought. He'd given her a direct order. He was the damn CEO.

"No, we don't. I'm shutting it all down. No investigators, no questions, no explanations."

"You can add to that, 'No general counsel.' Because I quit. I can't do my job in the dark, with ethically questionable things going on. Fire them yourself."

Hartsburg swallowed his need to lash back. He didn't need Nguyen suing the company for wrongful termination or talking to regulators after she was gone. "Nancy, you need to calm down. Don't do anything rash."

"My mind is made up. I've been uneasy with this whole situation since the first questions were raised about the 4750."

"Let's talk—"

"I can't be a part of this, Stephen. I'm leaving."

He sighed. "If you're really determined to do this, I can't stop you. I appreciate your service, and we'll give you a nice package."

"No doubt with an ironclad NDA."

"A nondisclosure agreement is standard. You know that better than anyone."

"All right. I'm gone, effective immediately. My people will be in touch with your people." She hung up.

Hartsburg replaced the phone and leaned back in his chair, facing the crackling flames in the stone fireplace. *Having Nguyen gone could be a plus,* he thought. She could create problems, and he wouldn't miss her obstruction and self-righteousness. Now he could return to the checklist. After terminating Napolitani and Wilkinson—there were plenty of loyal managers who would do that—he could begin a discreet process of finding out what was wrong with the 4750 and fixing it before the FDA found out. Then he could deal with the extortionist, with Marilyn Applewhite, and with his soon-to-be-ex-wife. He exhaled and allowed himself a small smile. The world was beginning to make sense again.

Chapter 13

Gina

This was too easy, as if some puppeteer was pulling all the strings in her favor.

She had made a quarter million dollars from Voyageur short sales just from being in the right place at the right time.

A weather-induced flight cancellation had provided the time, and with a hunch as the impetus, she had investigated Voyageur and found the company's stock value depressed far below the value of its patents, and its management in chaos.

And then, out of the blue and at minimal cost, she could get a foothold in the company, perhaps a seat on the board of directors.

Karma.

If she made this happen, it would establish her as a major international corporate raider, not just a facilitator who received the dribs and drabs from the mega-million-dollar deals she pulled off. It would put her on the same level as her Russian and Middle Eastern clients, the leering, groping, sadistic oligarchs and sheiks who treated her like . . . like . . . they treated all women. It would give her the platform to make them pay for all the slights and insults and condescension . . . and to avenge her parents.

Only one box was left to be checked. She knew, from the online research she had done at the airport, that there were no lawsuits against Voyageur related to the VC-25-4750, although she had learned that in Minnesota, civil actions didn't have to be filed in court right away; the lawsuit began when it was served upon the defendant. She needed to track down Justin Biggs, the jerky IT guy mentioned by Marilyn Applewhite, and find out how serious the issue with the ICDs was.

She called Biggs and introduced herself as Molly Burris from the finance department, wanting to set up a meeting to discuss a sensitive problem "that was best discussed off-site to avoid prying eyes and curious ears." Reluctant at first, Biggs agreed to the meeting when Gina said she was the assistant CFO.

"I'm guessing that you want to talk about VC-25-4750," Biggs said as he slid into the seat across from Gina. "Everybody and their cousin wants to talk about that. What's your interest?"

"I've been tasked with the job of assessing the extent of the damage and advising the risk management division on the cost of reparations and repair of the problem," Gina answered. "I'm told that you are the person in IT to talk to."

Biggs snorted. "I could fix it if they wouldn't keep me in the dark like everybody else. The rest of the programmers are lame. So are the engineers. Whatever this problem is, I'm the only one who can fix it."

Gina thought back to the flight with Applewhite, who, in her tipsy state, had described Biggs as a "cocky asshole." Gina silently agreed.

"Let's start with the scope of the problem," she said. "Can it be fixed, or will we need to discontinue the model and recall all units?"

"It would have already been fixed if they had come to me," Biggs groused, pausing to take a swallow of beer. "Instead, they ignored the fucking problem."

"What *is* the problem?"

"I don't know for sure until I'm allowed to dig into it, but I think something is hinky with the software."

"How do you know that?" Gina asked.

"How? Because that dipstick, Ralph Calder, got pissed and started tinkering with the software. Now it's a cluster fuck."

"Tell me about Mr. Calder."

Biggs described Calder, his former role in the company, and the death of his wife.

"What did he do with the software?" Gina asked.

Biggs hesitated, looking uncertain for the first time. "I don't know for sure. Like I said, they don't tell me jack shit. But I can tell you this much: he's been monkeying with the system. I don't know what he did, but it's not good. A couple more patients have dropped dead, people right in this area. I know Calder had something to do with it. I just *know* it."

He lowered his voice. "It's the updates. He had to be embedding something into the updates. Or he made some sort of transmitter that can externally manipulate the implants. And now Hartsburg is hiding his mistress, who I know has a 4750 implant."

Biggs chewed the inside of his lip, nodding his head. "Whatever is going on, I can fix it. All I need is full access to the product; the databases, all the code."

*   *   *

Gina was convinced that Biggs was neither the cause of the device's failure nor the blackmailer, notwithstanding what she had been told. He had been only too happy to trash his employer and throw his former colleague, Calder, under the bus. With his ego, Biggs would have been bragging about it if he had been responsible.

Nonetheless, she had learned several important things from the meeting with the brash IT whiz: there had been at least one more death, in addition to the one she had seen at the airport, and

Hartsburg's mistress had the faulty device implanted in her chest. That, alone, was a game-changer. Maybe she didn't need to come up with $35 million to gain control of Voyageur.

Chapter 14

Weezy

Weezy pushed back from the monitor, stood, and stretched. Her neighbor in 87A, Kalina, grinned at her and turned back to her monitor. They shared a silent, woman-to-woman bond formed by dislike of Justin.

She had been on the project for three days. Most of the time she'd been left alone. Choudhary seemed to be more manager than tech, checking Weezy's progress in the system but rarely talking with Weezy herself. Justin popped into her cubicle several times a day to peer at her screen or down her blouse. Usually both. But she was in a good rut: do a reasonable amount of work on the interface in the morning, then turn on her cover ID and search for the system breach for an hour, then back and forth between the two tasks. To a casual observer, she would seem a competent programmer, slogging away at a routine job.

She was down to finishing touches on the Carson EXV v2 interface work, but she needed more time to work on the Hartsburg project. She'd confirmed that the Voyageur database could be hacked, but initially saw nothing suspicious during the period Hartsburg had told her the theft took place. Obviously, the data had been stolen by someone working in the system, so the grab would look like regular work. The day before, the flaw in her thinking had come to her while she was writing a particularly boring routine as part of the cover project: people with the right credentials could grab the data, but they didn't. The patient acquisition was almost always done by the software under strict usage rules. People at Voyageur rarely looked at individual patient data. Confidentiality rules, she supposed. She wrote a string of instructions that looked like a test of the interface. It told the system to find any access not directed by the doctors' office software. She ran it back to the timeframe the theft must have occurred and buried it in the other test runs she did for the cover project.

She was tempted to drag her feet on the interface. Dishonest, yes, but Hartsburg was her real boss, and his work justified cheating a little on the cover project. She had sent him a message at the secure address saying as much and offering to expand the time frame, but she hadn't heard back.

While she waited, she began a search for any indication that someone might have tampered with the software that controlled the ICDs. She had initially dismissed the idea that someone might deliver an instruction to harm a person to an ICD as too sci-fi to believe, but it intrigued her, too. Then Pen Wilkinson had mentioned it.

She liked Pen. She realized she should be careful; nothing in the project so far had been as it seemed, but she wanted to trust Pen. She was smart and sophisticated in a way Weezy wished she could be. And she hadn't blown Weezy off for acting like a jerk.

Weezy sat back down and clicked on her cover identity. The script she had set to run during backup last night had produced results. Normal updates of the doctors' office software had to be done in a prescribed manner. Her hacker background told her to check the size of instructions of those updates. Hackers often added a caboose of code to a routine update as a way of getting into a system. Kind of basic, but worth a try. The doctors' office software updates always had the same four-letter code on their first instruction, so before she left the night before, Weezy had set a routine to find all those four-letter codes and report the length of the first handshake instruction associated with each of those identifiers. Probably a waste of time, but . . .

She sensed a presence behind her. She hadn't opened the file and switched back to her assigned identity. She smelled Justin's cologne. At least she'd worn a turtleneck today.

Paper slapped on her desktop. It took her a second to recognize the *Wired* article.

"So, we have a celebrity on the temp row, huh, Nardelli?" Justin pronounced the name slowly, emphasizing each syllable. "Or should I say Napolitani?" He smirked. "Always thought there was something bogus about your assignment. Who hired you?"

Pretend innocence, or meet him head on? The *Wired* article didn't have her picture, but online chat had added it to the gusher of gossip after the article. If he only knew. He hadn't mentioned Hotcakes, the scourge of black hat hackers, so her dark net web identity was safe. But her notoriety was just what she'd warned Hartsburg about.

Weezy sighed. She hated to play nice with this dweeb. "So, you figured out the security audit. Congratulations. I suppose it's too much to ask you to keep your insight to yourself."

Justin moved from the door frame to the cubicle and put a butt cheek on the edge of the ell of the desk in lieu of sitting. "I'm asking myself who would hire a famous hacker to work in a high-security area."

"What better way to do a security check?" Weezy said. "And, if you read the article, you know that IdeoPulse fired me. I'm out of a job, and I need the work." She shrugged. "Simple as that."

He lowered his voice. "So, what have you found?"

Weezy gave him the dumbass look. "See you later, Justin. Much later, please."

"Don't know what you think you're doing," he continued, "but you can't be stupid enough to think it's legal. You really want to risk jail time 'cause some suit thinks it's a good idea to test our security?"

Justin had a point. She could be pretty far out on a limb. She had only Hartsburg's verbal assurance that what she was doing was okay. She didn't have to answer, because Justin gave a chuckle that convinced her he must have enjoyed pulling wings off flies as a kid and meandered down the corridor.

As soon as she was sure he was pestering another contractor and therefore not back in his office watching her work, she opened the file from last night. Sure enough, there were several software updates with larger code blocks than the majority. She wrote a script to compare the shorter with the longer and extract the differences. She began reading what fell out, not immediately recognizing much except that it did perform some operation, presumably on ICDs embedded in patients. Understanding that it was a longer project, she encrypted it, hid it in her work in progress, and opened the conversion project.

Before going back to the grind, Weezy stood to stretch. She glanced across the cubicles and saw Choudhary standing in her doorway talking to a tall, professionally-dressed woman. Close-cropped dark hair with a streak of gray and an air of authority. Probably a Voyageur executive of some sort. As she prepared to take her seat, she realized the woman was walking toward her.

"Ms. Nardelli?"

"Yes."

"Olivia Holmgren. We have to talk."

Weezy cocked her head. "What subject?"

"The project you're working on."

The woman had a Voyageur badge, and it agreed that her name was Olivia.

"Probably best for you to talk to Ms. Choudhary for a status on the conversion."

Holmgren gave her a tolerant smile and looked around the area. "I'd like your report. We can use one of the conference rooms," she said, then turned and strode toward the glass-walled rooms at the far end of the programming area.

Weezy's first thought was to ignore her. Let her get wherever she was going and realize Weezy hadn't followed. But she had been talking to Choudhary, which gave her some legitimacy.

Weezy negotiated the maze of cubicles to Choudhary's office and knocked on the door frame.

Choudhary looked up, what might pass as surprise—no, irritation—on her face. "Yes."

"I've just been approached by a woman named Holmgren who has asked for an update on my project. I suggested you could give her the update, and she preferred to have me do it." Weezy sensed a presence behind her. "Do I have your okay?"

"Good call, Nardelli." The presence was Holmgren. "But I'd prefer not to drag Samira into this."

Choudhary said, "You should report to Dr. Holmgren and then continue your work on the conversion."

"Yes, ma'am."

Weezy turned to follow Holmgren.

Choudhary held up a hand to stop her. "Where are you on the conversion?"

"Almost finished. Should be ready to benchmark tomorrow."

"Can you finish today?"

"I can, but you'll want to run the benchmark overnight, because it was those overnight runs that caused problems with the older version."

"Okay. Let's get the basic work done by the end of the day."

"I wasn't aware of a time constraint."

"Executive committee review. Just got scheduled." Choudhary was unreadable, but something was different in her demeanor.

"Okay, I'll get on it as soon as I finish my report to Ms. Holmgren."

*   *   *

Weezy followed Holmgren to the conference room. As she held the door for Weezy, Holmgren glanced down the path they'd just followed, then closed the door. What was she concerned about? She turned to Weezy, her demeanor now less formal, extending her hand.

"Sorry to be abrupt," Holmgren said. "I want to draw as little attention to this conversation as possible."

Weezy shook her hand, thinking, *Another damn mystery.*

Holmgren turned to gaze out the window, rubbing her hands as if they were cold. "I work in the medical research division of Voyageur. I specialize in the interface between our devices and the human body. When devices fail, that hardware-to-human connection is most often at fault. That kind of failure happens, but only rarely. When it does, the company goes full throttle to figure it out." She turned to Weezy. "My mother had a Voyageur ICD. Arrhythmia, not too uncommon in people her age. Otherwise, she was in good health. Three weeks ago, she died in the Twin Cities airport. Heart failure."

Weezy tried to keep her voice steady. "I'm . . . so sorry."

"I am, too," Holmgren said. "And angry, and puzzled, and scared. It's possible that it was a fluke—sometimes, the best devices can't prevent the worst outcomes—but there wasn't any indication that the device failed. And there was no rush to investigate, because the company wasn't informed of anything unusual. A couple of people who witnessed my mother's death are digging into what might have happened. They have visited me here at Voyageur. Then I found out that there's some hush-hush project

163

about the database going on, probably started by Stephen Hartsburg. That led me to you. At least, I think to you."

Holmgren paused.

Weezy's defense wall rose but then hesitated. How should she navigate the twists and turns?

Wait a minute. Weezy realized she'd been swept up by the romance of having a seriously high-level person ask her to do an exciting job. There was the pay, sure, but also the encoded link, the airline ticket appearing with such ease. Warsame the driver, the cover story so carefully put together. It read like a spy novel. But now it seemed like it was falling apart. The silence from Hartsburg. Choudhary intuiting a cover story. Not a suave, good-looking tech guru, but creepy Justin. And now, the unexplained device failure of the mother of a company official. The whole thing looked like a house of cards, collapsing. How much did she really owe Hartsburg?

She chose the middle ground. "Yes, I am doing a data security audit. As is common with these audits, I don't know the purpose, other than to find out whether security has been breached. As is also common, the audit has not been announced. A programmer, Justin Biggs, has figured out what I'm doing."

"Has there been a breach?"

"I believe so. Probably an employee taking data. I believe, but have not yet proven, that the software used to control Voyageur's devices may have been selectively altered."

Holmgren's face blanched. "That means someone might be able to interfere with normal operation?"

"Yes."

"That could be catastrophic."

"Yes."

"We need to stay in touch," Holmgren said. "Can I have your contact information?"

"Got a pen?"

Holmgren raised an eyebrow. "You techies still write things dow—" but nodded. "Of course. No personal electronics in the programming area."

Weezy looked around the room. "Umm. No paper. Do you have . . ."

Holmgren dug in her pocket and produced a business card and a pen. Weezy jotted a number on it.

"Do you have a personal phone that Voyageur doesn't know about?" Weezy asked.

"No."

"Husband, boyfriend, girlfriend have a phone Voyageur doesn't know about?"

"My husband."

"Good. Have him join WhatsApp if he's not already a member. It's easy, and WhatsApp messages are encrypted. Then send a message to this number," she said, pointing to what she'd just written. "It's my phone, and Voyageur doesn't have the number. That will allow us to talk privately."

Weezy handed over the card.

Holmgren took out another of her cards. "The woman I mentioned who is looking into my mother's death is Sierra Bauer. I've written her phone and email address on my card," Holmgren said. "At some point, all of us should talk."

Another twist. The solo operation was suddenly crowded.

Weezy left Holmgren in the conference room. She walked slowly toward her cubicle. As she arrived at 87B, a jolt of fear startled her. She couldn't put a finger on what caused it, but it made her want to return to her comfortable, safe cubicle at MIT and forget this convoluted mess. She slipped into her chair, pondering next steps. She tapped the Return key, and her monitor woke.

She keyed in her project ID.

Access denied.

What?

A text appeared center screen: *See me in my office. Choudhary.*

She stood, puzzled. Then that jolt again, this time a chill, like a cold blanket thrown over her. She scanned the area and saw Justin staring at her across the cubicles, sardonic grin triumphant.

*   *   *

Weezy knocked on Choudhary's door frame, and Choudhary said, "Sit."

Eloquent, as usual.

Weezy took a seat and said, "Glad you texted. I'd like to go over some of the changes in the new release with you, and—"

"I've been with Voyageur for twenty-three years," Choudhary said. She took off her glasses and polished the lenses with a tissue. "During that time there's never been an issue with data security. I don't know exactly what this project of yours is, but a system audit by a talented hacker concerns me. Given your skills—Biggs has made your identity public knowledge, and I read the *Wired* article—management must suspect our database has been hacked."

She paused and replaced her glasses. "Have you identified the problem?"

Weezy met her eyes, saw anger, and realized that Choudhary took an attack on Voyageur's database as an attack on herself. She answered, "Data was taken from the secure patient database, probably by an employee. I'm trying to find how it was done and who did it. I have a partial answer."

"Who hired you? Hartsburg? Nguyen?"

"Yes."

Choudhary sat back in her chair, opened the lap drawer, extracted an envelope, and made a note on it. She looked up and said, "It concerns me that the project is being abruptly terminated."

"Terminated?" Weezy mentally backpedaled. Why would Hartsburg stop the project before he got a result? "That makes no sense," she said.

Movement at the office door caught Weezy's eye. A uniformed security person stepped into the room.

"Yes. Right. Makes no sense," Choudhary said. She slid an envelope across her desk. "But you are terminated from this project. You'll be paid through today by wire transfer. There's an expense report form for your meals and other expenses. Your hotel is covered through tonight. You have a flight to Boston tomorrow morning."

*   *   *

The guard had escorted Weezy back to 87B. She convinced him to let her shut down her terminal, which gave her a few keystrokes to sever her project files and hide them. She had no chance to capture them. She scooped up her wallet from the desktop, and the guard escorted her down the row toward the main aisle that led to the security area. Justin's office was on the way, and of course he was watching. Now the chill was gone, and she wanted to slap the superior smirk off his face. At the main aisle, as they turned toward security, Weezy caught a glimpse of Holmgren standing next to Choudhary's door, a look of shock on her face.

The guard directed Weezy back through the security area, where she collected her phone and pad. They passed through the main building to reception. Weezy expected the car that had driven her regularly to be there, Warsame at the wheel, ready with conversation.

Nothing.

She pulled up Uber on her phone and ordered a car to her hotel. The guard told her to stay in the waiting area, spoke to the woman at the reception desk, and left.

She tore open the envelope Choudhary had given her. Sure enough, there was a ticket to Boston, leaving the next morning. And a blank expense report. She almost crumpled the envelope, then remembered Choudhary had written something on the side she'd concealed from the security guy. "wa/me/16123559580." *Hmmm. Contact her on WhatsApp?*

The Uber was due in ten minutes.

How clever of them to do everything so rush-rush, leave me no time to grab any of my work from last night. Why has Hartsburg suddenly called off the project? Think, Napolitani.

She texted Hartsburg, asking what to do, then checked the Uber app. Five minutes.

A message popped up on her phone:

I've been denied entry to the building. My contract is terminated. I'd hoped to meet with you again. Give me a call. Pen.

Weezy saw the Uber pull up. She left the warmth of the reception area for a blast of cold air, got in the Uber, waited until they were well away from Voyageur, and texted back:

I've been let go, too. Back to Boston tomorrow.

Her phone rang almost immediately.

"Weezy? Where are you?"

"In an Uber on the way back to my hotel. I finished my contract at Voyageur, and I'm going home tomorrow."

"I get that you can't talk openly. We need to meet. Text me your address at the hotel, and I'll pick you up. We can talk over dinner."

The call ended, and Weezy texted the hotel address. Talking to Pen took away some of her tension. She realized that even though part of her was relieved to be done with the project, the lack of a conclusion bothered her. Hartsburg hadn't responded at all to her earlier message, and being shut out of the Voyageur system left so many questions unanswered. It would be good to at least talk to Pen before returning to Boston.

*   *   *

The Uber dropped her at her hotel. She didn't have much packing to do, so she spent the hour or so before Pen picked her up for an early dinner fidgeting and trying to figure out how she would get to the file she had hidden in the Voyageur system. She didn't have the computer resources to hack in. There was the WhatsApp address Choudhary had printed on her termination envelope, which might be a resource, but could just as well be a trap. *Probably better to drop the project,* she told herself. She'd been fired. She owed no one anything.

Best to go home.

Her phone peeped like a chicken, the signal for an incoming call on the encrypted link. Hartsburg, finally?

Keep it professional, she thought. She heard herself practically shout, "What is going on?" She hadn't realized how angry she was.

There was a short pause. "Ms. Napolitani, I apologize for my silence. There have been some developments in the case, and I've had to call it quits."

"I'm sorry to hear that. Do you want my report?"

"Thank you for your work, but no."

"Not even though it looks as if your ICD devices may have been—"

"No. Submit your expenses. Go back to Boston." His voice changed. She heard concern. "For your own safety, go back to Boston and discuss this project with no one."

She clicked off, angry and disgusted. Restless, she texted Pen:

Looking forward to dinner. Talked to Hartsburg and it's final. I'm done.

Pen replied immediately:

Yes, dinner should be nice. Unemployment is always worth celebrating.

Chapter 15

Hawke

There was something troubling about the Voyageur transaction, and its name was Gina Apate. Hawke had no leverage with her, other than to kill the deal, but that was contrary to his own economic interests.

He could, however, make sure that outside forces didn't interfere, so he hired Applewhite over the phone rather than wait until he arrived in Detroit.

"Find out what's going on at Voyageur with regard to management and the faulty implant device," he instructed. "Get on this right away. I can assure you that you will be handsomely compensated."

He drummed his fingers on the armrest of his first-class seat as Lufthansa Airlines flight 1139 gained altitude over Barcelona. He expected, or at least hoped, that her investigation would make the upset in his stomach go away. He would call her for an update when his flight landed in Frankfurt. Until then, he would occupy himself by worrying about Gina Apate.

Maybe she's Interpol. The possibility made Hawke pause.

But my three-million-dollar fee should not be so easily relinquished, he thought. *The loan might not pass the smell test, but there's nothing illegal about it, unless you consider the now-you-see-it, now-you-don't sleight of hand with the thirty million. But that is for the purpose of apprehending a blackmailer, and the thirty million will be returned to the lender immediately.*

Three million is my reward for apprehending the criminal, Hawke mused. *Or, perhaps, it is my fee for providing the lender the opportunity to acquire a position in Voyageur, or the chance to bilk the cardiac device industry.*

He chuckled to himself at the beauty of his own logic. He was, after all, only taking advantage of an opportunity. He had done *nothing* illegal. He allowed himself a sly smile and ordered a glass of wine from a passing flight attendant to celebrate.

The wine came, and Hawke's face puckered when he tasted it. *THIS should be illegal,* he thought, staring at the wine glass, *not my transaction.*

*   *   *

As soon as Hawke emerged from the jetway into the Frankfurt terminal, he dialed Applewhite. No answer. With two hours to wait until his connecting flight, he found a bar, ordered a bourbon, and tried Applewhite again. Two bourbons and three calls later, his flight to Detroit was called.

He tried Applewhite one last time before boarding. This time she answered.

"You have been difficult to reach, madam," Hawke cooed into the phone. "When you are in my employ, I expect you to be available at all times." The words, and the tone in which he delivered them, told two entirely different stories.

"Uh . . . um . . ." Applewhite stuttered.

"But we are together now," Hawke said, taking her off the hook. "Tell me what you have learned."

"I've told you about the attorney and this Nardelli woman . . ."

"Yes, I have them under surveillance," Hawke interrupted.

"But there's another person nosing around, using the name Molly Burris. She's a phony; the real Burris is an employee of

172

Voyageur who's on maternity leave. This person is apparently passing herself off as Burris, trying to pry information from Voyageur employees. I don't think she's got any connection to Hartsburg, so I'm not sure what her game is."

"What sort of information is she seeking?"

"Mostly about VC-25-4750, I think."

"A reporter, perhaps?" Hawke speculated. "See what else you can find out about this woman, and what information she desires. Have there been any other incidents involving that device?"

"None that I've heard of."

"What can you tell me about Hartsburg?"

"He's still shacked up with his mistress in his Northwoods mansion; hasn't made a personal appearance at Voyageur in over a week. The company seems to be running okay without him."

A second call for his flight reverberated in the background. "I must go," he said. "I will see you at the Detroit airport in eight hours."

"Wait. One more thing," Applewhite said. "One of Voyageur's employees is . . . was . . . the daughter of a woman who died from a faulty implant. The employee's name is Olivia Holmgren. She has gotten a couple of people from outside the company involved."

"Police?"

"No . . . maybe . . . I'm not sure."

"Please look further into that, as well. And stay close to your phone."

*   *   *

Hawke mulled the information as he boarded the plane. A meeting with Hartsburg was definitely needed in order to impress upon him that the three million dollars was owed regardless of whether this lawyer, Wilkinson, was able to find Calder. *And what*

173

of this person masquerading as an employee? News media, or maybe Interpol? Or a bureaucrat skulking around? Perhaps people from outside the company meddling, trying to take advantage of the situation?

Or, maybe, a mysterious heiress trying to be sure her thirty-five million dollars is safe?

He chuckled to himself. He loved puzzles. Especially when he knew where all the pieces were, and how they would all fit together.

Chapter 16

Gina

Gina activated the Zoom session and waited for Hartsburg to join her. She had considered driving to northern Minnesota to meet with him in person but, prompted by the weather, had opted for the efficiency of a video call.

The email she had sent to set up the meeting had simply introduced her as the person who was providing the money "to solve your problem" and who needed to go over a few details before the loan closing. Hartsburg had accepted her invitation immediately.

An icon appeared on the screen, indicating that Hartsburg was in the Zoom waiting room. Gina took a deep breath, sat up straight, and clicked on the icon. Hartsburg appeared on the screen, tanned and relaxed with a smile on his face, wearing a flannel shirt over a turtleneck.

"Ms. Apate, I presume," he intoned with a lilt in his voice.

"Mr. Hartsburg, I am Gina Apate. I have tentatively agreed to lend you thirty-five million US dollars, but I have learned that your implant device, VC-25-4750, has been compromised and that two people have died as a result. What would you do if you were in my position?"

"I . . . uh . . . I . . . uh," Hartsburg stammered, caught off-guard by the frontal assault.

"I am going to withdraw my loan offer," Gina said, without waiting for Hartsburg to utter a cogent sentence, "unless you meet certain conditions."

"What con—"

"Perhaps you should ask Ms. Doran to join you. These conditions affect her as well as you."

"What? Why?"

Gina stared at him through the screen. "I am not a patient person, Mr. Hartsburg."

Hartsburg, his tanned face now ashen, slowly turned in his chair. "Tricia," he shouted. "You'd better come in here."

Gina watched as Tricia, an attractive, middle-aged woman, appeared in the background and walked toward the screen, her expression puzzled.

"Ms. Doran, my name is Gina Apate. I am the person who is keeping you alive by lending the money to pay your boyfriend's blackmailer."

Tricia staggered back one step, her mouth open but speechless. She looked at Hartsburg with a deer-in-the-headlights expression.

"There are certain requirements that must be met for me to make this loan," Gina continued. "They are non-negotiable. Unless you both agree to all of them, I will not make the loan and, depending upon the circumstances, I may have to alert the proper regulatory authorities about the deaths caused by your VC-25-4750 device."

Paralyzed, they sat staring at Gina, mouths agape.

"First," Gina said, "you must immediately terminate all investigations, and all personnel involved in the investigations, related to the blackmail attempt, to the database hack, and to the flaws in VC-25-4750. Next . . ."

"I've already done that," Hartsburg interrupted, relieved to have something to which he could respond.

Gina glared at him. "Next," she repeated, "you will resign from the board, and as chief executive officer of Voyageur. You will, of course, be given an exit package sufficient to allow you to lead your current lifestyle."

She held up her hand, palm out, to stop either of them from interrupting. "You will name me as your preferred replacement on the board of directors and will convince the other board members to elect me as your replacement and as chairman. I will provide you with a complete written authorization and power of attorney, which you will execute and return to me promptly. You will include a letter explaining that you are indisposed and stepping aside temporarily in favor of me, a respected international business consultant."

"How could I . . . I can't . . . the outside directors—Reverend Leighton especially—wouldn't just accept that. They'd want details, background on why this is happening."

"Not my problem," Gina replied. "Threaten them if you have to."

"I'm supposed to intimidate *Sterling Leighton*? The guy marched in fucking Selma when he was a kid. He's faced down dogs, fire hoses, cops with truncheons—"

"If you want the deal, use your persuasive powers to make it happen."

"But they will never—"

"You will place all your Voyageur stock, and stock options, in a voting trust that I will control . . ."

"That's not part of our deal," Hartsburg sputtered.

"It is now," Gina said.

She addressed Tricia. "You will quit your position at Voyageur. You will be given a severance package commensurate with your time of service. Most importantly, your cardiac device will continue to function normally."

"I won't . . ." Hartsburg started to rise from his chair.

Gina's reply was calm and steely. "These terms are *non-negotiable*. You have seventy-two hours to call a board meeting, tender your resignation, have me elected chairman, and sign the voting trust that will be delivered to you tomorrow. Unless all of that happens, there will be no loan to pay off your blackmailer, and you, Tricia, will be condemned to a life of fear, wondering whether your implant is going to work."

Hartsburg sat back down.

"You have my contact information," Gina said. "Let me know the time and place of the board meeting."

The screen went black as the Zoom session ended.

Chapter 17

Gina/Biggs

Although Gina had given Hartsburg seventy-two hours, she had no time to wait. She needed to find Calder and learn how he'd been able to make the 4750 devices fail on command.

Using the stolen Molly Burris credentials to secure entry, she brazenly walked into Biggs's third-floor cubicle and sat down in the extra chair.

"What the . . . what are you doing here?" a surprised Biggs stammered.

"Justin, I lied to you," she said, loud enough for adjacent cubicles to hear. "I am not Molly Burris. My name is Gina Apate, and I am about to become the CEO of Voyageur. I need to locate Ralph Calder, and you are going to do it for me. How quickly you perform that task will determine your future in this company."

Biggs hesitated. "You . . . what? I haven't heard anything about any change in CEO."

"Well, how do you like being privy to inside information? You're privileged, Mr. Biggs. But if you don't get with the program in approximately two seconds, you'll be privileged to be unemployed."

Biggs, blinked, gulped, nodded. "What do I do when I find Calder?"

"You bring him to me," Gina answered, her voice now several decibels lower.

"Listen, I'm all in," Biggs whispered, "but why me?"

"When we met, I couldn't let you know who I am or what is happening with Voyageur," Gina responded, ignoring Biggs's question. "Now things have progressed so that it is no longer necessary to keep it secret."

"What about Hartsburg?"

"He'll be resigning. I'll be in control."

"Wow. How did—"

"There are some things you do not need to know at this time. Just bring me Calder. Then we'll take the next step."

Gina began to rise.

"Wait."

She stopped in mid-rise and fixed Biggs with a stony glare.

"I may have something for you that's better than Calder."

Gina sat back down.

"I can get the complete list of people who have VC-25-4750 implants; over five thousand of them. There might be some people on the list who would be of interest to you."

"Why would they be of interest to me?"

"Because knowing who's on the list would provide you leverage, if you get my drift." Biggs paused, a smug look on his face.

"As CEO, I'll be able to get that list any time I want it. Find Calder!"

Biggs bristled. "I'll find Calder for you, but he's not the only one you need to keep an eye on; there's also that lawyer Hartsburg hired. She's still screwing around in Voyageur's internal matters, causing trouble. And you need to get rid of Olivia Holmgren. Having the daughter of someone who died from one of our implants as an employee is insanity."

Gina's answer was terse. "The lawyer has already been taken care of. I'll handle Dr. Holmgren at the appropriate time." She rose. "Here is my new contact information. Let me know when you have located Calder. You have twenty-four hours."

Chapter 18

Pen/Weezy

"It's early for dinner, even for Minnesota," Pen said. Indeed, the dining room in the restaurant tucked away in what seemed like a cozy neighborhood was mostly empty. Dusk was gathering, and the lighting inside was low. *Good for conspiracies,* Weezy thought.

"What's funny?" Pen asked.

"Oh, I was just thinking of my original conception of this project as a high-level, sophisticated data-sniffing job, and here I am at four thirty in the afternoon, in a restaurant across from a small body shop in a neighborhood in . . . which twin city?"

"Minneapolis. I believe we're in the Longfellow neighborhood."

"—in Minneapolis, my cover pretty much blown since the first day, nothing to report, a lot to suspect, a plane ticket home, and a blank expense report."

She paused, then continued, "And some tantalizing information that suggests someone might be tampering with Voyageur ICDs in a way that kills people. In fact—"

She saw the warning in Pen's eyes.

The *maître d'* had become their waiter and was hovering, pad in hand.

Weezy picked up the menu.

Pen shook her head. "Order the walleye sandwich."

The waiter nodded agreement, and Pen said to him, "Two."

*   *   *

Dinner was delicious. Weezy had been skeptical about ordering fish this far away from either ocean, but the walleye was as good as anything she could get on the wharf at home.

Weezy had briefed Pen about the stolen data, Holmgren and her comment about the other people involved, as well as the tantalizing hints about ICD control software that she'd hidden in the Voyageur system. And the call from Hartsburg, telling her the project was over.

"He didn't even want a report. He sounded different from when we'd first talked, maybe scared, and he told me to talk to no one about this for my own safety."

"Glad you ignored that last part," Pen said. She then gave Weezy a capsule version of her own research to date. Weezy listened, impressed at the amount Pen had uncovered in the short time since they'd met.

"And for learning all this, you got fired," Weezy said.

"I got canned," Pen agreed. "But who knows why? My ID card didn't work to get me into the building. So, I called Nancy Nguyen and found out she quit. Then I spent half an hour making phone calls to people in HR and Legal and finally learned that my contract has been terminated. Classy."

They skipped the luscious-looking ice cream cake and ordered coffee. The restaurant was filling, the noise level rising. Weezy was suddenly anxious to go back to the hotel. She enjoyed Pen's company, her agile mind, a budding friendship. But it would go nowhere—there was no more to do. And Hartsburg's warning about her safety had been picking at her all night long. Time to cut and run back to her comfortable, if slightly boring, life in Boston.

Weezy took her last sip of coffee and said, "It bothers me that something awful might be happening here, but I don't know what to do about it besides pack up and go home. I've enjoyed working with you, and—"

"Don't go home."

"Like I said, I don't know what—"

"Don't go home. There's more work to do here." Pen leaned forward. Weezy pulled back from the intensity in her gray-green eyes. "I need you to help me."

"If I stay, I have a whole lot of logistics problems, Pen. Until just now, Hartsburg and company have been very professional. If I try to change my ticket, will they see? They know where I'm living, so if I stay, I have to find a different place. Hartsburg warned me not to talk—like I've just been doing with you—for my own safety. And I have to do it with my own money. Furthermore—"

"Weezy, this is something big. It's not going to conveniently evaporate. It runs through technology and data. I need you."

"Yeah. Technology and data, and there's the other problem with me staying here: I've got this peashooter"—she dragged her pad out of her bag— "and we're trying to bag an elephant. In Boston, I have computer power and the fully functional version of my own software to crack Voyageur's database."

Pen sat back, chewing her lip. The waiter brought the bill. She took it and waved off Weezy's credit card.

"You bribing me?"

Pen chuckled. "Sure, if that would work. But let me make a call. I think I can solve the computer power problem."

*   *   *

Weezy cracked the door of her hotel room and listened. She opened the door slowly. Her suitcase was on the rack where she'd put it, with the "Harvard Sucks" T-shirt flopped over the edge

183

where she'd left it. She entered, feeling stupid. This was just a temporary contract, and it had been terminated. No big deal. Except . . . If someone was messing with ICDs, they probably wouldn't hesitate to kill to cover it up. Hell, they might already have done so. She closed the door and double-locked it.

Pen had convinced her to stay. She'd made a reservation for the next night at a hotel Pen suggested. They'd decided to make a serious effort to make it seem as if she'd gone home. She would go to the airport in the morning, go through security, to the gate, wait until boarding, plead emergency and not get on the plane. Pen would pick her up and take her to the new hotel.

She considered sending a note to Choudhary on the WhatsApp address but decided it should wait until she was out of this hotel with its too-easy-to-identify server.

Tomorrow.

*   *   *

The next morning, Weezy took an Uber to the airport. She carried only her backpack, no luggage to check. She sat in the waiting area at the gate, and as boarding began, she sidled near the service desk. The call from Pen came in just on time and, hoping she wouldn't hurt her new friend's ears, nearly shouted "What?" then a pause and "I'm on my way."

The rest went smoothly. The gate agent told her the hard truth that her ticket was about to become worthless, confirmed that she'd checked no baggage, and told her she hoped things would come out all right.

Pen picked her up and told her about her nephew Kenny, the computer jock. "I'm afraid he knows who you are," Pen said. "I didn't know you were famous."

"More like infamous."

"Well, Kenny's excited to meet you. I asked him if he had a big computer. He chuckled and spouted a bunch of techno word salad—a Ryzen nine something-or-other, Risk Five something, thirty-two gigs of—"

"Internal memory, probably," Weezy said. "Yeah, he's got a big computer." She hid her skepticism. Anyone could put together a big computer, but a whiz-kid to Pen might be what Weezy's friends on the internet dismissively called a script-kiddie. But Pen had been a problem-solver extraordinaire so far, so maybe . . .

Which brought up Choudhary's note.

"I have a dilemma," Weezy said.

Pen glanced at her.

"My supervisor at Voyageur was Samira Choudhary," she continued, glancing at the skyline of Minneapolis as they drove north. "She seems like a company person; she learned about my job and was angry that someone was messing with the database. Also, she directed Holmgren to me, and Holmgren seems to trust her. When she terminated me and passed over the envelope with the ticket home, she wrote a WhatsApp address on the back. I sense that she sees the violation of Voyageur and wants to help me, but it could be a trap. I encrypted some files I think are important and stuffed them into a hidey-hole on the Voyageur system. I believe she's willing to help; she could get us those files."

"I think she's okay if Holmgren trusts her."

"I also gave Holmgren a way to send encrypted messages, and she said we should maybe get everyone together."

"Sounds like a good idea," Pen said. She took an exit. "I'll drop you at the hotel. Kenny can meet you there this afternoon and the three of us can talk."

*   *   *

185

The hotel was on the edge of downtown Minneapolis, near one of the lakes, she was told. They let Weezy check in early. Her room smelled new and apparently used the same not-unpleasant cleaning chemical the last one had. She was relieved that it wasn't too expensive, at least by Boston standards. She could relax for an hour, but that would put off the decision on whether to trust Choudhary.

Weezy dropped into a leather easy chair next to the bed, closed her eyes . . . and her pad chimed. Incoming WhatsApp message. She opened it:

Ms. Napolitani. This is Olivia, and this is a safe phone. Understand you were terminated yesterday. Are you in Boston?

Weezy tapped back:

No, I'm still in Minneapolis. Working to finish the work on ICD manipulation. I have been offered help by Samira Choudhary.

Her fingers paused. *Am I getting ahead of myself? If I'm mistaken about Olivia or Choudhary, I could be in danger. So could Pen. But this problem is too big to dodge.*

She finished her message. *Can I trust her?* And pressed send.

The answer came almost immediately:

I've talked with Samira about this. She's loyal to Voyageur. She thinks Justin Biggs is up to no good. Yes, I think you can trust her.

Weezy shot back:

Great. Thanks. I'll tell you when I know more.

Kenny knocked on her door at 2:00 as promised. He was a good-looking kid, maybe not a lot younger than Weezy. He had naturally dark, curly hair with a wide blue streak. Six feet tall and slight of build. Tasteful ear hardware. An appealing combination of preppy and geek.

"Ken Sellars." He put out his hand. He seemed nervous, but the shake was strong, confident. "What an honor to meet you."

Was she blushing? *Crap!*

"You too. I don't know your aunt well, but she is very impressive. She thinks highly of you." She couldn't think of any more small talk, so she dove right in. "Has Pen told you about our situation?"

"She says you have found some problem in Voyageur's ICD software and maybe a list of names that someone copied out of the database."

"True. I ran a test that I haven't analyzed. It's in an encrypted file in my work area. I may have a way of moving it with some help, but it would take more computer power than I have to analyze it. Also, I figured out a way to penetrate the company's database security, but, again, I don't have the power to do it."

Kenny gave Weezy the specs of his computer.

"Phew! Did you build it?"

"I did."

"Then I think we're in business."

After half an hour, Weezy knew Kenny was definitely not a script-kiddie, and they had built a plan to hack Voyageur. They Zoomed Pen into the conversation.

Pen listened to their plan, then considered. "There are several people critical to this. With a realistic shot at getting the data we need from Voyageur, we need a group meeting. Weezy, you said Olivia Holmgren gave you contact information for Sierra Bauer. Let's give her a call."

Chapter 19

Hawke

As the plane taxied toward its gate at Detroit Metropolitan Airport, Hawke picked up messages that had accumulated during the flight. Only one stood out: a call from Ralph Calder. His call-back went to voicemail. Hawke left a message.

Applewhite waited for him at an airport watering hole just outside security. She gave him an address for Pen Wilkinson and a report on Louise "Weezy" Napolitani, celebrity hacker.

"Apparently they've both been fired by Hartsburg." Applewhite shrugged. "Guess he didn't need them anymore."

"What about this Molly Burris imposter?" Hawke asked.

"I don't think she's a media person, unless she's freelance," Applewhite answered. "I know most of the locals, and they would have no reason to give a false identity. They'd just barge in and ask the question. Might be an undercover cop."

"Or a securities regulator," Hawke suggested. *Or maybe it's Gina Apate,* he thought. *She knows a lot about Voyageur.*

Hawke slid an envelope across the table toward Applewhite. "For your services," he said.

Applewhite slid the envelope into her purse. "Should I keep digging?" she asked.

Hawke shook his head. "I'll let you know when I need something further."

After she was out of hearing range, he dialed the number he had been given for Apate. There was no answer, no voicemail.

As Hawke waited for his connecting flight to Minneapolis, his phone buzzed. It was Calder.

"Monsieur Calder, how can I be of service?" Hawke answered.

"I've been getting calls from a Voyageur employee," Calder responded, his voice agitated. "Justin Biggs. He had a small part in developing the 4750 implant device."

"And why does that alarm you?"

"The guy is a pain in the ass and a troublemaker."

"Might he have some legitimate reason to call you? Perhaps to consult on how to fix the flaw in the device?"

"Not him," Calder answered. "He wouldn't ask me to consult. His ego's too big. He thinks he's smarter than everyone else."

Another unpredictable moving part. Hawke thought for a moment. "I suggest you leave town. Do not meet with this Biggs person," he said. "Check into a hotel room somewhere under an assumed name. Pay cash. Don't use your cell phone. We don't want anyone or anything to interfere with the completion of our transaction."

Chapter 20

Matt

Matt quickly learned that finding someone using the internet and technology was far from easy if the person you were looking for knew how to drop off the cybergrid. Not surprisingly, Ralph Calder was one of those people.

After performing multiple generic searches on various people-finder websites and sifting through a few dozen "Ralph Calders" from across the country, Matt had found nothing constructive. He even paid two of the several websites that dug up dirt on people for a fee. That search hit a wall because Calder had apparently dropped off the map or somehow blocked those websites from compiling his personal information.

Sighing, Matt muttered, "Time to call in the cavalry." In his case, it meant calling Zach Perez. He hated to impose yet again, but Danilson's death weighed on him more and more each day. He waited until he knew Zach was at home so as not to disturb him at work. After explaining his frustration at not finding Ralph Calder's address, Matt said, "So, that's my situation. Got any suggestions?"

Another long silence on Zach's end of the connection told him he did, but Zach was reluctant to share that information.

"I know I said I'd stop asking you for help after the employee records help you gave me," Matt said. "But Danilson was my mentor, a true inspiration. I owe him my career. I want to help his family. If there was *anything* suspicious about his death—either malfeasance on the device or something worse—I want justice for his wife and son."

"I get it," Zach said. "Loyalty and family are damn important to me, too. It's just that finding someone who doesn't want to be found and has the computer skills to erase their online existence won't be easy. It could take days of digging."

"Days?"

"All depends on the searcher's skills and ability to access information not available to most hackers."

Matt perked up. "But *you* have that sort of access, don't you?"

More silence.

"Come on, Zach. Let me buy dinner and we can discuss it. Maybe you can give me a few hints on how to access that special information so you can stay out of it."

Zach laughed. "Your tech skills have come a long way since I first met you, *amigo*. But ain't no way I'm giving you some *hints* and you not going to jail."

Matt immediately comprehended the statement. "FBI-type hints? Classified or something?"

"Or something."

"Okay. But let's do dinner no matter what. I owe you that from last time."

A sigh. "All right, Matt, but I'm worried about gaining weight."

"What?"

"By my count, you owe me three dinners now."

*   *   *

Matt sat in his car that night, watching a house In Eagan, not far from the VCS campus. It was the kind of neighborhood where doctors, lawyers, and CEOs insulated themselves from their worker bees. Finding Ralph Calder's house, a near-McMansion, had proven ridiculously easy. If Calder had tried going off the grid and erasing all traces of his life, he had made an obvious mistake: he owned a house and had left it in his own name. Zach's quick search of property tax records had turned up the house in less than two minutes, leaving the young man annoyed and Matt embarrassed. The endeavor had hardly required the efforts of a world-class hacker.

Matt got out of his car and strode boldly to the door, eager to confront Ralph Calder about the threatening emails, and perhaps even get a believable explanation of who or what had caused Magnus Danilson's death from someone who understood the Voyageur ICDs more thoroughly than Biggs did.

Predictably, no one answered, so Matt returned to his car and drove it to a spot where he could see Calder's house but was far enough away so Calder couldn't easily identify him. He doubted Calder would recognize him, but he took no chances, wanting to gain the upper hand in a surprise confrontation. Then he settled in for a long, yet hopeful, wait, running the engine frequently to avoid freezing in the January cold.

He remained in position until darkness fell and nature called. Matt drove a few miles to a nearby Kwik Trip, used the restroom, and bought coffee and a microwaveable sandwich. He returned to his station within ten minutes and observed no lights on in Calder's house. Odds were small that he'd come and gone at exactly the time Matt had taken a break, so Matt was still hopeful.

But after three more hours of impatient waiting, Matt gave up. His options were to keep on surveilling, hire someone else to watch Calder's house, or try something else. His gut told him Calder would not soon return home, that he was probably hiding from someone or something. Finding the house had been easy—perhaps too easy. Why would someone with Calder's skills leave his house open to discovery? Unless, Matt thought, he had vanished and didn't intend to return.

As far as Matt knew, the most likely person to know Calder's whereabouts was Justin Biggs. He inwardly sighed, knowing Biggs wasn't likely to talk to him again, but he refused to give up. Maybe he'd call it quits after doing everything he could think of to solve the riddle of Dr. Dan's death. But that time was a long way off. And it might never happen.

*　　　*　　　*

Matt tried lying in wait for Biggs outside his Minneapolis condo once again. Unfortunately, Biggs had grown paranoid and constantly looked around and behind him as he headed for the building entrance. Upon spotting Matt rapidly approaching, Biggs bolted inside the foyer and hit the panic button that had been installed primarily for women worried about their safety from stalkers, but also for anyone in distress. An alarm blared, catching the ears of several people in the parking lot. Someone coming out of the building quickly reversed course and retreated to the foyer. When Biggs stood there, glaring and gloating at him, Matt knew his photo had been taken from probably four different angles.

Deciding to retreat and regroup, Matt quickly got into his car and drove out of the lot, using the farthest exit from the building entrance. He'd been outsmarted that time but wasn't ready to concede victory to Biggs.

The answer to the confrontation issue was to catch Biggs in neutral territory. He rented a different car, returned to Voyageur Cardiac Systems late the next afternoon, and waited where he could see Biggs's car and follow him when he left work. He hoped Biggs would go out to dinner again and was proven right after following him to a different restaurant. This one was a pizza place closer to VCS.

Once Biggs was inside the restaurant, Matt followed. He looked around more than usual, taking a page from Biggs's paranoia playbook in case the programmer was setting him up. But no one intercepted him before he went inside. At the hosting stand, Matt scanned the room and saw Biggs sitting at a table in the far corner, chatting with the waitress.

When a woman arrived to seat him, Matt pointed at Biggs and said, "I'm with the guy at that corner table."

She nodded, and Matt headed toward Biggs. He caught Biggs's look of surprise and stared him down. But then Biggs's surprise changed to a smug smile that seemed far too confident for a man literally trapped in a corner. When Biggs pointed at him and said, "This is the asshole," Matt spun around to see two extremely large, muscular men striding toward him with intense expressions.

Biggs *had* set him up. He should have known that someone with Biggs's intelligence and cunning would not blithely ignore Matt's earlier confrontations with him and assume that all was well in his world. Matt raised his hands in mock surrender and faced Biggs.

"Bodyguards, Justin? Isn't that a bit of overkill? I just want to know where to find Ralph Calder. He's dropped out of sight. All I know is his most recent address. And he's not answering."

Biggs sneered and glanced at his two bodyguards, who circled around Matt to stand on either side of the seated Biggs. "Looks like you're shit outta luck, Larson," Biggs said.

At least Biggs still believed Matt's fake name was real. Unfortunately, with the abundance of cameras filming people in public places, Matt knew Biggs could easily identify his photo and then connect it to his real name through some legal database or another.

"Look, Biggs, I don't have a beef with you anymore other than your disrespecting Dr. Danilson. But I got my punches in and that's over. I don't want any trouble. Just tell me how to find Calder."

"Go fuck yourself," Biggs said.

When the bodyguards took a step forward, Matt beat a humble retreat. Getting into a fight would not help the Danilson family. But the fact that Biggs needed bodyguards implied he was either more important than Matt had first imagined, or had a severely overblown ego. Or was there a third reason?

*   *   *

Floundering for a way to proceed, Matt returned to Calder's house. He felt the perfect fool for thinking this time Calder would magically show up, invite him inside, and answer all his questions over a snifter of cognac. With no other ideas to pursue, what could it hurt? He parked a safe distance away from the house in case Calder arrived home and got suspicious. An hour passed with no activity other than neighbors coming and going in cars. But when it was fully dark, other than streetlights, house lights, and starlight, a car pulled up in front of Calder's house and stopped.

Shifting into high alert, Matt stared at the person exiting the car. In the darkness, he was pretty sure it was a woman but wasn't positive. She walked to the front door as if she were a friend calling on Calder. As expected, no one answered the door for two minutes after she'd knocked. But when the woman pulled out a small flashlight, turned it on, and crept around to the back of the house, Matt got out of his car and followed her at a safe distance. Fortunately, her boots crunching on the snow masked his own steps. He waited until she was in the backyard before inching to the corner and peering around it. She knocked on the back door and waited for thirty seconds. Then she went to each first-floor window and shone her light through the panes.

Matt sprang around the corner and strode toward the woman. "What the hell are you doing?"

She jumped and gasped, then flashed her light in his eyes. Matt thrust up his hand as a shield, then crouched, trying to get a clear look at her.

"I'll ask the same thing, buddy," she said defiantly.

"I'm waiting to talk to the guy who lives here," Matt retorted. She hadn't pulled a gun yet or attacked him with some sort of karate or Taekwondo move, so he felt relatively safe.

"What guy is that?"

"You first. You seem more eager to talk to him."

"You a cop or something?"

"No. Are you?"

"No. So tell me who you're here to see." She seemed ready to play serve-and-volley all night.

Matt was about to give in and answer her question when her gaze shifted past him. He tensed but couldn't move until he heard a sonorous male voice say, "Is there a problem here?"

He spun to face a man about his height, decent looking, whose body language screamed "cop." How had he not heard the man's footsteps? Matt mentally kicked himself for letting his danger radar relax and his awareness of his surroundings falter.

"I don't think so, Quinn," said the woman.

Matt turned back to her. "You know him?"

"Yes, and he *is* a cop, so I'd be careful about what you say and do."

Matt raised his hands and checked to see if Quinn was holding his sidearm. He was. "Whoa now, I'm not looking for trouble. I just want to know why you're here. And I'm hoping to talk to someone who lives in this house."

"Who?"

"A guy named Calder."

Her mouth opened perceptibly. "What for?"

"None of your business. Are you here to see him too?"

"Yes. Why else would I be here? Who are you?"

"Just a guy who wants some answers for a dead friend's family."

She raised a brow. "Strange coincidence. That's why I'm here too." She hesitated for a long moment, then reached out a gloved hand. "I'm Sierra Bauer. This is Quinn Moore."

Matt shook her hand and then Quinn's. "Matt Lanier." He motioned for them to follow him. "Let's ring the doorbell again, just in case he was taking a nap earlier."

Sierra and Quinn followed him to the front door, where he pressed the doorbell again. A two-toned chime sounded from within the house.

"I don't think anyone is home," Matt said. He eyed the two strangers, still not trusting their motives. "Does this have anything to do with Voyageur Cardiac Systems?"

"It has everything to do with VCS," Sierra said.

"I think my friend and mentor was killed by a faulty ICD made by VCS."

"I have similar suspicions about another ICD wearer who died in front of me."

"In that case, maybe we should talk."

She nodded slowly. "Maybe."

Matt stomped his boots on the stoop and shivered. "I don't know about you folks, but I'm freezing out here. What say we get a cup of coffee and compare notes?"

Sierra nodded. "Good idea. All the decent coffee shops are closed in the evening, but I know a Denny's not far away that might have something one level above sludge."

Matt followed Sierra and Quinn to the nearby Denny's, where they found a vacant booth, ordered barely drinkable coffee, and began discussing Ralph Calder.

Quinn asked, "How do you think Calder was involved in your friend's death?"

"Why do you want to know?"

"Oh, for Pete's sake, Lanier, lighten up," Sierra said. "Because we think he might have had something to do with the death of my dad's mentor's wife. We just aren't sure how yet."

Matt furrowed his brows. "How did she die?"

"Collapsed after she got off a plane at the airport. She had an ICD—implantable cardioverter-defibrillator—that the autopsy showed malfunctioned."

"They actually determined that?" Matt asked.

"Yes," Sierra said. "Weird thing is, she'd just been in for a checkup, and everything was fine. They updated the device, but there were no signs of any issues, at least according to the family."

"That *is* weird," Matt said. "My professor also had an ICD. He'd recently been to his doctor, who said he was in excellent health. I don't know if he'd had his ICD checked at that appointment. But his family told me it stopped working, and he died because of that."

"So why do you think Calder had something to do with it?"

Matt hesitated, as if he was weighing how much to disclose. "Let's just say someone I know suggested Calder has more information about what happened to our two victims."

"Mind if I ask who?"

"Actually, I do mind." Matt wasn't about to falsely implicate anyone in a potential crime. He'd been on the wrong end of a cop-killer accusation that compounded his troubles staying alive and out of jail. This situation didn't seem quite as serious, but the principle was still valid. "I'll tell you later if necessary to help our investigation."

Sierra scrunched her mouth into a wry smile—a mixture of mild surprise and distrust. She gave Quinn a sidelong glance before saying, "Let me ask you this: You said your professor died in front of you. Did you see anybody suspicious lurking around at the time?"

"There was a guy . . ."

Sierra and Quinn waited.

"He looked like he didn't really belong there. He wore a suit, but he behaved a little strangely. He wore a tie with Seahawks colors."

"Holy—" Before Sierra could answer, her phone rang. She answered it, then excused herself and walked away after saying, "Yes, okay . . . One sec, please."

While she was on the phone, Matt asked Quinn, "If you're the cop, why is she asking all the questions? Seems to me you're the professional interrogator."

Quinn gave him a wry smile. "There are two reasons. One, I'm a cop at the airport, so that's where my jurisdiction begins and ends. Second, Sierra's a bit, um, how do I put this, *headstrong*, and doesn't like to sit on the sidelines—especially when she has me for backup."

Matt nodded appreciatively. "I've known a few women like her."

Sierra returned a minute later and sat down. "Interesting call I just took. You ever hear of a woman named Pen Wilkinson?"

Matt's expression remained unchanged. Wilkinson was the attorney Biggs had told him about. He decided to evade the question. "Who is she?"

"She's an attorney who was hired by VCS to look into problems with the VC-25-4750."

"That's right up our alley," Matt said.

"Yup. I told her about you and about Calder. She asked if we'd run across a guy named Justin Biggs. We did—how about you?"

Matt recoiled against the booth's padded backing. If Sierra and Quinn knew about Biggs, then his reluctance to share what he knew about the man was a moot point. "Um, yeah. I've run across him."

"Is there any chance he and not Calder could have caused the deaths of these people?"

Matt shook his head. "He has a solid alibi. He was at an anger management retreat up north. But I wouldn't rule out some involvement. He's an asshole."

Sierra smirked. "First, asshole's a little too polite a description of that walking bag of slime. Second, Pen called to ask me to meet her about the situation at VCS. When I mentioned I had just met you, she said, 'Bring him along too if he's interested.'"

"Hell yes, I'm interested," Matt said. "When and where?"

"I told her Quinn and I can host the meeting. Give me your cell number, and I'll let you know the time."

Matt did so, and they all agreed to keep in touch in case the meeting fell through. He fished his wallet from a pocket, pulled out two business cards, and gave one to each of his new acquaintances. "Here's my contact information."

Quinn read the card and raised his eyebrows. "So, you're a musician, huh?"

"Yeah," Matt said. "The man I was talking about whose ICD failed was my college orchestra director and mentor." He tossed a five-dollar bill onto the table to cover his bill. "If you learn something, anything, about what might have happened to him, please contact me."

"Sure," Sierra said. The couple pocketed the cards and watched as Matt left. He felt their stares on his back until he was out of the restaurant.

*   *   *

Quinn paid their check, and he and Sierra left. As they headed for their vehicle, Sierra said, "Well, that was weird."

"What's weird is, someone else is looking for Calder because someone they knew died when their ICD stopped working. Talk about coincidence."

"With something like an ICD?" Sierra said as they headed down the road. "This doesn't feel like a coincidence."

Chapter 21

The Group

Sierra puttered in her living room, straightening, waiting for her guests. Quinn walked in.

She turned, holding a magazine. "Have you read this yet?"

"Just toss it."

She nodded and began to walk away. Quinn gently took her arm, steering her to the couch and sitting down next to her. "Give it a rest, hon. Everything looks fine."

"Did you put more salt on the front steps?"

"Yes, they're clear now."

Sierra exhaled. "What am I doing, Quinn? I've invited these people I don't know, looking into something I don't understand, based on a wacky theory . . ."

"You're doing the right thing."

"I hope so—"

The doorbell rang. She glanced at her watch—seven on the dot. Matt Lanier stood on the doorstep.

"Come on in," she said. "Pretty punctual for a musician." She opened the door, letting in a blast of icy air.

"Just a fluke," Matt assured her.

Quinn stepped forward, holding out his hand. "Nice to meet you again, Matt. Welcome to beautiful Apple Valley."

"Thanks. I don't get out to the suburbs much." They shook.

"Something to drink?" Quinn asked, taking his guest's heavy parka.

"How about a beer?"

Sierra and Quinn looked at each other, uncertain. "I think we have one left over, on the bottom shelf," Sierra said.

"Forget it," Matt said. "Diet Coke, if you have it."

"Sure." Quinn left, and Sierra showed their guest to a recliner next to an entertainment center.

Matt looked around. "Nice place."

"Thanks. A better meeting venue than a car staking out a house, I guess."

Quinn returned with Matt's soda, but the doorbell rang again before he could sit down. Sierra joined him at the door, where two women waited outside, one in a wheelchair.

"Hi," said the blonde in the wheelchair. "I'm Pen. This is Weezy."

"Oh," Sierra said. "I didn't—" She caught herself.

"It's okay," Pen said. "I should have told you about the wheelchair."

Sierra ran a hand through the streak of white in her dark hair. "So . . . what do we do?"

"Maybe somebody could pull me up."

Quinn stepped through the door. "I think we can do that. I'm Quinn." He shook hands with both guests.

Sierra joined them on the sidewalk. "And I'm Sierra. But I guess that's obvious. I'm sorry. I just . . ."

Pen laughed. The laughter was soon joined by Weezy and Quinn, and finally by Sierra herself. "Don't worry about it," Pen said. "I'm sort of an awkwardness-producing machine."

Matt appeared at the doorway.

"Come on out," said Sierra. "Join the party."

"How about if you all come in? It's like the Ice Age out here." Matt introduced himself to Weezy and Pen. Then he and Quinn turned Pen's wheelchair around and pulled her backward up the three steps while Sierra held the door. In the entryway, Pen produced a small rag, which she used to wipe the snow and salt off the wheels of her chair. Pen and Weezy struggled out of their winter coats, and everyone got situated in the living room.

Pen tried to break the ice. "Are you a native Minnesotan, Matt?"

"Yes."

"How do you handle the cold?"

"It doesn't bother me much. I once spent most of a winter camping outside, up in the Boundary Waters."

Weezy and Pen shivered involuntarily. "What do you do for a living?" Weezy asked.

"I'm a musician."

"Who trains for polar expeditions in your spare time."

Matt shrugged. "Not exactly. It's a long story. Didn't end well."

"What kind of music do you play?"

"Jazz and classical. I'm on the sidelines at the moment." He held up his hands. "I just finished rehabbing an injury to some fingers. Gives me more time to find out what happened to Magnus."

Sierra arrived with sodas and cookies, setting them down on the coffee table. "How about you, Weezy? You're a programmer, right?"

"Actually, a cybersecurity specialist."

"Sounds impressive," said Matt.

"Weezy is more than a 'specialist,'" Pen said. "She's a legend in the cybersecurity world. That's why Stephen Hartsburg personally hired her."

Sierra and Quinn sat down, and everyone reached for the goodies. "Your turn, Pen," said Sierra. "Tell us about yourself."

"I'm a lawyer. I started my career handling personal injury cases and then spent a couple of years as a federal prosecutor. But in recent years I've worked mostly on freelance investigations, like the one Nancy Nguyen hired me for."

"Have you worked here in Minnesota?"

"Yes—all over, really. I live in California, but Minneapolis has become my second home."

"I'm an aircraft mechanic," Sierra said. "And Quinn is a cop. We're just working folk."

"You're professionals," Pen replied. "And you've made some astute observations about this situation. Speaking of which . . . we appreciate your hosting. I know this is a little unusual, forming an unofficial group like this, but it looks like the situation we've been exposed to is literally life-and-death. Until we've got enough to turn it over to the police, we'll have to do what we can. As I understand it, Quinn is a police officer but doesn't have jurisdiction here and needs to stay in an advisory role."

She looked to Quinn for confirmation. He nodded.

"Is Olivia Holmgren coming?" Pen asked. "She's the one who brought us together."

"She's not coming," Sierra replied. "She's still a Voyageur employee, and I think she wants to distance herself from our efforts."

The room went silent. "I guess we feel a little awkward," Pen said. "We don't really know each other. Maybe we need to just get started, and we'll get more comfortable as we work together."

"Sounds good," Sierra said. There were nods from the rest of the group.

"Sierra, I think you were the first to realize that something was wrong. Why don't you summarize for us what you know?"

Sierra took a breath, put her glass down, and described her involvement, along with Quinn's, beginning with Alice Holmgren's death, her conversations with Olivia, and their suspicions about Ralph Calder.

"He thought the ICDs were defective, even before he allegedly tampered with them," Pen suggested. "And the defect might have killed his wife?"

"Correct. So Olivia asked us to look into this, but Quinn and I don't think we have enough to go to the police."

"I agree," Pen said. "We don't know what we're dealing with here. Is it intentional weaponization? Or is it just a defect, albeit a fatal one, that the company is trying to cover up?"

Matt rolled his eyes. "You're telling me there's nothing nefarious here? Just a defect? Give me a break."

"It could be a defect somebody is trying to exploit."

"So Calder is just hanging around, waiting to exploit a defect? I'm telling you, this was deliberate. It was murder."

"Let's not jump to conclusions, Matt."

"How much proof do you need?"

"Hold that thought, and let's figure out how it might work. Weezy, what do you think?"

Weezy began, her voice carrying the strains of a New England accent. "Stephen Hartsburg contacted me to check out VCS's patient database; he said he suspected some kind of breach. And Pen found out that he was being extorted for a gazillion dollars, probably by Calder. Anyway, because somebody was interested in the patient database, I figured they were trying to find people with a specific type of device. I also thought maybe they might be using the software updating process to slip some kind of malware or vulnerability onto the device. And I've come to believe that both of those things are true."

There were nods around the room.

"I found extra code being slipped into some of the updates."

"Could that extra code actually control the device?" Pen asked. "Tell it to shut down or give the patient a shock?"

"Theoretically, yes. And with access to the database, Calder or another bad guy might be able to zero in on the serial numbers of specific devices, or maybe on the doctor's office of specific patients."

"My God," Pen exclaimed. "That's it. The kill code."

The group paused for a few moments to let this sink in. "Sierra," Pen finally asked, "if Calder has the information on the patients and their devices, what would he do next? Would these commands—the extra code—work automatically? Or with a few clicks on a keyboard?"

"I suppose you could plant a time bomb with the code," Sierra answered. "Set it to go off at a certain time. But that's not how it's worked so far. It looks like Calder is physically present and activating the commands with a radio signal. He wants to see it happen."

Quinn Moore sipped from his soda glass. "So he would presumably have a transmitter of some type."

"Right. He could build one from scratch, or . . ."

The group waited.

Sierra explained her theory. "Patients get a station—a receiver—with their ICD that receives data from their device, and the station sends that data—encrypted, of course—back to the hospital via a network cable and the internet. Thing is, it wouldn't be that hard to turn a wireless receiver into a transceiver—a transmitter and receiver combination. In fact, I wouldn't be surprised if they're built that way for future use. I also know that a power boost would extend the range of a transmitter."

"What would the range be?" Quinn asked.

Weezy answered, "Hard to say, but with a power boost and signal amplifier, maybe a few hundred yards."

"And," Matt added, "Calder would probably have one of those stations sitting around from the days when his wife used one."

Sierra nodded.

"So," said Pen, "Calder was apparently at the scene of both the Holmgren and Danilson deaths."

"Right," Matt said. "If we find Calder, we should get some answers."

"True," Pen said. "But maybe not *all* the answers. Something is rotten in the company—more than just Ralph Calder going rogue and fiddling with the code and database. Both Weezy and I were fired without explanation. Nancy Nguyen was forced out, too. And Hartsburg has pretty much vanished."

"According to Olivia, Hartsburg's girlfriend, Tricia Dolan, isn't coming into work," Sierra added.

"I—well, tried the database after I left," Weezy said. "I wanted to try to identify people who received the extra code. People who might be at risk."

"And?" Matt asked.

"It's been locked down, by somebody good." She leaned forward. "With database access, you'd be able to look up the kind of heart problem the patient suffers from. Then you might be able to tailor the attack to the patient. You could give the patient a shock, or you could just cause the device to cease functioning. Whatever would be more effective for the type of cardiac condition."

"Holy shit," Sierra exclaimed. "That's terrifying."

"It might be happening already."

Pen threw her hands up. "This is crazy. Who the hell is pulling these strings at VCS?"

"How about Justin Biggs?" Sierra suggested.

"I've met him a couple of times," Weezy said. "He's a miserable excuse for a human being and a general dumbass."

Matt nodded. "I'll second that. I've had a couple of encounters with him, too."

"He may be involved somehow," Pen said. "But is he the mastermind?"

Nobody answered.

Sierra turned to Weezy. "Where are you on finding names of people at risk?"

"I don't have names yet. I'm still working on getting back in."

"What *do* you know?"

Weezy paused just long enough to let everyone know she'd swallowed a retort. "I found that modified code—the extra stuff slipped in—is in fact being sent to doctors' offices for updates. Fortunately, it's not every doctor's office."

"Do we know which offices?" Quinn asked.

"Before I got locked out of the system, I saw a list of about twenty offices whose software has been modified. It looked like most are located around the Twin Cities and outstate Minnesota. Some in Wisconsin, a cluster in Florida around Tampa, and a few in Arizona. Assuming the doctors' offices aren't complicit, this means that everyone whose ICD has been checked or updated in those offices after insertion is compromised. And, I hate to say this, but the list may not have been complete."

"Can you give us the list?" Matt said.

"I couldn't capture it, but I wrote down as many names as I could remember. I'll send it. What's your WhatsApp handle?"

"Uhhh . . ."

The blank stares and raised eyebrows sent a shiver of fear down Weezy's spine. She stifled her inclination to flame on the group. Instead, she said in what seemed to her a calm voice, "We are going to share a lot of information amongst the group. We cannot just drop it into email. The person who is keeping me out of the database is a black belt in hacking. Everything we share"—she scanned the room—"*everything* . . . must be encrypted. If you don't have one, get a WhatsApp account and let us all know your handle."

"So, you know something bad happened, but you don't know who it affects?" Weezy heard a hint of acid in Quinn's voice.

Once again, Weezy took a breath and responded patiently. "Right, but the good news is, I am working with Pen's nephew, Kenny. He's a talented hacker who owns a big-ass computer. We're going to get into that damn system and find the names of people who might be affected."

"Let's sum up," Pen said. "The evidence for a defect is nearly ironclad. The evidence for deliberate weaponization, not so much."

Matt exploded. "What the hell do you want?"

"Everything is circumstantial. We don't have an airtight case."

"This isn't a courtroom."

"And we are not a bunch of self-appointed vigilantes," Pen shot back. "We're just concerned people trying to learn the truth and turn it over to the authorities."

"Self-appointed," Matt sputtered. "That sounds an awful lot like you."

The doorbell rang. Sierra and Quinn gave each other quizzical looks, then both rose and went to the door.

The man who stood outside was short, wearing an elegant overcoat and a fedora. "Good evening," he said, handing each of them a business card.

Sierra read from the card. "Henri Hawke. Attorney. What can we do for you, Mr. Hawke?"

"I know you are meeting with several people tonight regarding matters at Voyageur Cardiac Systems. I believe I might be able to be of assistance." He spoke with an accent Sierra couldn't quite place. Spanish, but somewhat different.

Sierra looked at the business card again, then at their visitor. "How did you know about our meeting?"

Hawke smiled. "Sources. Might I come in? Minnesota in January unquestionably has its charms, but warmth, alas, is not one of them."

Sierra and Quinn glanced at each other. Quinn gave the attorney a not-so-subtle once-over and nodded. Sierra motioned for Hawke to come in.

Hawke entered the house, slipped out of his overcoat, and handed it to Quinn, along with his hat. Quinn tossed the items onto the back of a chair, keeping an eye on the lawyer. Sierra walked him over to the group. "Guys, this is Henri Hawke, an attorney. He somehow found out we were meeting and says he can help us."

On hearing the lawyer's name, Pen grabbed the wheels of her chair. "Search him," she said. "This is the guy who threatened Marilyn Applewhite with a gun."

Hawke raised his hands. "That was a most unfortunate misunderstanding. I assure you, I am unarmed and intend no harm."

Quinn stepped forward. "Let's confirm that." Matt stood up, poised to help, but Hawke submitted without objection to a pat-down by Quinn, who nodded. Matt sat down.

"I guess you can sit down, and we'll hear you out," Sierra said. No chairs remained in the living room, but she retrieved one from the dining room. Hawke sat down, and Quinn stood off to the side, watching him closely. Sierra quickly introduced the group.

"How did you know we were meeting?" Pen demanded.

"I had you followed, Ms. Wilkinson. My sincerest apologies."

"How do you know who I am? And what's your relation to these events at VCS?"

Hawke held up his hand. "Please allow me to explain. I have my reasons to be interested in these events. I am sure each of you does as well."

"Damn right we do," Matt said. "My mentor, a great man, was murdered, before my eyes. I may not be a high-powered lawyer or IT whiz or a cop or aircraft mechanic or whatever. I'm just a lowly musician. But I won't let this go."

"Well said, Mr. Lanier. A defective product certainly requires accountability."

"Defective? How about weaponization?"

Hawke shifted in his chair. "Perhaps that is a possibility that should be investigated. But as I understand the situation, there is no evidence of such a scheme."

"No ev—" Matt began to stand up, fists clenched, then sat back down. "There are some pretty damning things that need to be checked out."

"Ah, then—you are all prepared to report this 'crime' to the police?"

No one spoke.

Finally, Pen rolled forward slightly. "Speaking of accountability, we're entitled to some information, Mr. Hawke. Who are you? We know you've been working with Hartsburg to pay off Calder by setting up some kind of charitable foundation. And we know you enlisted Marilyn Applewhite to help. Who do you really represent? And what's your objective? Last but not least, why have you been following me?"

He nodded formally. "Of course—allow me to elaborate. I am an attorney. My home is in Barcelona, but my workplace is—" he spread his arms— "the world. I help clients solve difficult and unique problems."

"You're a fixer," Pen asserted.

Hawke shrugged. "A rather crude term, if I may say so. One of my clients is Mr. Stephen Hartsburg, who was troubled by reports of possible defects in one of his company's devices. I was able to bring him and the person alleging such a defect—"

"Let's say his name," Weezy interrupted. "Ralph Calder."

"That is correct. I was able to bring them together, to reach an accommodation."

"How much did Hartsburg pay?" Weezy demanded.

"Alas, I am not at liberty to disclose details. However, I must clarify that not all the consideration was paid by Mr. Hartsburg personally, nor was it received personally by Mr. Calder."

Pen rolled her eyes. "Of course not. Way too straightforward, too transparent."

"In fact," Hawke continued, "the payment is being used to establish a nonprofit watchdog organization to prevent future medical device failures, to do what the FDA sometimes fails to do."

Quinn gave Hawke a skeptical look. "That sounds like an expensive project. I find it hard to believe that Hartsburg paid for it out of his own pocket."

"I was, in fact, able to procure financing from a third party, an international business financier. It should be a beneficial arrangement for all parties."

"Who's the financier?" Pen asked.

Hawke paused, as if pondering whether to divulge the information, then said, "Her name is Gina Apate. She is a Greek national with a large trust account."

Sierra set her glass down and leaned forward. "Sounds like you've got this deal all wrapped up. What do you want from us? And why did you have Pen followed?"

"I heard from Mr. Hartsburg that VCS had employed Ms. Napolitani and Ms. Wilkinson to investigate the alleged defects in the VC-25-4750. I inquired further and learned that others may have been involved on an informal basis. Perhaps it was impertinent of me to rely on surveillance to discover your identities and location, and for that I do apologize. But it is in the interests of everyone that the settlement I have negotiated proceed smoothly and without interference."

"Come on," Matt said. "You want Calder to go scot-free?"

"If Mr. Calder is ultimately proven, after due process, to be guilty of the crimes of which you are accusing him, he will of course have to answer to the law. But we must not get ahead of ourselves. We have a most important and worthwhile transaction in progress, which must not be derailed."

Matt leaned forward, resting his elbows on his knees. "You say he's clean, despite all the evidence against him. Maybe if we could talk to Calder, he could convince us. Can you make that happen?"

"Regrettably, I have been unable to communicate with Mr. Calder in recent days. I am sure there is nothing amiss. But I think your suggestion is a good one, and I will be happy to advise you when I reestablish contact with him."

Hawke stood up. "Of course, I cannot tell you what to do. You are all very capable individuals. But I implore you to think of all the good that my transaction will accomplish, as well as the stability and goodwill that will flow from a result that meets everyone's needs. Thank you for a most lively and fruitful discussion." He made a little bow. Quinn handed him his hat and coat, then followed the attorney to the door, peering through the window after he had left.

Quinn returned. "He had a car and driver. I couldn't read the plate."

"What kind of vehicle was it?" Matt asked.

Pen, who was not sitting by the window, answered. "A white Mercedes SUV."

"How did you—"

"Hawke admitted he had me followed. That's the vehicle."

There was silence in the room. Then Weezy's voice: "What the hell was *that*?"

"*That*," Pen snapped, "was a steaming pile of horseshit. That 'charitable foundation' doesn't remotely pass the smell test. I don't know who the hell this guy is, but I'm going to make some calls tomorrow and find out. Same with Gina Apate."

"What have we gotten ourselves into?" Sierra mused. "With patients dying and VCS a total mess, now we've got these people running some kind of hustle. What is Hawke's game?"

"He was pretty straightforward about wanting the Hartsburg-to-Calder payoff to go ahead," Matt answered. "He undoubtedly gets a nice cut of the action. This watchdog organization sounds like a cover or a scam. Look, I sight-read him during the meeting, and I think he's holding back. Reminds me of a virtuoso pianist who only lets you hear him play a masterful version of 'Chopsticks.'"

"It's interesting that Hawke can't reach Calder, either," Weezy observed. "But he's still out there. We may not be able to prove yet that he's weaponized the devices, but it certainly looks like he has. That's a terrifying prospect. And Ralph may have his own agenda relating to his wife, but if he's really controlling the devices, what if somebody else gets hold of whatever he's using to do it? There are thousands of patients at risk, millions if the device can act on any ICD."

"And," Sierra added, "there's the possibility that somebody could enhance the transmitter. What if the range wasn't so limited? Or what if you could use it on other types of devices, like pacemakers?"

Quinn sat down on the chair vacated by Hawke. "Maybe Hawke just wants our help in finding Calder. I think it's safe to say Hawke will be keeping an eye on us in case we run across him."

"That doesn't mean we shouldn't look for Calder," Sierra said. There were nods around the room.

Pen glanced at a notebook and then looked up. "First of all, are we all agreed that we don't tell Hawke a damn thing?"

The group responded with vigorous nods.

"It seems to me," Pen continued, "that we need to proceed on three tracks. First, we need to find Ralph Calder, along with that transmitter he might have."

Sierra raised her hand. "Quinn and Matt and I have already been working on that. Maybe we should continue the job."

Pen looked around the circle. "Any objections? Fine. My only thought is that you'll need cyber help to find Calder. My nephew, Kenny, could help."

"I've got a guy, too," said Matt. "Zach is good, and Kenny is busy helping Weezy."

"Why don't we have them work together?"

"Not necessary. I prefer to use Zach. He works for the FBI but helps me on his own time. He's not sharing anything with his superiors."

Sierra raised a hand, palm out, to interrupt. "Hold on. Calder might still be at home, but if he thinks someone is following him, he'll bolt. He's a computer guy, so if he suspects someone like your cyber-geeks or that jerk Biggs is looking for him, he'll try to stay off the grid. You can hardly rent a room at a hotel without a credit card these days. If it were me, I'd probably try to find a relative or friend to crash with, at least for a day or two. Matt and I can ask around, check with his neighbors." She looked at Quinn, and her brows rose. "Heck, maybe his family has a cabin somewhere. If I wanted to hide out, that'd be a perfect place to go."

Quinn chuckled. "Yes, but you'd freeze your ass off up there this time of year."

"How would we find the place?" Matt asked.

"If you don't want to use your buddy Zach, you can start with public information, otherwise known as property records," Sierra said. "All we need is a name and we should be able to check online for any property that person owns. I've used that before to find a friend of mine who, ah, went missing with the help of someone she trusted. Long story."

Pen worked her jaw back and forth. "I'll give you the contact information for Kenny, in case you change your mind. Now, the second track is finding out what's going on inside the company. That's tough to do, but I think getting electronic access, especially to the patient database, is a critical first step. That database presumably contains the names of people who could be the next targets. And maybe getting inside would give us some clue as to what they're up to. Weezy, do you agree?"

"I do. And I hate the thought of Justin Biggs messing with the system, trying to do who-knows-what."

"Nobody likes Biggs," Quinn said. "But we need to avoid making this personal."

Pen held up her hands. "Okay, okay. We're all professionals, and I expect we'll all behave that way. The third track is finding out what we can about Henri Hawke and Gina Apate. I'll take that one."

"Does that mean talking to the police?" Sierra asked.

"It might mean talking to law enforcement." She paused, glancing at Quinn. He was a cop, but he didn't object. She continued. "But they don't need to know—nobody needs to know—who I'm working with, or any details."

"Let's keep it that way for now," Quinn said. "We can't start making accusations without some solid evidence."

Matt stood up. "Then let's go and get some."

*　　　*　　　*

Pen drove Weezy to her hotel. They shivered in the wheelchair van's inadequate heat. "What do you think?" Pen asked as she turned onto I-35W.

"A good group. Sierra and Quinn are very nice."

"And pretty capable, I think. And Matt?"

"He's—well . . ."

"Cute?" Pen suggested.

"Um, yes. Maybe not like Kenny, but . . ."

217

"Focus, girl."

"Okay, okay. Matt doesn't seem to like you much."

"He doesn't need to." She drove on. "I did a little research on Matt."

"And?"

"What if I told you he killed a guy?"

"*What*?"

"How about two guys?"

"Holy—"

"Self-defense. All legit. It happened last year. Actually, he was a hero. He brought down this conspiracy called Millennium Four, some kind of massive, shady land grab in southern Minnesota. I found out in another article that his ex-wife was killed in a shootout with the baddies."

After a brief silence, Weezy asked, "Do you trust him?"

"The jury is still out. He's obviously smart and perceptive. My concern is that he might be messed up from all he's been through, especially the ex-wife's death. And he's certainly got a serious burr under his saddle about Danilson, which may be clouding his judgment. He seems to be more of a lone-wolf type than a team player."

"We have both personality types in the cyber security business," Weezy said. "Either can get results."

"We'll need every skill set we can get to unravel this mess. God help us."

"Do you really have any doubt as to whether the devices have been weaponized?" Weezy asked.

"Not much," Pen confessed. "But this is serious business and potentially an incredibly nasty crime. We *have* to have proof."

They were silent for a couple of miles. "So," Weezy said, trying to lighten the mood, "you've done investigations, right? Have *you* ever killed anybody?"

Pen took a long time to respond. "Once."

"For God's sake, I was just kidding . . ."

"I shot another guy the following year, but he lived."

The mood did not lighten.

"What the hell have I gotten myself into?" Weezy said at last. "Who *are* you people?"

Pen smiled to herself. Someday, she might tell Weezy about her exploits, about all the reasons the anti-anxiety pills had ended up in her purse. How she'd solved several murders, jailed a crooked Congressman, gone undercover to thwart a Russian spy ring, rescued Kenny from nasty mercenaries. Glancing at the younger woman beside her, Pen felt a strong and somewhat sad premonition that in the years to come, Weezy would be doing very similar things herself.

But for now, Pen just smiled. "Weezy, I think we've got one hell of a team here."

Chapter 22

Matt/Sierra/Quinn

Over the next couple of days, Matt staked out Calder's house a few more times, with similar results as before. Then he got a call from Sierra Bauer.

"Quinn thinks we can make the case to do a welfare check on Calder. No search warrant needed if we can persuade one of his neighbors to admit he or she hasn't seen Calder in days and it's not normal for him to be absent for so long without telling them."

"Sounds good to me," Matt replied. "When do we do this? And can I come along?"

"I'll talk to Quinn," she said.

Half an hour later, Quinn, Sierra, and Matt stood on Calder's front doorstep. "Are you sure this is okay?" Matt asked. "Given you're not on airport property?"

Quinn shrugged. "I'm law enforcement. I've got a badge."

"And a neat-looking gun," Sierra added.

Quinn rang the doorbell and pounded on the front door. "Mr. Calder! Police! Open up!"

No response. Quinn pulled out a pry bar.

Sierra stopped him. "Wait. Let's try the obvious before we go and ruin the door." She grabbed the doorknob and twisted.

The door swung open. "Hmm. That's not suspicious at all." Sierra stood back to let Quinn take the lead.

Quinn stepped into the house, then motioned them inside. "Don't touch anything," he warned.

Sierra and Matt entered. Sierra surveyed the room. Books and notebooks were scattered around a bookcase, pages torn out and strewn about like debris. Drawers in the narrow console table near the door were pulled out and the contents emptied onto its surface. She indicated a small desk in a corner, its top buried under paperwork inches thick, the drawers still open. "Damn. And I thought Quinn had a messy desk."

"You're one to talk," Quinn said.

"Hey, at least I know where everything is."

The threesome searched the house, finding no trace of Calder.

"I didn't see anything suspicious," Matt said. "Except the guy isn't a neat freak."

"It's been searched," Quinn said. "I haven't seen many tossed houses or apartments in my career, but this certainly fits the mark of a pro. Organized, thorough, but fast. Check everything, but don't clean up at all. They were looking for something valuable."

"The big question is, did they find it?" Matt said.

"That I can't answer," Quinn said.

"Any signs of a struggle, injuries, blood, violence?" Sierra asked.

Quinn shook his head. "No, but if the ransackers were here to both kidnap Calder and get something of value that he possessed, they could have surprised him or drugged him and avoided any damage or evidence of injury."

"So we're no better off than we were before we broke in," Matt said.

"We didn't break in," Sierra said. "The door was open."

"Next step will be to talk to neighbors and try to find some family members to interrogate," Quinn said. "Maybe he told someone where he went."

"Divide and conquer?" Sierra asked as she looked at Matt.

He nodded. "I'll take the odd address numbers. You do the evens. Let's go a block in either direction."

"Deal," Sierra said.

"I have to get back to my real job," Quinn said. "The welfare check ends now. And I can't officially proceed despite the ransacked house because there was no proof of forced entry. We actually have no proof Calder didn't do it himself. But keep me in the loop."

"Of course," Sierra said and gave him a discreet peck on the lips. Quinn left, Matt crossed the street, and he and Sierra began knocking on doors.

An hour later, they reconvened in front of Calder's house. "Any luck?" Matt said.

Sierra shrugged. "Got a neighbor to confirm a family cabin somewhere up north, owned by some unknown relative. You?"

"That's more than what I learned. Calder has an ex-brother-in-law way out in the 'burbs. I'll look him up, give him a call, see if he knows where the cabin is. If he doesn't, maybe he can connect me with a family member closer to Calder."

"At least get a name of who owns the cabin. We can check property records from there. I guess we're done here for now," she said.

"Need a ride somewhere?"

She nodded. "Thanks." They left in Matt's car and drove without speaking until Matt dropped her off in front of her house.

Sierra got out. "Thanks for the ride. Keep in touch, and let one of us know if you find out anything about the cabin."

"Will do," Matt said and drove away.

*　　　*　　　*

Calder's ex-brother-in-law wasn't able to add anything to what his neighbor had stated about the family cabin: located in northern Minnesota; owned by an unknown relative; used

222

primarily as a deer hunting lodge by Calder and other family members.

Unsure how to proceed, Matt called Pen and let her know what he and Sierra had discovered—not much, in fact. "I'm at a dead end here. Got any suggestions?" he asked.

"Let me talk to Weezy and see what she's learned so far. She's trying to break into the patient database and gain some leverage over Biggs if we can corner him without his bodyguards getting in the way."

"Got it. I'll see if Zach or Kenny can find an address for Calder's cabin. I thought Zach could work on his own, but he welcomed Kenny's help because he's already full time and then some with the FBI."

"Kenny is world class," Pen replied. "He's done things you don't want to know about, for people you'd never want to meet. He's helped me several times with cases. He's done some work for the FBI, too."

"Keep in touch then," Matt said and clicked off.

Chapter 23

Pen

Pen woke up early and then proceeded through her laborious morning routine. She had left a message last night for her FBI contact in Los Angeles, asking for information on Henri Hawke and Gina Apate. Now, as she finally finished with the bathroom and dressing, she rolled out to the kitchen. She was rummaging through the refrigerator, searching for breakfast, when her phone chirped with a text notification.

Weezy: *Still at it. No luck yet.*

Pen finished breakfast, puttered around the condo, talked to James. She was contemplating a shopping trip in the early afternoon when her phone rang. She checked the caller ID: Wendy Nomura, the FBI friend she'd called last night.

Pen answered. "Hey. Did you get my message?"

"I did," said Wendy. "I'd like to talk about it in person."

"Okay. How should we—"

"Could I come up?"

Uh-oh, Pen thought.

Special Agent Wendy Nomura appeared at the door a couple of minutes later, carrying a paper bag. "I brought lunch," she said, putting the bag down on the counter and leaning down to embrace Pen.

"You're looking good," Pen said. Wendy, in fact, looked spectacular, as she always did, strikingly beautiful at six feet tall. "Recovery still proceeding well?"

"I'm just about back to normal, I think." A couple of years earlier, Wendy had been shot and seriously wounded.

They sat at the kitchen table, next to the window overlooking Nicollet Mall, eating sandwiches and soup.

The small talk didn't last long. Pen began. "I'm assuming my innocuous little request—"

"Was the opposite of innocuous."

"Since it caused you to immediately hop on a red-eye and fly halfway across the country, I guess it must have set off some alarm bells."

"Yep, it was *ding, ding, ding* when I put the names into the system," Wendy said and bit into her turkey sandwich. "I was told to get out here and find out where you got those names, pronto. And I'm supposed to—"

"Tell me nothing."

"Right."

Pen remained silent, eating her broccoli cheddar soup.

Wendy put her food aside. "You first."

Pen sighed, put her spoon down, and gave her a detailed account of her involvement in the VCS matter, omitting the names of those she was working with. Wendy took no notes.

After Pen had finished, her friend thought silently for several minutes. "I was sent here to shut you down," she said at last. "There are multiple, sensitive investigations of Hawke and Apate being run out of New York. We can't just come charging in here with interviews and subpoenas. You spook them, and they'll scurry back down the rathole and everything will be lost."

"Wendy, people are dying here. We're supposed to just ignore that?"

"Of course not. But to disrupt these other investigations, we'd need something very solid to show an actual link to the deaths."

Pen took a spoonful of her now-cold soup and put it back down.

"We won't be ignoring this," Wendy assured her. "You've got two shady characters hanging around Minnesota in January, circling a company that's in trouble. That's not enough in itself to open a new investigation, but our people can start working on this charitable foundation right away, see if there's any paperwork on it. If we could pierce that, or get evidence of the extortion scheme, that could get us started. But we need something to sink our teeth into."

"And that's where we come in?"

"Yes, assuming you can trust these people you're working with."

"I don't know them well," Pen admitted. "But I've been impressed so far. So, tell me about these shady characters."

Wendy pulled a tablet out of her bag, logged in, and began reading: "Henri Hawke, forty-eight. A Spanish attorney who also has French heritage and education. He maintains an office in Barcelona but operates worldwide. Basically, he's an international fixer. Puts together dubious deals and takes a cut."

"Does he cross the line?"

"Yes, but nobody has been able to prove it. In fact, he's been active here in your neck of the woods. Remember that nutty senator who busted out of jail in Red Wing?"

"Sure."

"We think he set it up. We know he had done business with the senator—he also helped her back in Boston. There were a couple of deaths there that we believe he had a hand in, but as always, he managed to avoid leaving any fingerprints. He's dangerous, Pen—not just a paper-pusher."

Pen exhaled. "What about Gina Apate?"

"While Hawke moves easily in the legitimate world, Apate is more of an actual gangster. She's a Greek national and a former field operative for EYP, the Greek national intelligence service. She's a chameleon—turns up everywhere, in different guises and with different names, speaks half a dozen languages. And she's deadly—proficient in Silat, one of the nastier martial arts out there."

"What's her cover?"

"International business consulting. She runs a trading company out of Dubrovnik, Croatia, which also has an office in New York. She can't cross the border under her own name, so she maintains a set of fake identities."

Pen let it sink in. "Holy crap. And now she's got her sights set on Voyageur Cardiac. What about Ralph Calder?"

"I checked him out, and he has no record. He's just an IT guy. He may have a grudge concerning his wife, and he may or may not have been seen in the vicinity of a couple of deaths, but there are no grounds to move on him."

"We'll fix that," Pen snapped. "And Justin Biggs?"

"Clean."

"Damn."

"Pen," Wendy said with exaggerated patience, "we need your discretion. *I* need it. I've told you these things in confidence. You've never burned me before. In fact, you've bailed me out a couple of times."

"So, are you shutting me down?"

"For the record, yes."

"And off the record?"

Wendy stood up and smiled. "It was great seeing you, Pen."

They embraced. Wendy paused at the door. "For God's sake, be careful."

Chapter 24

Pen/Weezy

Two o'clock. The bar downstairs was closing, and sounds of laughter and music filtered up to Weezy's hotel suite. Pen, hanging out in the little kitchenette, considered pouring another glass of wine. That would be a second another, though. She sighed and pushed a glass under the refrigerator's water dispenser. The spot in her back that tightened up when she stayed in the chair too long was speaking to her. Sixteen hours was definitely too long.

She really should keep Kenny and Weezy company. They'd been at it for hours, too, pausing only for pizza. They spoke a language made up of acronyms and terms she'd never heard. Apparently a dialect of English, if the connectives and pronouns were to be believed.

Pen rolled into the small living area, now converted to a technology den. The dining room table held three monitors. Two computer enclosures nestled together under the table. A cable ran to the coat closet, where the router lived. Two chairs were pulled up to the table, facing two keyboards. Hunched in the chairs, staring into the monitors, were two hackers, Weezy and Kenny.

Weezy had stopped tapping on her monitor and was looking over Kenny's shoulder.

"Yes!" Weezy exclaimed.

Kenny pushed back, rolled his shoulders. "Halfway there."

"I have a backdoor," Weezy said, turning to Pen. "Olivia and you both think Choudhary wants to help us, right?"

Pen nodded.

"Well, then, let's do it." She tapped her keyboard, then waited several seconds. Pen watched the worry muscles bunching around her shoulders. Then an exhale. "We're in."

Kenny looked at her. "Your rootkit?"

Apparently not salacious, because she said, "Why not? Try it."

A long pause, punctuated only by *uh-huhs*, *un-uhs*, and Anglo-Saxon expletives.

Then "Yes!" exploded from both simultaneously. "Yes, yes, *yes*."

Weezy put her arm all the way around Kenny's shoulder and gave him a kiss on the cheek. She turned to Pen and said, "He did it. We're in."

*   *   *

To: Group

From: Weezy

Subj: Found 'em

We, mainly Kenny, snuck ourselves right the hell into Voyageur's database early this morning. I found that list I mentioned of doctors' offices. It's 23 offices, 15 in Minnesota and Wisconsin, five in Tampa Bay area, and three in Arizona. I'm attaching it. The poison software goes to doctors' offices via scheduled software updates, but it's not automatic—someone has to hang the little sucker on the end of the regular software for each office, a fairly common hacking trick. Good news: They targeted relatively few offices, about 10% of the total in the update log. Bad news: We have to assume the doctors' offices aren't complicit, so they will probably unwittingly be adding the bad software to every ICD they update. Also, unless we stop them, whoever it is can corrupt every office in Voyageur's network, and ultimately every device. Voyageur has 10,000 of the 4750s installed, but it's a relatively new product. There are over 200,000 Voyageur devices in place just in the US, and who knows whether this flaw is in only the 4750s. We gotta stop 'em, gang.

Kenny and I are currently working to cross-reference the docs' offices with people in the database who have recently visited for a regular checkup.

Love, or at least a handshake,
Weezy

att: {Targeted names}
    {Doctor Offices}

Chapter 25

Gina/Ralph

Ralph Calder was not cut out for this. His world consisted of ones and zeroes, straightforward, precise. His personal life had been the same: work, family, church. Even after Lois died and he developed the cardiac transmitter, his life was laser-like. No cloak-and-dagger stuff, no interference, none of this intrigue, no anxiety. But then his test of the transmitter on Alice Holmgren had gone terribly wrong. Now there was Biggs, and Hawke, and Hartsburg, and the police, and . . . and . . . alcohol.

He poured another tumbler of cheap whiskey from the bottle on the bed stand. *Screw Hawke. Screw them all. I don't need them to tell me what to do.*

He looked at his phone and stabbed his finger at the blue call-back icon. Justin Biggs answered. "Ralph, thanks for calling me back."

"Whaddaya want?" Calder's words were slurred.

"Just want to know how you're doing," Biggs answered. "We really haven't talked since you left Voyageur. I thought maybe we could have lunch."

"What?" Calder tried to process the invitation. He and Biggs had worked together, but they were not friends. While he had to admit that Biggs was a good programmer, he'd never liked the brash younger man. So, lunch? Why would Biggs want to have lunch with him?

"Yeah, sure," he answered.

*   *   *

Hung over, Calder parked his car and walked across the parking lot toward the entrance of the restaurant. Why had he agreed to do this? He was tempted to leave, but he had driven all the way from his cabin, and his curiosity about what Biggs wanted, plus the prospect of another swig of the hair of the dog, propelled him forward.

He entered the restaurant and spotted Biggs sitting with a woman.

Calder hesitantly walked to the table. "Am I interrupting?"

"No. Not at all," Biggs said, standing and extending his hand. "Good to see you, Ralph. I'd like you to meet Gina Apate. She's about to become Voyageur's new CEO, and she has some questions for you."

Calder's eyes grew big. "N—nice . . . to meet you," he stuttered, his hand held in mid-air just short of Biggs's handshake.

"Sit down," Gina said, nodding toward an empty chair.

"Can I order you something?" Biggs asked.

"A shot and a beer. Rye," Calder answered, too stunned to think. He thumped down on the chair across the table from Gina.

"I've been wanting to meet you," Gina said. "I understand you are one of the primary architects of the VC-25-4750 software."

"What happened to Hartsburg?" Calder asked, ignoring the question.

"He's out of the picture."

"I don't understand."

"Hartsburg has resigned. I am about to be named as his replacement, both as CEO and chairman of the board."

"But . . . but . . . I had a deal with Hartsburg . . ."

"I am well aware of your deal. I am the one who will provide the funds that will make your deal work, and it is the deal that has resulted in my taking control of Voyageur."

The shot and the beer arrived. Calder downed the shot in a single gulp. "Another," he rasped. "That's not . . ."

"I am also aware that you have developed a device that can externally manipulate the implanted VC-25-4750s," Gina continued. "I know that two people have died as a result of your handiwork. I know that you will go to prison if this deal does not go down; that is to say, if I do not provide the money."

Calder looked at Biggs, a helpless, questioning look on his face. "You set me up. What . . ."

"But I am willing to provide the money," Gina interrupted. "I do wish this deal to go down. However, I have run into a tiny obstacle; an obstacle that you and your little zapper device can remove."

"No." Calder shook his head, holding up both hands as if to ward off a curse. "I won't . . ."

"Just so we're clear." Gina stopped him in mid-sentence. "If this obstacle is not removed, there is no deal. I walk away from Voyageur, you don't get thirty million dollars. Instead, you go to jail . . . forever."

They sat for a moment without speaking as Calder took a swallow of beer and then downed the second shot as soon as it arrived.

"What do I have to do?" he finally asked.

"Nothing you haven't done before. And the good news is that it will be the last time you have to do it. There is a member of the Voyageur Board who is standing in the way of our transaction. He must be removed . . . permanently."

"Who's the board member?"

"Sterling Leighton."

"Reverend Leighton?" Calder's voice rose. "He's—I mean, respected, a leader in the community. Why . . ."

"It has been confirmed that he was directly involved in the cover-up of VC-25-4750." The lie came easily to Gina. "My sources say that he opposed a recall of the product because of the financial loss that a recall would create for the company."

"I thought it was just Hartsburg," Calder exclaimed. "You mean . . ."

"Oh, the cover-up went higher than Hartsburg. Key members of the board of directors, led by Reverend Leighton, were involved. Once Leighton is removed, and I am chairman, I will deal with the other guilty board members."

She paused, letting her lies do their work.

"What do you say, Mr. Calder?" she said. "Do we have a deal?"

Ralph slowly nodded his head. "If I do this, does the thirty million dollars still go to the watchdog company? Does Hartsburg still get nothing?"

"Hartsburg gets nothing except disgraced, and maybe a jail sentence for his part in the cover-up," Gina assured him.

"Then we have a deal." Calder extended his hand across the table.

"My word is all you need," Gina said, ignoring the offered hand. "Work out the logistics with Justin. You have forty-eight hours. After you've removed the obstacle, you will hand over the device, the software, and all the notes and material involved in making it to Justin." Gina looked at Biggs without smiling and then back at Calder.

"Here's Leighton's address," Biggs said, sliding a piece of paper across the table to Calder. "As soon as you're done with your mission, call me and I'll meet you somewhere to pick up the transmitter and your programming notes."

Calder left, feeling the effects of his double whiskey lunch, and not entirely comfortable with how the meeting had ended. But if what Apate said was true, with Hartsburg headed for prison and the watchdog agency soon to be established? Leighton should not be allowed to stand in the way of Lois's legacy.

*　　*　　*

"Do you have another minute?" Justin asked as Gina started to rise.

"This hacker that Hartsburg fired is still trying to break into the database," Biggs continued. "I've been successful in keeping her out, but she's really resourceful. She might get lucky and get through."

"That's a nuisance we don't need. Thanks for telling me," Gina said. "I'll take care of it. What about that attorney? The cripple? Is she still snooping around, too?"

"More than likely."

Gina nodded. "I'll take care of them both."

"You know," Biggs said, "when I get my hands on that transmitter, I could do a lot of things with it: increase the range, possibly even make it usable against other types of implant devices, not just the VC-25-4750."

Gina gave Biggs a half smile. "I'm counting on that," she said.

And once that's done, you'll no longer be needed, she thought as she walked away.

Chapter 26

Ralph

Calder walked along 12th Street on the outskirts of downtown Minneapolis, head down, glancing up occasionally to check for surveillance cameras. He turned and shuffled down Yale Place, sweating under his heavy Seahawks jacket in the icy wind. The street was sparsely populated in the evening darkness, with only an occasional dog-walker braving the cold. Thin streams of snow blew across the sidewalk. Calder slowed even more as he approached Greenway Gables, a townhouse development on the edge of Loring Park.

His mission was not a pleasant one, but it was necessary. He owed it to Lois. His plan had gone seriously sideways, but there was still a chance to salvage it. He reached around and felt the transmitter in his backpack. One last time, to use the weapon he had fashioned. He longed for a drink but hadn't brought anything with him.

Ralph walked past the complex's main entrance to the parking lot of an adjacent condo building. Shuffling into the lot, he could see the line of townhouses perpendicular to the street. He counted: two, three, four units from the street and walked into the condo parking lot, trying to look purposeful. Lights were on in the unit he sought, on both the second and third floors. The garage occupied the ground level. He looked around; there was no one in the parking lot. He stopped at a random car and pantomimed unlocking its door. Meanwhile, he looked at the townhouse. He could see movement through the curtains on the second floor. A human form.

Gina Apate damn well better be right about Reverend Sterling Leighton, the pastor and civil rights leader who had spent ten years on the VCS board. He hoped Leighton was in fact part and parcel of the cover-up of the VC-25-4750 defect, and that he now was working to derail the watchdog agency.

He had no reason to disbelieve Apate. She worked with Hawke and seemed to know a lot about finance. More to the point, she knew all about the deal he had negotiated with Hawke and Hartsburg and had every incentive to see it succeed. But if Apate possessed an air of mystery, she also emanated, even more than Hawke, a bit of menace. These were not people to be trifled with. At least they were better than Hartsburg, who was utterly indifferent to the value of human life.

The movement behind the sheer curtains took human form. The figure looked like a man, judging from its size and shape. Ralph moved to a different spot, three cars away, for a better look. The figure moved back and forth, leaning over, carrying things. Cleaning up after dinner, Ralph guessed. He watched for a few more minutes; then the figure disappeared.

The man—he could see clearly now that it was a man—re-emerged up on the third floor, walking slowly in front of one of the windows. Ralph could see him even more clearly in this position.

This man was evil, Calder told himself. He was complicit in the deaths of cardiac patients. He was blocking the formation of a lifesaving organization. It had to be done.

Leighton bent over, then stood up. Ralph could see his face now, and it was smiling. He bent over again, then stood up.

Ralph pulled the transmitter from his backpack, thinking of all the VCS patients who'd been cheated out of experiencing happiness like Leighton's. And thinking of Lois. It was time.

And then Leighton stood up again, this time holding something, something he lifted up toward his face.

A baby. Probably a grandchild.

Oh, God.

Chapter 27

Gina/Hawke

"Calder never delivered the transmitter. Worse yet, he never took care of Leighton."

Biggs's words hung in the air as Gina glared at him. They sat at a table in a conference room at VCS headquarters, two doors down from Stephen Hartsburg's office.

"Do you know where Calder is?" Her words were cold, brooding.

"He's not answering his phone, and he's not at home."

"Find him! And his little zapper. My associates will help you, and they'll also help you track down the whiz-kid programmer and her paraplegic attorney friend," she added. "Maybe they know where Calder is."

And when you find them—Calder, the whiz-kid, the attorney— they will all disappear. Russians are good at that.

"You know, if we can't find Calder, I can build you another transmitter; better than his," Biggs said.

"So you've said," Gina responded, "but not finding Calder is not an option."

"He's probably at the bottom of a bottle somewhere."

Gina picked up her phone and punched in a number.

"Viktor," she said when her call was answered. "I have a level-three job for you. Meet an associate of mine, Justin Biggs, at Manny's in an hour. There will be a reservation in my name. There are three people, and Mr. Biggs will have the information on them. Bring Maksim."

She ended the call and looked at Biggs. "Manny's. One hour. Find them."

After Biggs left, Gina dialed another number. Receiving no answer, she left a message. "Hawke, this is Gina Apate. I need to talk to you about Ralph Calder. It seems he is not reliable, and I am having second thoughts."

*   *   *

Hawke listened to Gina's message with a smirk.

He already knew about Calder, and he knew that Gina had no intention of going through with the loan, because Calder was sitting in Hawke's hotel suite, sweating and shaking.

"She's going to take over Voyageur. She wanted me to kill Reverend Leighton," Calder repeated. "I couldn't do it. My God, what have I started?" He sat on a chair, elbows on knees, head in his hands, staring at the floor, moaning. "I'm sorry, Lois. I didn't want it to go this way. I'm sorry. I failed . . ."

"It appears that we may both have underestimated the avarice of Ms. Apate," Hawke interjected.

Calder looked up, haggard. "I'll have to let go of Lois's legacy. I want this to stop. I don't want the thirty million dollars."

"That ship has sailed, Mr. Calder. If what you say is true, your little blackmail scheme has mushroomed like the cloud of a nuclear bomb. It is no longer in your control."

"But don't you understand?" Calder cried. "This won't be the end of it. Once she gets her hands on my transmitter, she'll have Biggs, or someone like him, make it universal. Then she'll be able to manipulate every cardiac device, not just Voyageur's. No one with an implant will be safe!"

"Once she gets her hands on your transmitter, you will be dead. I suggest you destroy your transmitter and go into hiding. If there is a place you can go that no one will find you, do it."

"But . . . but . . ."

"Mr. Calder, you have unleashed a fury that is beyond even my ability to control. I suggest you leave immediately."

Calder rose and staggered to the door.

Dead man walking, Hawke observed. *The poor fool.*

The hotel door clicked shut behind Calder. Hawke stood for a moment, stroking his chin between his thumb and forefinger, then turned and walked to the bar. He uncorked the half-full bottle of cognac, poured himself three fingers, and swirled the amber liquid. He inhaled the pungent scent, took a sip and rolled it around in his mouth, savoring the taste.

He thought of Gina Apate, without emotion. *Being double-crossed is a risk of doing business, but it must not be allowed to occur without repercussion. There is a code that must be honored.*

Chapter 28

Matt/Sierra/Quinn

Matt yawned and stretched as much as he could behind the wheel of his Toyota, feeling the numbness in his ass and the aches from his various "war wounds" inflicted on him by members of the conspiracy he'd battled almost two years ago now. He was parked behind a copse of evergreen trees some fifty yards down the road from the cabin that belonged to Calder's relative, a detail Zach had provided after a little cyber-digging. A small break in the screen of pine boughs allowed him a narrow view of the cabin. Sierra Bauer was in her small SUV somewhere out of sight on the other side of the cabin.

They were in north-central Minnesota, five miles outside the tiny town of Aitkin, a two-hour drive from the Twin Cities, north of Lake Mille Lacs and embedded in an area ripe with hunting land and some good fishing lakes.

They'd arrived early that morning under cover of darkness and parked where they had a partial view of the windows of the cabin that faced the road. The hope was to find Calder there, contact Quinn, and the three of them would confront Calder and find out exactly what his role in the compromised ICDs was. Unfortunately, since they'd arrived, they'd observed no signs of life in the cabin.

Matt called Sierra with his cell phone, which was receiving a good signal despite some spottiness in coverage on the drive up.

"Did you find a good place to park? Can you see the cabin?"

"Yeah, I'm at the neighbor's place. There's a shed between the driveway and Calder's cabin. I've got a pretty good view."

"Anything on your end?" he asked, already knowing the answer.

"Nope," Sierra said. "Stakeouts aren't nearly as exciting as the cop shows make us think they are, huh?"

"Especially when it's below freezing, and we can't run the engine for fear of being noticed."

"At least our tracks aren't the only ones out here; who knows how many ice fishing houses are out on the lake. And it looks like it hasn't snowed for a while. If you're getting cold, do some chair aerobics to keep warm."

"Chair aerobics in a car? I got about two inches of clearance between my knees and the steering wheel and no room to move my left arm."

Sierra chuckled. "You need to modify the exercises. Scale 'em down. Wiggle your fingers. Make fists and relax ten or twenty times. Flex your ankles and toes. Lift your butt off the seat a bunch of times. Rotate your neck. Use your imagination."

"You got this pretty well figured out. Have you been on stake-outs before?"

"Hah," she said. "Not me. But Quinn tells me all this stuff. He's been on dozens of stakeouts."

"Really? An airport cop?"

"He was with St. Paul PD for ten years. I learned how to be a cop by osmosis."

"So, where the hell's Calder? If he's not here, that tells me he went on the run to someplace far away and warm that doesn't have an extradition deal with the US."

"Relax. It's not even eight; the sun's just coming up. Don't you know crooks are notoriously late sleepers?"

"Never thought of that," Matt said. "But if nothing happens by nine, I say we cut our losses and get some hot breakfast and even hotter coffee."

Sierra said, "I'll call Quinn. See if anything's changed from our original stakeout plan. He said he'd come up after his overnight shift. He should get here before nine."

"Great," Matt said. "What if something goes down before he gets here?"

"Quinn said don't approach Calder or anyone with him until he arrives. If someone leaves, one of us will follow. The other will stay and watch the cabin."

"All right. But I'm really getting tired of this. I want answers. Calder's our answer man."

When Sierra didn't reply, Matt realized she'd clicked off and called Quinn. A female airline mechanic and a cop. Interesting relationship. Of course, being a musician implied that any romantic relationship he had would also be considered "interesting."

Matt pocketed his phone and tried some chair aerobics. He felt silly moving and wiggling in place like a toddler who needed to pee, and soon. But his blood flowed faster, which tempered his chilliness.

After another minute, his phone rang. It was Sierra. "Whatcha got?" he asked.

"Quinn'll be here in twenty. You notice anything at the cabin?"

"Noth—wait. Someone switched on a light. Maybe a bathroom or kitchen. Hard to tell when I don't know the floor plan."

"Our plan hasn't changed. We wait for Quinn."

"I figured." Matt hesitated. He stank at making small talk but wanted to do whatever he could to put Sierra's mind at ease about him. His past was hardly reassuring. Once it had become clear to his new allies—Sierra, Quinn, Pen, and Weezy—that he was the same Matt Lanier who'd brought down the Millennium Four conspiracy and admitted to killing two men in self-defense, they'd all seemed nervous and tentative around him. Like he might explode at the slightest provocation and blow away the group with an Uzi.

"So," he began, "I'm glad we were able to track this place down. I'll have to remember the property records trick."

"No trick," Sierra said. "At least Zach was able to find us the name of Calder's great-aunt. From there it was a piece of cake to look up the property.

"As Quinn would say," Sierra continued, "most crimes are acts of passion—anger, love, greed. Whatever crimes Calder might have committed fit the story Justin Biggs told you about a VCS employee going off the deep end, pissed that a loved one died from a defective ICD."

"My thoughts exactly," Matt said. "That also implies Calder won't be armed. Or if he is, he won't be a trained shooter."

"Agreed," Sierra said. "I'm surprised you thought we needed two computer geniuses to track Calder down. Turned out to be light duty for a hacker to track a family tree."

"I wouldn't know," Matt said. "I'm pretty techno ignorant. Just got my first smartphone a year ago." He visualized Sierra's eyebrows raising in disbelief.

"I'm like most folks," she said. "I use it regularly, although I don't consider myself hooked. Working as an airplane mechanic ten hours a day keeps my hands busy, anyway."

Matt was about to ask what she did on her phone, but she continued. "Hey, a light flicked on in Calder's cabin on this side."

"Okay, someone's definitely inside and waking up."

Sierra said, "I'll let Quinn know," and clicked off.

As she called Quinn, Matt stiffened. A set of vehicle headlights approached from Sierra's side of the cabin. Ice fisherman? Who else would be out here this early? The lights turned into

Calder's drive, and Matt could see they belonged to a large SUV. His pulse quickened as the vehicle pulled up and parked in front of the cabin.

Sierra called back and said, "I told Quinn about the lights and the SUV arriving. He's ten minutes out. Said to wait, but text him if anyone leaves."

A slight pain welled up in Matt's head. Dammit. *Go away, PTSD headache.* He'd been relatively pain free for several months, but the situation with Dr. Danilson dying and his getting involved in finding out why he'd died had stirred up old, violent memories and feelings from the past. Including more frequent headaches. He breathed slowly and deeply several times, the best remedy he'd found after trying many relaxation techniques. At least he wasn't going into a gunfight and being forced to kill or be killed.

Or was he?

Three men exited the parked SUV and headed for Calder's front door. The winter sun was still low in the sky, so he and Sierra would have difficulty identifying anyone from afar. Biggs and his bodyguards? Matt checked his watch. Quinn should arrive in five minutes now.

"How's this gonna go down, Sierra?" Matt figured Calder wasn't much of a physical threat, being a middle-aged man who'd sat behind a desk most of his life. But what if he or one or more of the other men were armed? Was this going to be a shooting situation?

"Not sure," Sierra replied. "Quinn rarely goes into a situation without backup. But this isn't his jurisdiction. Maybe he requested a local sheriff's deputy to help."

"I hope so," Matt said. "I've been in enough shootouts to last a lifetime. I don't want to add to the total."

"Does that mean you're packin'?"

"Got my concealed carry permit six months ago. Not going to make it easy for anyone who tries to mess with me again."

The momentary silence on her end of the line was deafening. "You've, um, done this kind of thing before, right?"

Matt chuckled. "Long story. Trust me. If you're on my side, I'm harmless."

"And if I'm not?"

He made a pistol with his fingers and pointed it in her direction, knowing she couldn't see it. "Then . . . watch out."

The minutes ticked by too slowly for Matt. He sensed something bad was happening and wanted to stop it, but if he and Sierra went up against three men who might be armed, they'd lose that fight in seconds, even with the element of surprise. If Quinn showed up soon and waved his badge in their faces first, the good guys might have a chance of getting Calder safely away. Then again, seeing a badge might panic the three men into doing something desperate or reckless—like shooting at them.

But what if the three men were just friends coming to Calder's cabin for breakfast? Matt almost laughed out loud at that thought. Calder was on the run after probably killing two or more people who had ICDs from Voyageur Cardiac Systems. The visitors were either allies or enemies who weren't concerned with breakfast.

He called Sierra. "I can't keep sitting here. I'm going in to take a look."

"What? Are you crazy? Quinn'll be here in a few minutes. We wait." Her strident tone didn't deter him.

"I'm only going to peek through an uncovered window, listen at the door, try to find something. Anything. I'll be careful."

"Matt!"

He clicked off without replying and got out of his car. Matt winced as snow crunched under his boots as he made his way toward Calder's cabin, but with the windows closed, he hoped his footsteps couldn't be heard. The cabin and surrounding woods were silent; most cabin owners closed their cabins during winter unless they were into ice fishing, skiing, or snowmobiling. The only cabin in the area with wood smoke or furnace exhaust curling upward was Calder's. Matt only needed to worry about someone from the inside glancing out a window and seeing him.

In less than a minute, he was at the edge of the property. Drawing his Beretta 9mm from his coat pocket, he crept up the drive. Ten feet from the front sidewalk, he spotted a flash of movement through the slit in the curtains. He ducked behind the SUV in the driveway, tightened his grip on his Beretta, and focused on the movement, trying to identify the figure in the window. He got his answer immediately as a hand parted the curtain from one side and a head peered out.

Justin Biggs.

Matt's heart raced as a surge of adrenaline energized his senses. He crept to the rear fender of the car and signaled to Sierra. Unsure whether she saw him, he fumbled for his phone just in time to feel it vibrate with an incoming call.

"Whatcha got?" Sierra asked before he could even say hello.

"Biggs is inside," Matt whispered.

"Holy shit."

"The other two must be the goons I ran into last time I tried to talk to him."

"What else do you see?"

"Nothing. There's only a slit in the curtains. I haven't heard anything, either."

"Biggs must be here for the transmitter," Sierra said. "We need to stop him."

"But how?" Matt asked. "What if Quinn doesn't get here before they leave?"

"Speak of the devil. He just drove up."

"Bring him up to speed fast, then let me know what to do. I'll drop back around the corner of the garage in case they come outside."

"Roger that," Sierra said. "Hold on."

From his new hiding spot, Matt saw Quinn's SUV disappear past the neighbor's shed and assumed he pulled up next to Sierra. Seconds later, Quinn parked his car across the road from Matt's parking spot behind the copse of evergreens. He lowered his window and gave Matt the two-fingered, V-shaped gesture that signaled him to keep his eyes open. Matt gave him a thumbs up, then raised his gun hand to show Quinn that he was armed. Seeing that, Quinn did a quick, angry wave. Reluctantly, Matt nodded and returned his pistol to his coat pocket.

His toes were starting to go numb, along with his cheeks and the tip of his nose, after a few minutes of staying still in the frigid January air. He tried to redirect his exhales, but the steam kept drifting across the driveway toward the front door. Hopefully, it wouldn't be noticeable to anyone looking out the window.

Just then, the front door creaked open, stiff on its hinges from the freezing temps. One large man led the way, followed by Biggs, Calder, and the second goon. Biggs held a package in his hand. The trailing goon had his hand at Calder's back. A real gun or was he faking? The goons had flashed no weapons in his previous encounters with them, but that didn't mean they weren't armed. Calder was certainly in no shape to put up a fight against anyone, let alone two younger, stronger men.

If they were going to make a move to stop Biggs from leaving, Matt saw no signal from Quinn to make that happen. Matt sight read the situation and realized Quinn might be hesitating because he was out of his jurisdiction and didn't have any authority here to arrest or even detain Biggs and his cronies. Not good. That situation needed changing—now. Time to improvise.

Matt sprang from behind the garage and charged the group. No one noticed him until he was almost upon them. Then the lead goon shouted, "What the fuck?" and crouched, preparing to take on Matt's charge.

But Matt was a second too fast for the man. He barreled into him at full speed, tackling and sending him crashing into the car. Matt released his arms, grabbed the man's head, and slammed it into the car as hard as he could, two, three, four times, until the man slumped against the car door, motionless.

By this time, Biggs had recoiled from the charge, slipping on the packed snow and losing his balance. The goon behind Calder seemed to grope for a weapon. Matt lunged for the package in Biggs's hand, presuming it was the transmitter everyone was so keen to get their hands on. But Biggs was quicker and spun to protect the package from Matt's grasp.

Biggs yelled, "Viktor, get this guy off me!"

Where the hell are Quinn and Sierra? Matt thought as he grappled with Biggs. Then Viktor was on him, gripping his collar, tearing him off Biggs and groping for a handhold with his other hand. Matt spun, twisted, trying to wrench himself free, but the goon landed a gloved punch to his head, which knocked Matt to the ground, his head throbbing from the impact. Matt's ears rang and the world spun from the blow.

"Let's get outta here!" Biggs yelled at Viktor. The first goon was still groggy and unable to stand.

"Police! Hold it right there!" It was Quinn, approaching from the pines, holding up his badge.

"No, you hold it!" Biggs said. "Stop there, Viktor."

The scene went silent. Finally able to focus, Matt saw Viktor shove Calder ahead of him with a gun to his head. Calder's face was frozen with fear and panic. "Don't shoot me!" he exclaimed.

Quinn said, "I'll only say it once. Drop the weapon! Let's talk."

"Unh-unh. Ain't gonna happen," Biggs said with a sneer. "You got no uniform on, no squad car, no backup. That means you're a cop out of his jurisdiction, which means you can't legally shoot me unless we shoot at you. And you can't even be sure my associate is holding a real gun on my friend Ralphie boy. It could be a plastic toy." Biggs's sneer turned into a smug smile. "Besides, if you want to arrest anyone, arrest this asshole for battery," he said, jerking his thumb toward Matt. "He started this fight with no provocation whatsoever."

Matt staggered to his feet, still woozy. He was fifteen feet away from Calder but wasn't sure about the weapon jammed against the programmer's head. "Quinn, I can't confirm if the weapon is real or a fake!"

In a flash, Sierra appeared from the far side of the SUV and lunged for Viktor. She came down hard on his gun hand with an object Matt didn't recognize right away. A foot-long socket wrench? Viktor dropped the gun, screaming in pain as he grabbed his injured wrist. But Sierra lost her balance after striking him and dropped the wrench.

Matt sprang forward, his gun redrawn, and thrust it into Biggs's chest. Quinn raced up the driveway, pulling his service weapon. Viktor reacted after the initial shock and picked up his gun with his uninjured hand. He stood and thrust it against Sierra's head, then wrapped his free arm around her neck. Matt's thoughts flashed back to the image of the woman he'd loved and lost to violence and he froze, momentarily panic-stricken. From across the driveway, he saw similar fear and trepidation in Quinn's eyes.

Quinn pointed his gun at Biggs. It shook slightly. "Stand down, Lanier. I've got this."

After quick glances at Sierra's situation, Quinn's firing range and angle, and the first goon—who might be faking his injury and ready to pull a weapon—Matt stepped back two paces but didn't lower his Beretta. He didn't trust his aim enough to shoot Viktor and not hit Sierra. But he held his pistol at the ready, able to turn and fire at any of the three foes if necessary.

Quinn nodded and stared at Biggs. "We got us a little stalemate here, Biggs."

"You got that right, pal." Biggs glanced at Matt. "You brought some friends along, Larson? Or is Lanier your real name?" Matt's flimsy cover was blown, but he doubted he'd have to deal with Biggs after today, whether they won or lost this showdown.

"Look, Biggs," Matt said. "We don't want this turning into more deaths. We just want Calder and the transmitter."

"Transmitter? What transmitter?" Biggs tossed the package in his hand up and down like he was tossing a baseball. "This is just a personal gift from Ralph. A late Christmas present. We're headed out for breakfast now. That's all. You two are waaay off base if you think something criminal is going down here."

"Can the crap, Biggs," Quinn snapped. "We know what's going on at VCS. We know Calder started this mess, and we're going to stop it. So just give us the transmitter. If you do, I promise the authorities will go easy on you. I'm guessing you haven't killed anyone yet, like Calder has. That means you haven't committed a crime . . . yet. Why not keep it that way?"

Biggs glanced around at all the players in this game. "Promise? Yeah, right. The way I see it, we each have a hostage. I'm guessing this pretty little thing is the girlfriend of one of you two losers. No one needs to die as long as I get what I want."

"Which is?" Quinn asked.

Biggs held up the package. "Just this. Let me go and the girl goes free. You can even keep Calder. Turns out I don't really need old Ralph here. He already told me everything I need to know about the software and the transmitter. I was just going to bring him along for insurance. Looks like the best thing for me to do is cash in that policy right now."

Quinn glanced at Matt, then gazed at Sierra. Matt saw the anguish on his face as he weighed his choices. He knew what he'd do in this situation. He wondered if Quinn would do the same.

After a long hesitation, Quinn said, "How do you propose we defuse this?"

Biggs gestured at the goon still lying on the ground, the one Matt had dispatched. "Let Maksim here get in the car and start it up. As a show of good faith on my part, Calder can go inside. Viktor and I will slowly get into the car. He keeps his gun on the girl. Lanier here can keep his gun on me. Once we're in the car, on the count of three, each gunman lowers his weapon, and we drive off. You have the extra weapon, so if you think something hinky's going down, you can shoot."

He paused to let Quinn think it over. Then Biggs continued. "However, you won't shoot me because I know too much to be of use in the remote possibility that you figure out who the real brains and power are in this situation. But by that time, I'll have a few million dollars and a luxurious condo on a beach somewhere in the Caribbean."

Again, Quinn looked at Sierra. "Make the deal and let them go," she said. "I'll be okay. If they were that kind of muscle, they would have shot Matt already."

Matt said, "We have no choice but to trust him on this. We at least get Calder, which is who we came for. We can figure out the transmitter issue faster with his help than we can without it. I say we make the deal."

Without hesitating, Quinn said, "Deal."

Calder scurried inside as if he were running from a tsunami. Maksim staggered to his feet and got into the driver's seat. Then, as if they were executing an awkward snow ballet, Matt and Biggs sidestepped to the front passenger door, while Viktor and Sierra did the same and went to the right rear door. Both men got in slowly. Both weapons stayed trained on their targets. Quinn held his at the ready, keeping it trained on Viktor. He had the look of a man who was not about to let the love of his life die a cold, brutal death. If he needed to shoot Viktor to save Sierra, Matt was pretty sure Quinn would gladly face the consequences with his superiors.

Once Biggs and Viktor were seated but with the doors still open, Biggs said, "On three. Guns down. We leave. Everyone lives. Agreed?"

"Agreed," Quinn said.

"Okay then," Biggs said, looking nervous for the first time during the encounter. "One. Two. Three."

Matt lowered his Beretta. Viktor lowered his weapon. Quinn kept his aimed at Maksim, the driver. As Biggs and Viktor closed their doors, Maksim gunned the engine and reversed out of the driveway, executing a sharp backout onto the road, then a controlled spin to reverse the car and drive away from Calder's cabin.

"We're not through with you, assholes!" Quinn yelled. "Damn it!"

"A pretty slick maneuver for a guy who probably has a concussion," Matt said, pointing at the disappearing vehicle.

Quinn waved a hand dismissively. "They'll probably switch drivers once they're out of range." Sure enough, they saw brake lights flash on as the SUV rounded a curve in the road. Then the sound of doors slamming and the engine revving again. "Anyone get the license plate number?"

Matt slapped his forehead with his palm. But before he could speak, Sierra said, "Yeah, memorized it while he had the gun to my head. Give me a piece of paper before I forget it."

Quinn grabbed her around the waist. "Let's get inside, warm you up, and have a friendly, low-key chat with Mr. Calder."

Chapter 29

Weezy/Pen

Weezy and Pen exited the elevator on the ground floor of Weezy's hotel.

"Nice to get out for lunch," Weezy said. "Holed up in that room, you forget what day it is. Are you on the street or in the garage?"

"Ramp. Uhh, garage."

"Ready to greet what the weather forecaster said was a 'pretty tolerable' day?"

Pen chuckled. "Above zero is good."

The hotel abutted the garage. A creaky elevator took them up three levels. Chill wind whistled through the spaces between buildings and through the ramp's open sides. Weezy watched Pen as she turned toward her van, a short distance away. After several steps, Weezy realized this older ramp had a steep grade. Pen had fallen behind her. She wondered if it would be polite to offer to push, turned toward Pen, and realized it wouldn't.

Pen, using the fob on her keychain, opened the van, wheeled in, and began securing her chair. She raised the tailgate for Weezy, who stowed her suitcase. As Weezy tapped the *Close* button on the tailgate, she noticed two men getting out of a car below the entrance she and Pen had just come through.

Weezy jumped into the passenger seat and closed the door, and Pen backed out. As Pen prepared to straighten and drive toward the exit, Weezy realized the two guys hadn't turned into the exit door but were walking toward them, one on each side of the drive aisle. The one on Pen's side held up a wallet with what looked like a police shield. The other guy, substantially overweight, trailed his partner on Weezy's side.

Pen stopped the van and glanced at Weezy. "Looks bogus," she said. "Let me handle this. Sit tight and keep your window up. If they're real cops, we play nice."

Pen lowered her window about halfway. The police shield guy on her side began the standard license-and-registration riff. "Lower your window, ma'am," he said. "All the way." He tried the door, which was locked. *Would a real cop do that?* But Pen lowered the window.

The guy on Weezy's side caught up, puffing. He knocked on Weezy's window. She shook her head *No*, like Pen had said. The guy pulled his jacket aside to show a waistband gun, which the guy's paunch forced to point at his testicles. She swallowed. The gun changed everything, didn't it? She felt in her pocket for the pepper spray Petey had insisted on, silently thanking him for his caution. She pulled out the small black pouch.

The fat guy rapped on her window again. She turned to Pen and said, "He's got a gun," which came out about an octave higher than she'd expected.

Pen's face fell.

Time for improvisation.

Weezy lowered her window and said, "Dude, the way that gun's pointing, you slip on the ice and you're going to be singing soprano."

The guy looked confused. "Huh?"

The shield guy reached into the van and grabbed Pen's door handle. "Out," he yelled. "Get out of the car."

Weezy brought up the pepper spray. Fat guy's eyes widened, and he reached for his gun. The spray hit him full in the face, and he dropped to his knees screaming not particularly inventive four-letter words.

Pen hit the gas and leaned on shield guy's arm, trapping it. The van backed up the ramp, dragging the guy on Pen's side. He stumbled along as best he could, yelling "No no no no no." He'd just got his feet under him when they passed a Ford stretch cab pickup, its butt a bit farther out in the lane, trailer hitch protruding, which hooked the guy at knee level as the van sped by. Just like the train used to pick up mailbags in the olden days.

Pen jammed the shift into Drive and shot forward as the fat guy, shaky from the pepper spray, drew his gun. As they closed, Weezy whipped her door open, which slammed into the guy. She shouted "Stop" to Pen, jumped out, and stomped the guy's wrist. The gun flew away, and Weezy did a mazurka on the guy's ribcage. At 113 pounds and wearing Nikes, it wouldn't put him in the hospital for long, but it gratified the adrenaline surge.

"Enough!" Pen shouted. "Get in!"

Then they were down the drive aisle, out of the ramp.

Pen pulled over, stopped, and turned on Weezy. "Are you crazy? I told you to keep your window up. You could have been killed."

"Sorry."

Pen exhaled. "Anyway, good job. Glad you brought that pepper spray. Now we need to call the cops. The real cops."

*   *   *

The "investigation" didn't take long. The police directed Pen and Weezy to return to the hotel. They arrived promptly, canvassed the area efficiently, and took statements politely and respectfully. They lamented that there had been a rash of carjackings in the city during the past couple of years. Pen and Weezy, after declining medical attention, were of little help; they described their assailants as best they could but hadn't clearly seen their car. The police mentioned that Weezy and Pen might want to "watch it a little" going forward, but clearly believed they were in no further danger.

Weezy and Pen knew better. "Let's get out of here," Pen said as they stood in the lobby after the police had left.

"Where to?"

"My place, downtown."

"Won't they find us there?"

"It wouldn't be easy. It's not in my name. It's also a security building."

Weezy sighed in relief. "All right, you've convinced me."

They quickly collected Weezy's belongings, retrieved the van, and headed for downtown. Pen arranged for Kenny to come and pick up the computer equipment. On the way, Pen's phone rang. She checked the caller ID: "CANDIOTTI A."

Pen exhaled and picked up the call from Minneapolis police lieutenant Lexi Candiotti.

"Welcome to Minneapolis," Lexi said. "Thanks for letting me know you're in town, and thanks for bringing your usual boatload of fun with you."

"Sorry. It's been busy. I've only been in town a few days."

"And already you and a friend are a victim of a random carjacking attempt. Just so you know, we picked up two bozos sitting in a car a couple of blocks away from the hotel who fit the description you gave the uniforms. Two guys hired from Craigslist under Muscle. They were sort of banged up and teary-eyed. We'll need to have you come down and identify them."

"Fine," said Pen, but she didn't know when they'd get a chance to do it.

"They didn't know anything," Lexi continued. "They were hired anonymously. Level with me, Pen: Did it have something to do with your latest project?"

Pen stopped at a light on Lake Street. "No way to know."

Candiotti wasn't buying it. "This is me you're talking to. What are you working on?"

"A project for Voyageur Cardiac." She paused. "There may be some corporate shenanigans going on."

"Your specialty."

"Yeah. But listen—I've talked to the FBI. They're on it." She glanced over at Weezy, who raised an eyebrow at the misleading-but-not-a-lie statement.

"Well, why didn't you tell me?" Candiotti said with heavy sarcasm. "I'm sure the Bureau has it all under control and would prefer to let us local gomers stick to carjackings and parking violations."

"I may need your help before it's over."

"For God's sake, Pen," said Candiotti, exasperated.

"I'm sorry. We'll have dinner soon, and I'll give you the play-by-play."

A sigh at the other end. "Just be careful. And stay the hell out of trouble."

Fifteen minutes later, Weezy and Pen arrived at the condo, downtown on Nicollet Mall. On the 22nd floor, Pen unlocked the door, and they stepped inside.

Weezy surveyed the unit. "Wow. This is way nicer than my hotel."

"Let's hope it's safer. You can put your suitcase in the spare room," Pen said. "Down the hall, second door on the right."

"How about the computer?"

"I'll have Kenny put it over on the dining room table, I think."

Weezy returned, joining Pen at the table. "This should work," she said and began unpacking her laptop, which she'd brought with her. "Have you talked to any of the others?"

"No, but we'd better. They could be attacked next. And I have no idea if they're making any progress."

"Sounds like we need another meeting," Weezy suggested.

"Agreed. Let's invite everybody here for tomorrow night at seven. But in the meantime, I'm going to call Hawke."

Weezy stopped her unpacking, gently setting the laptop down on the table before staring at Pen. "Are you serious? That sleazebag?"

"A sleazebag who might know something useful."

"You think he'd tell you if he did?"

"It's worth a try." She punched in Hawke's number, putting the call on speaker.

Henri Hawke picked up Pen's call immediately. "Ms. Wilkinson," said the syrupy Catalan voice. "So nice to hear from you."

"Louise Napolitani is here with me. Somebody just tried to abduct us."

"They—oh, my. How dreadful. Are you injured?" His surprise sounded genuine, Pen thought.

"No, we got away. I thought you might have some idea who was behind it."

A pause. "I may have some thoughts about it. Before I express them, could you be so kind as to tell me whether you have located Mr. Calder?"

"As far as I know, we haven't. We haven't checked with the others recently, but I'm sure they'd tell us if they'd found him."

"One additional question: Do you think you might be able to make contact with Mr. Hartsburg? To ask him to call me?"

Pen glanced at Weezy. "It's not inconceivable," Weezy said. "I've dealt directly with him."

"Ah, then—"

"Of course, we'd want to be in on the call."

Weezy smiled, and Pen could sense Hawke's frown over the phone connection. "That may be acceptable," he said. "I will wait to hear from you on that."

Pen resumed: "Now, you say you might have some idea who attacked us."

"Regrettably, I believe it was probably Gina Apate, a person I worked with toward a worthy goal."

"Why would she want to go after us?"

"My source informs me that Ms. Apate is using internal machinations to attempt to take control of Voyageur Cardiac Systems."

"Holy—what 'machinations'?"

"She has co-opted various VCS officials and employees, using bribery, threats, or promises of reward."

"Is Justin Biggs one of those people?" Weezy asked.

"I am afraid so. But there are others, including members of the board of directors. I am advised that within a couple of days, there will be a vote on measures that will give Ms. Apate complete control, replacing the current board with members friendly to her."

"Wouldn't Hartsburg be able to stop that?"

"I regret to say that Mr. Hartsburg appears to be subject to coercion."

Weezy and Pen gave each other knowing looks. Gina was threatening Tricia's life. "Who's your source?" Pen demanded.

Silence.

"You rebribed Marilyn Applewhite, didn't you?"

"I reached an accommodation with her," Hawke said.

"All right. We're putting together a meeting of the group again, probably tomorrow night. You're welcome to come if you want. I'll be in touch with details."

"Thank you, Ms. Wilkinson and Ms. Napolitani."

Pen clicked off. "What do you think?" she asked.

"I think VCS is in deep, deep trouble. And I think you might take some heat from the group for inviting Hawke to the meeting."

"We learned more from him in a five-minute call than we have from beating our heads against the wall for two days."

"If what he said is true."

"Even if half of what he said is true. Actually, that ratio sounds about right."

"Are you convinced now? You wanted proof that somebody has weaponized the 4750—is the attack on us enough?"

Pen nodded. "I'm convinced. I've always thought that was the case. But we couldn't go off half-cocked, accusing people. Now we know for sure what we're up against."

Weezy resumed setting up the computer while Pen sat silently. After a minute, Weezy glanced over at her friend. "Pen?"

No response.

"Are you all right?"

Pen was struggling to breathe, her chest heaving.

Alarmed, Weezy came around the table and took her friend's hand. "Pen?"

"P-purse," Pen gasped.

Weezy wheeled around, spotting Pen's purse on the counter leading to the kitchen. She grabbed the purse and opened it. "What do you need? An inhaler?"

"Pills." Pen managed to get the word out as her face reddened.

Weezy found a bottle of prescription medication and handed it to Pen, along with her water bottle, which had been clipped to her backpack. With shaking hands, Pen managed to take one of the small pills. Weezy watched, terrified.

"I'll be okay in . . . a few minutes," Pen said. Gradually, her breathing returned to normal, and she leaned back, exhausted.

"Are you okay?" Weezy asked. "What happened?"

"I'm okay. It was a panic attack."

"A panic—wow. How long have you been getting them?"

"I was treated for PTSD several years ago. I haven't had an attack in more than a year."

"What caused the PTSD?" She stopped herself. "I'm sorry. It's none of my business."

"I had some sticky situations like the one we had today. It's been a while since somebody stuck a gun in my face. I thought I was past this, but . . ."

"Nobody's bulletproof, Pen. Not even you."

Pen forced a smile. "The truest statement I've heard today." As she leaned back in her chair, calming herself, her fists clenched as she thought about the diabolical plan they faced, no longer conjecture but a certainty. And she thought about the thousands of patients threatened by an unimaginably perverse evil: life-giving devices being used to threaten, control, and ultimately to kill. She and her group had to stop the scheme.

They couldn't fail.

Chapter 30

The Group

Sierra, Matt, and Quinn arrived separately at Pen's condo building. All came to a back door, next to the service entrance, and then texted Pen, who went down to let each of them in. Upstairs, in the unit on the 22nd floor, Weezy sat at the dining room table in front of Kenny's pumped-up, homemade computer. A printer churned away on the counter as Kenny took sheets from it, collating and lining up stacks of paper on the table, as well as on a card table a few feet away in the living room. The coffee-maker had been moved to the counter between the dining room and kitchen, with cups next to it.

The group assembled in the living room. Pen introduced them to Kenny, who gave a brief nod. Weezy remained in the dining room, at the computer. "Help yourself to coffee," Pen said. "It could be a long night."

The group headed for the kitchen counter, grabbed mugs of coffee, and returned to their seats.

"Where's Ralph?" Pen asked.

"We've got him stashed," Matt replied.

"Where?"

"Better you don't know, for now."

"I guess you're right. But sooner or later we'll have to figure out what to do with him."

"Believe me, he'll pay," Matt said.

"Well, what did you get out of him?"

"Basically nothing," Sierra admitted. "He was in rough shape, almost catatonic, after what happened at the cabin."

"What happened?"

Sierra quickly described the altercation with Biggs and his thugs. "Ralph just kept shaking his head and muttering. He kept saying 'baby,' and something else we didn't quite understand, like a name." She turned to Matt. "What was he saying?"

"It sounded like 'Leighton.'"

"The name sounds familiar," Pen said. "But I can't place it. Ralph didn't admit to killing anyone?"

Quinn answered. "No, but he's been up to something. He's stonewalling, acting guilty as hell."

"He's holding something back," Matt agreed. "But unfortunately, we didn't get squat out of him."

Pen's green eyes bored into him. "You think he's killed someone else?"

"Could be. Or maybe he tried."

"How are you and Weezy doing?" Sierra asked, changing the subject. "That carjacking had to be a terrifying experience."

"We're okay. We're just lucky they sent a couple of stumble-bums instead of serious muscle."

"And the police?"

"They're treating it as just another carjacking attempt."

"Even though it was probably Apate," Quinn said.

Pen nodded. "It almost had to be, but we can't prove it. My question is, what is she up to? Who's her next victim?" She put her coffee mug down. "What about you three? You had a hair-raising experience of your own."

A grim-faced Sierra answered. "Yes, it was an adventure of the wrong kind, and I'm still kicking myself that Biggs and those thugs, probably Gina's people, got away with the transmitter."

"But do they know how to use it?"

"We have to assume they do," Matt asserted. "All indications are that Justin Biggs is working with Gina, and he's probably sharp enough to figure it out. Plus, Biggs has muscled up. Those goons had to come from somewhere, and my money is on Apate."

Sierra sipped from her coffee. "What did you learn about Hawke and Gina?" she asked Pen.

Pen summarized what she had learned from Agent Wendy Nomura. "We're dealing with some bad people," she concluded. "However, I've asked Hawke to join us at eight."

Matt exploded. "Are you serious?"

Pen nodded.

"I don't know which is crazier, spilling everything to an FBI agent or inviting that crooked shyster Hawke. What on earth were you thinking?"

Pen remained calm. "I don't trust Hawke a bit. But at this point, our interests are aligned with his."

"He's turned against Apate?" Sierra asked.

"Yes, as far as I can tell. I actually think she turned against him first."

"But you involved the FBI," Quinn said. "This is our case."

Pen rolled her eyes. "Listen to yourself. This is not 'our case.' It's not even your case, and you're a cop. We're trying to dig up enough to turn it over to the authorities. And we're trying to do it before there's another victim. Speaking of which . . ." She turned to Weezy, who was still working at the dining room table. "How's it going?"

Weezy didn't look up from her screen. "One last batch to print," she said. "Then we need to start going over the names."

"We have good news," Pen said to the group. "Weezy has finally cracked the rest of the database." There were murmurs of approval and excitement around the circle. Pen allowed herself a brief moment to ponder how the group took Weezy's hacking, and Kenny's and Zach's, for granted. What they did was extraordinary, world-class.

"What did Weezy find?" Sierra asked.

"She's accessed the names and addresses and basic medical information of people with the VC-25-4750 devices who have received updates within the past six months. But that's all we have."

Sierra frowned. "Don't we know which doctors' offices were affected?"

"Unfortunately, no. We weren't able to cross-check this list versus the list of updates that included the extra code."

"What are we looking for?" Quinn asked.

Sierra answered. "Potential targets. We could look for recognizable names of powerful people. Politicians, business executives, labor leaders."

"Or law enforcement," Pen added.

"We don't know the names of everybody who might be a threat to Gina," Matt pointed out. "It will just be intuition—hit and miss. Shots in the dark, especially since we don't know what she's up to."

"Then we'd better get started."

Weezy and Kenny handed out stacks of printouts. "They're arranged by zip code rather than alphabetically," Weezy said. "We're looking at about eight hundred names. Enjoy."

The group scanned the printouts intently, stopping frequently to Google names on their phones.

"This guy's a corporate CEO," Sierra said. "But he's in California."

"Is there an obvious connection to Gina or Voyageur?" Pen asked.

"None that I can see."

"Then put a mark beside his name for follow-up and move on."

"Here's a Justice Department lawyer," Quinn reported. "She's based in Washington."

"Mark that one, too. We'll have to see if she's investigating or prosecuting Gina."

Pen's phone rang; it was the front desk downstairs. She answered. "Yes? Now?" She sighed. "All right, send him up."

Pen clicked off and looked up at the group. "Hawke is here now," she said. "An hour early."

"Aw, hell," Matt said, disgusted. The rest of the group responded with exasperated looks.

Quinn walked over to the door to admit Hawke, who looked uncharacteristically worried.

"Come on in," Pen said to Hawke. "The more, the merrier."

Hawke entered the room, nodding to each of the guests.

"We're looking through lists of 4750 patients who received Calder's altered updates," Pen reported. "But we don't know exactly what we're looking for."

"Perhaps I could be of assistance."

Everyone stopped, looked up, and turned toward Hawke. "Through my sources," he continued, "I have ascertained that Gina Apate has a most despicable plan in the works."

The group waited as the weight of his words sunk in.

Hawke continued: "Ms. Apate's initial objective was to profit from the plan developed by Mr. Hartsburg, Mr. Calder, and myself to develop a watchdog group to prevent defective medical devices. However, Ms. Apate is now in a position to seize the opportunity presented by Mr. Calder's device to take control of Voyageur Cardiac Systems."

"To take over the whole company?" said Sierra, incredulous. "How does she plan to do that?"

"By having herself appointed chair of the board of directors at a special meeting to be held tomorrow."

"How could she do that?"

"Stephen Hartsburg has resigned and endorsed her slate of candidates."

"Uh-oh," Pen said. "He's being coerced."

"Exactly," Hawke replied. "He is complying with Ms. Apate's wishes because of threats to his special friend, Tricia."

"That sounds farfetched. She can't just waltz in there and take over on Hartsburg's say-so. The directors and employees will be asking questions. So will the regulators and shareholders."

"I believe it will be a short-term operation. With even temporary control of the board, and the compliance of a handful of key employees, she would be able to loot the company, obtain the technology that enables the weaponization of ICD devices, and make good her escape before regulators and shareholders are able to respond."

"How do you know this?" Matt demanded. "Who are these 'sources' of yours?"

"I have spoken with Mr. Calder and with Ms. Applewhite. Both confirmed this scheme."

"Damn," Quinn said. "I knew Calder was holding something back."

"So that's it?" Pen said to Hawke. "You're telling us Apate already has a majority of directors lined up?"

Hawke hesitated.

"Out with it," Pen demanded.

"One director remains opposed," Hawke said at last. "Reverend Sterling Leighton. He is a respected pastor and civil rights leader. Regardless of Mr. Hartsburg's coerced recommendations, Ms. Apate cannot prevail over his opposition."

"Okay," said Weezy, who had joined the conversation. "So, what is Gina going to do about it?"

Hawke was silent for a long moment, then seemed to come to a decision. "Ms. Apate sent Ralph Calder to Reverend Leighton's residence with his transmitter."

"Holy shit!" exclaimed Matt. "Leighton's got an ICD? And Calder was supposed to kill him?"

"Regrettably, yes. However, Mr. Calder declined to perform the deed once he got there."

"That's consistent with his behavior when we found him," Quinn said.

"Right," Matt said. "He was mumbling something that sounded like 'Leighton.'"

"But that means Leighton is still vulnerable," Weezy pointed out. "And now Gina and Justin Biggs have the transmitter."

Pen sat up straighter. "First things first. Let's make sure Leighton's on the list."

Everyone returned to the lists. After only half a minute, Quinn looked up. "Here he is."

"And the meeting is tomorrow," Pen said. "We need to move now. Biggs or his people could be at his house anytime." She turned to Weezy. "Find his number and call him. Tell him to get the hell out of there. Kenny, do what you have to do to locate his phone." The young man nodded and began typing on his laptop.

"What about the police?" Sierra asked.

Pen responded. "Calling 911 won't work. We don't know that anybody is there to attack him right now, and how would we describe the attack to the officers? I'll call my detective friend and have her get somebody over there."

"How about the FBI?" Matt asked.

"I'll call my friend there, too," Pen said, "but that will take even more time."

"Where does Leighton live?" Matt asked. "We need to get over there and protect him."

Pen turned toward the dining room. "Weezy?"

"Voicemail," she said. "But I've got his address. It's 64 Greenway Gables."

"That's only about three blocks from here."

Matt stood up. "Then let's go." Everyone reached for their coats.

Weezy's phone rang. She looked at the number. "Wait, everybody," she called out. "It's Hartsburg." She came back into the living room. "I'm putting him on speaker."

She answered the call. "This is Napolitani."

"It's Hartsburg," said the frantic voice over the speaker. "You've got to help me."

"Slow down," Weezy said. "What's the problem?"

"Tricia. She's gone."

"Okay. Where did she go?"

"She's on her way to the Twin Cities. She's probably almost there now. She's headed to the airport."

"Why?"

"To leave town, so she won't be vulnerable to having her ICD used against her. Against *me*. She feels guilty. She called me from the car and told me she was on her way out of town. I told her it's not her fault that I'm being coerced, but she feels responsible."

"What's wrong with her leaving town?" Weezy asked. "In fact, that sounds like a good idea."

"She apparently slipped past the people Gina Apate had watching her up here at the lake," Hartsburg said. "But don't you think they could track her? Won't they try to intercept her at the airport?"

Nobody disagreed.

"Why did you call me?" Weezy asked. "What do you want me to do about it?"

"Look, I'm sorry I shut you down. I didn't have any choice. But I need help. I can't just call the police and explain all this. They won't understand. They'll want some proof. And, well . . ."

Pen wheeled closer to Weezy. "And you'd have to tell them some of the shitty things you and your company have done," she said.

"Who's that?" Hartsburg asked.

"Pen Wilkinson."

"The attorney. Look, you know people, right? Police or FBI? Nancy must know people, too, but she won't take my calls."

Pen looked at Quinn and Sierra. "Yes, I may know some people who could be helpful."

"And Ms. Napolitani. You could track Tricia, right? Hack her phone or something?"

"Maybe," Weezy responded.

"Please, help. They might kill her."

Pen looked around the room. "We'll do what we can, Mr. Hartsburg. But when this is over, you're going to come clean. And you're going to pay."

Silence.

"All right," Pen said. "First, you're going to give Tricia's phone number to my . . . associate, Mr. Sellars." She glanced at Kenny, who nodded. "Next," she continued, "you're going to give a description and plate number of Tricia's vehicle to another gentleman here, Detective Moore. Then you're going to sit tight and answer if we call you."

While Hartsburg relayed the information, Pen turned to the group. "Sierra, you and Quinn are familiar with the airport. You know people there—you should handle that end. And you're more likely to encounter Apate and her serious thugs—you'd better take Matt with you. I'm familiar with Leighton's neighborhood, and we're likely up against just one guy with a transmitter, so Weezy and I will go to Leighton's."

Matt looked inclined to argue but finally nodded and grabbed his jacket.

"Stay in touch, everybody," Pen said as Weezy helped her struggle into her coat. "Kenny will let you know if he's able to get locations. And for God's sake, be careful."

Pen spun and wheeled toward the door, then stopped so suddenly the trailing Weezy nearly fell on top of her.

"What?"

"Where's Hawke?" Pen asked.

Chapter 31

Weezy/Pen

Pen and Weezy hurried to the garage, still wondering how the sleazy little toad/attorney had left the meeting without anyone noticing.

They reached the garage, and Weezy fidgeted while Pen went through the tedious process of opening her van's side door, extending the ramp, wheeling on, transferring, and securing the chair. By the time they exited the garage, Weezy had pulled up the route to Leighton's townhouse, barely four blocks away. They drove down Yale Place as light snow began swirling around them in the cold breeze.

"Take the second left," Weezy said, looking at her phone and then up at the road.

"Okay. Start looking for Justin's vehicle," Pen replied. "It's a red Mustang."

They made the turn and cruised slowly through the complex's parking lot. "There's Leighton's unit," Weezy said, pointing to a two-story townhouse with a double garage underneath. A single dim light was visible in a first-floor window. After a second pass, during which they saw no trace of Biggs's vehicle, they returned to the street and then turned into the parking lot of an adjacent condo building. From there, they'd be able to see Leighton's house.

"Pen," Weezy said, "Are you sure we shouldn't have called 911?"

"Not a hundred percent sure. But what if we did? How would we describe the emergency?"

"I don't know."

"And if the police showed up, what would they find? The purported victim isn't here, and neither is the alleged criminal."

"Um, right."

"But that doesn't mean we shouldn't try to get help." She called Lieutenant Lexi Candiotti.

"Pen," the lieutenant said. "I've been waiting for your call."

"Really?"

"No, not really. I actually have a date tonight."

"We're in a bit of a bind here." Summoning all her lawyerly skills of exposition and persuasiveness, Pen summarized the problem.

After a lengthy pause, Candiotti said, "So, if I understand this correctly, you're afraid a bad guy with a radio transmitter is going to show up at a minister's house and kill him by remotely fiddling with his heart pacemaker."

"Well, yes," Pen said. "I know it sounds improbable, but—"

"I'm sorry, Pen. We could open an investigation, I suppose. Give me a call tomorrow. But at this moment, I'd need a lot more than that to get involved."

"Can you have some uniforms do a drive-by? It might deter the guy with the transmitter."

"All right, I can do that much. And, of course, if the guy shows up, call 911."

"Right," said Pen, knowing it would be too late by that time. "Thanks, Lexi."

She clicked off and looked at Weezy.

"What now?" Weezy asked.

"We find out if Kenny has located Leighton."

"He hasn't. I've been texting with him and giving him some pointers. If you can't slip malware onto the target's phone, it's a lot harder."

And even more illegal, Pen thought. "Can Zach help?"

"He's busy trying to locate Tricia." Weezy fidgeted while texting. "Do we have a Plan B?"

"No."

They waited. Twenty minutes passed. Pen kept her eyes glued to the street, watching either for Biggs's red Mustang or for a car approaching Leighton's house. She squinted through the snow, keeping the engine running for warmth. A police car cruised slowly by the complex entrance—Lexi's drive-by, Pen assumed.

Weezy stopped texting, exhaled, and looked over at her friend. "Justin is a little crazy."

"No argument there."

"I mean, who would do something like he's going to do? And he's going to have a gun."

"No doubt. But Sierra, Matt, and Quinn will be facing down thugs with guns, too, maybe even more dangerous than Biggs. We took the easy assignment."

Weezy glanced out the window. "Reassuring to know."

"It wouldn't have to be Justin who shows up to do this."

"My money's on him."

Weezy returned to her texting, then looked up. "The VCS board meeting is tomorrow morning. They could go after Leighton any time before then—maybe in the middle of the night."

"True," Pen admitted. "But I think they'll want to get it done soon. If the transmitter doesn't work for some reason, they'll want time to try something else."

"Like kick down Leighton's door and shoot him?"

"Probably something like that."

Another twenty minutes passed. Weezy looked up suddenly from her texting. "Kenny found Leighton. He's close."

Pen put the van in gear. "We can't let him get close to his house. Biggs could be lurking nearby."

Weezy glanced again at her screen. "He's approaching from the northeast on Yale Place."

"That's the street we came in on." They pulled out onto Yale Place and turned right. "What are we looking for?"

"There's a white Toyota SUV registered in Leighton's name. He should be coming toward us."

There was very little traffic on the street. Pen pulled over to the right curb to get a better view of approaching vehicles.

A pair of headlights came slowly toward them. They strained to see the vehicle.

"It's a pickup truck," Weezy said. They exhaled and resumed their vigilance.

Weezy glanced at her screen again. "Only a couple of blocks. What do we do when he approaches?"

"Try to get his attention and stop him."

"How?"

"I don't know."

"You know," Weezy said, "if we can track him—"

"Biggs might be able to do it, too. And he's out there somewhere . . ."

"There's Leighton." Weezy pointed to a vehicle—now visible as a white SUV—approaching from the northeast.

Pen began flashing her lights. The SUV didn't change speed or direction. She honked her horn several times. The SUV continued its approach.

"Hang on!" Pen yelled, pulling out of their parking spot and swerving left, stopping sideways across the opposite lane. The SUV skidded to a stop, horn honking. Then it started to pull out around the van. Pen backed up at an angle, blocking the other vehicle.

The SUV's driver's-side window lowered, and an irate, distinguished-looking Black man stuck his head out. "What's going on? Get out of my way!"

Weezy lowered her own window. "Reverend Leighton! Don't go back to your house. Get away from here, now! Somebody is waiting there to kill you. The police are on the way."

"What the—"

Pen looked out her own window, back down the street the way they had come, and saw a red Mustang turn onto Yale Place, headed their way. "It's Justin!" she yelled. "He might already be in range!"

Weezy yelled to Leighton, "Please! Go back, *now*! They're trying to fiddle with your ICD!"

"How did you—"

Pen didn't wait around for the response. She shifted back into Drive and gunned the engine, swinging around and racing back toward the Mustang, now less than a block away.

"Do we call 911?" Weezy asked.

"No time." Pen swerved to the left, trying to pin Biggs to the curb on the right side. The Mustang screeched to a stop, and Biggs jumped out, holding a backpack.

"Shit!" Weezy yelled. "He's got the transmitter. And Leighton is probably within range." They both glanced back down the street; the minister's SUV had not moved.

Biggs, standing behind the open door, had removed an object from the backpack.

Pen increased speed, aiming the van directly at the driver's door, and at Biggs.

Biggs looked up in alarm and, at the last moment, dived back inside the Mustang.

Pen sideswiped the driver's door with a bang and a loud screech. Her van's engine stalled.

Weezy opened her door.

"What the hell are you doing?" Pen screamed, trying to restart the van.

Weezy ran around the rear of the van. "We have to get the transmitter away from him!"

"Shit!" Just then, white-and-blue lights rotated across the landscape. Pen again honked her horn and flashed her lights.

Biggs then reappeared on the sidewalk, having come out the Mustang's passenger door. He carried an object the size of a cigar box and started to hold it up. A brief blast of siren sounded from the police car, now visible as it approached from the direction opposite Leighton. Lexi's drive-by unit, still in the area?

Weezy tackled Biggs, who went down to the sidewalk, dropping the transmitter. He rolled over and sprang to his feet, this time holding a gun.

Weezy backed off, raising her hands. "You stupid bitch!" Biggs screamed. "You're fucked! You and your cripple friend and all the rest of you!"

"Drop the weapon!" The voice came from the loudspeaker on the police car, which had stopped in front of Pen's van, beside the Mustang. Officers were getting out of the car. Pen raised her hands, so they would be visible in the windshield.

"Drop it now!" the voice repeated. Biggs hesitated, then turned and began to run.

"Stop and drop the weapon!" This time, the voice was not amplified. It came from an officer who was crouched beside the Mustang. Pen could see a second officer, crouching behind the police cruiser.

Biggs stopped, hesitated, turned around, then waved the gun wildly in the direction of the officers.

The police fired. One shot. Two. Three. Four. Weezy screamed and flinched.

Biggs went down, dropping the gun and clutching his chest. One officer, a woman, approached him cautiously, gun drawn. The other sized up the rest of the scene, spotting Weezy and Pen. "I need to see your hands," he shouted. "Come out slowly."

Both women already had their hands raised. Weezy came out from in front of the Mustang. Down the sidewalk, the female officer was calling for an ambulance.

The male officer, holding his gun at his side, turned to Pen. "Ma'am, get out of the vehicle slowly. Do it now."

"I'm sorry. I can't."

The officer tensed up, raising his gun.

"She's a paraplegic," Weezy said. "For God's sake, don't shoot!"

Pen, breathing hard, kept her hands raised.

"We're the good guys," Pen managed to say. "I'm the one who called Lieutenant Candiotti."

The officer kneeling over Biggs on the sidewalk looked up. "He's gone."

After further back-and-forth, the male officer eventually put Weezy in the back of the squad car and allowed Pen to transfer to her wheelchair, watching her carefully. After a pat-down and a check of her ID, she was lifted into the back of the squad car with Weezy.

"Are you okay?" Weezy asked.

Pen reacted with fury. "*Okay*? Are you crazy? You are incredibly lucky to be sitting here, alive. That was the stupidest damn thing I've ever seen."

Weezy looked out the window at the crumpled front end of Pen's vehicle. "Your van," she said at last.

"What?"

"Your van. The rental company is going to be pissed."

Pen let out an astonished chuckle. "You, my dear, are a certified dumbass."

*　　*　　*

It was nearly one in the morning when Weezy and Pen left the Public Safety Building in downtown Minneapolis, having given detailed statements dating from the beginning of their involvement with Voyageur Cardiac Systems. After the first hour, Lieutenant Lexi Candiotti, who was overseeing the investigation, let out a long sigh. "We'll need to get the FBI involved. They'll end up taking the lead."

The police had secured the device Justin Biggs had taken out of his backpack. Reverend Leighton and his family had been moved to an undisclosed location under police guard. During a break in the interview, both Pen and Weezy began texting rapidly, trying to get updates from Sierra, Quinn, and Matt. Pen looked up from her phone and glanced at Weezy. "You getting anything from the gang?

"Nope."

"Uh-oh."

Chapter 32

Matt/Sierra/Quinn/Tricia

Tricia Doran entered the small general aviation terminal at Castor Aviation and headed to the counter, where a woman with bottle-red hair finished a phone call.

"Tricia?" the woman asked. "Oh my God, it is you. I thought I saw your name in the computer. How long has it been?"

"Hey, Cherie. I didn't know you still worked here." Tricia glanced at the glass entrance doors, her head starting to ache from the tension she held in her neck and shoulders. "I'd love to catch up with you, but I'm here to catch my charter."

Cherie tapped a few keys on the computer. "You're early. I just called the flight crew in. It'll be a couple hours before they're ready to go."

Tricia tried to keep her voice calm when all she wanted to do was scream. She stole another look toward the entrance. "A couple hours? I thought when I booked the charter two hours ago it'd be ready by now."

"I wish I could say it worked that way, but unless you're Bill Gates or Warren Buffett, it doesn't. We have to make sure we've got a plane available, and then we have to find a crew who can fly. Pilots have strict time limits between flights, and we're short two crews right now. The soonest a crew will be ready is two hours."

"From now?" Tricia winced at the squeak in her voice. "Sorry. I just thought . . ."

"If we had another crew, it would be ready." Cherie leaned over the counter. "Hey, it'll give us some time to catch up. Are you still seeing that real estate guy?"

God, the last thing I need is small talk, Tricia thought. "No, we broke up ages ago. I found out he was seeing the woman who staged his houses." Tricia caught movement outside the entrance, but when she looked, she didn't see anything. Her nerves buzzed with anxiety, and she caught herself before she could gnaw her nails any shorter. Could she wait two hours? Should she just hop on I-494 and drive to Wisconsin now? Would that be far enough?

"Pity. He was hot. Are you seeing anyone now?"

"Um, yes." Unless Stephen's latest deal—the one he wouldn't talk to her about—blew up in both their faces. Maybe this whole thing was an opportunity to decide if he was worth it. He still hadn't divorced his wife, and he'd insisted that would be his Christmas present to Tricia.

"Ooh, do tell," Cherie said, rubbing her hands together. "Is he handsome? Tall and dark? What does he do?"

Dark shadows blocked the light at the entrance. Tricia froze, her pulse thudding in her ears.

Cherie patted her hand. "Hey, what's wrong?"

Two men, thick and tall, one in a long black wool coat and the other in a leather bomber-style jacket, both wearing black watch caps, opened the entrance doors and crossed the threshold side-by-side like a pair of thugs from central casting.

Adrenaline flared through her. "Shit. I have to go." Before Cherie could say anything, Tricia bolted toward the nearest exit: the door marked for boarding passengers only. January cold hit her in the face like a feather pillow swung by a pro ballplayer, stealing her breath for a moment.

Brilliant floodlights mounted on the terminal building and atop tall poles lit the apron like it was late afternoon. In the evening dark beyond the apron, blue lights traced the taxiways, weaving toward the runways lined with white lights.

She took a quick look around and cursed again. What the hell had she been thinking? Everything was flat—there was no place to hide. To her right, three rows of planes, a mix of small jets and propeller planes, were parked on the tarmac with a metal hangar overlooking them. To her left, under more lights, three de-icing trucks were parked in front of what looked like a garage for commercial trucks, all across half a football field worth of asphalt.

"Hey! You! Stop!"

Shit. The shout from behind her kicked her into motion. She dashed toward the planes, vowing if she got out of this alive, she was going to make Stephen's life a living hell.

*　　*　　*

Matt called Zach from the backseat of Quinn's SUV and put his cell phone on speaker as Quinn took the exit to the Minneapolis-St. Paul International Airport. "Did you find her?"

"No, man," Zach said. "She's not on any of the passenger lists."

"What do you mean?" Frustration laced Matt's voice. "Hartsburg said she was on her way to the airport to fly out of town. Why wouldn't she be on any of the passenger lists?"

"Maybe because she doesn't have a ticket," Zach answered. "I can't find what isn't there, dude."

Matt's voice held an edge. "Did Hartsburg say MSP or another airport? What if . . ."

From the front seat Sierra said, "Matt, chill. Pen said Hartsburg told her MSP, but most people don't realize how many airports there are in the Twin Cities. Zach, can you see the manifests for any charters?"

A moment later Zach answered. "No can do. They apparently don't use the same ticketing systems. I'd have to dig a bit."

"Wait," Quinn said, "what about her phone? Can you find it? Track it?"

"Got her number?" Before anyone could answer, Zach said, "Wait, Kenny's got it. Just a minute." Muted clacking from the other end of the call filled tense seconds. "Nope. She must have either turned her phone off or turned off the location services."

"Of course she thought to do that," Sierra said with a grumble.

"Good luck, guys. Sorry, but I gotta do my real job now." Zach clicked off.

"Now what?" Matt said, frustration sharpening his voice. "How the hell are we supposed to protect her if we don't know where she is?"

"If she's here at MSP and wants to get out of town," Sierra said, "there aren't many places she can go, especially if she isn't at the main terminals. Charters leave from the general aviation terminal halfway across the field. Quinn?"

Quinn headed out of the drop-off area of the main terminal. "I follow you. It's our best option at this point."

Matt leaned forward. "But what if she's not here yet? Or she hasn't bought her ticket yet?"

"According to Pen, Tricia should be here by now." Quinn accelerated onto the service drive that cut around the main airport grounds.

"Right, but it's not Tricia we should be worried about," Sierra said. "It's the goon squad Gina sent after her. And chances are this time they'll be more competent than the last ones we ran into." Quinn braked hard and skidded around a corner.

"Do you have your backup gun?" Sierra asked Quinn.

"You know how much I hate carrying that when I'm off-duty, but yes, I have my gun."

"Good. Here's hoping you don't have to use it."

"Don't worry," Matt said. He unzipped his parka and checked his waist holster. "I've got mine. Just in case."

Quinn looked at him in the rear-view mirror. "Please tell me you have a carry permit."

"I do. I once pissed off some nasty people, big-time. Don't worry, I'll only shoot in self-defense."

"Well, why didn't you say so?" Quinn said.

"Look." Sierra pointed ahead, where a large black SUV was parked in front of the general aviation terminal. "Dammit, they're here."

"I guess it's a good thing they follow the black SUV trope," said Matt.

"Yeah, we'd be in trouble if the bad guys started driving Priuses." Sierra braced a hand on the dashboard and cursed under her breath as Quinn braked hard to a stop behind the SUV.

"Seriously, Quinn? I know you want to get a new truck, but . . ."

"How else do we stop them from leaving? Let's go."

They ran to the terminal's entrance to find no one inside except the red-haired receptionist with a phone receiver pressed to her ear. Quinn reached the counter first, badge in hand.

"Quinn Moore, Airport Police. Was there a woman here waiting for a charter?"

The receptionist lowered the receiver, attention shifted to the exit to the airport proper. "I was just going to call the police. Yes, Tricia. She was here, waiting—I'd just called the flight crew in—and then these two big guys came in. As soon as she saw them, she ran out onto the tarmac. They didn't say anything, they just took off after her."

Sierra suppressed a sudden surge of icy fear. She'd been chased by thugs in the confines of the hangar here before. "How long ago?"

"They just … just now."

Matt bolted through the door onto the tarmac before either Sierra or Quinn could say anything. "Aw, hell." Sierra couldn't decide whether to follow him or try to loop around and come at the general aviation apron from another direction. She spotted the Authorized Personnel Only door that she knew led to the hangar and another door to the apron.

Quinn was already on the phone, calling for backup, she assumed. She waved to get his attention, then ran through the Authorized Only door and down the hall she remembered from her last—and only—ill-fated visit to this hangar. She'd survived that nightmare years ago and prayed she'd get out of this one, too.

*   *   *

Tricia wove around airplane wings, stealing a glance over her shoulder. Only one of the men was behind her. Where did the other one go? She didn't bother to look. She dodged around the tail of a twin-engine propeller plane in time to see a tall, lean man lunge at the other brute she'd seen enter the terminal. The men tumbled to the ground, and the newcomer launched fists at his quarry. She stopped. *Who the hell . . .*

A hand that felt like a vise clamped onto her arm. "Gotcha."

Tricia almost choked on the guy's halitosis as he pulled her. She resisted as much as she could, but the guy was twice her size. He yanked her back around the tail of the plane like she was little more than a toddler with a tantrum. "Let me go!" Panic fed terror, kicking her pulse into overdrive. She pounded on his chest, tried to pry his fingers off her.

He slapped her. Pain exploded behind her eyes. She tasted a metallic tang of blood. It was like being hit with a two-by-four. "Settle down, or I'll get rough with you."

*   *   *

Sierra found the door that opened onto the tarmac at the very back of the hangar, where the familiar, sharp scent of jet exhaust and deafening roar of a 767 taking off greeted her. She burst through the door at a run toward the rows of planes parked outside the terminal, assessing the situation.

Matt chased down one of the goons—*Ooh, nice flying tackle, but damn, that must have hurt.* One down, one to go.

Quinn ran into view from the direction of the terminal. "Stop! Police!" He stopped short of the first row of planes, badge in one hand, gun in the other. "Let her go."

Now Sierra saw them. The other goon had caught Tricia at the tail end of what looked like a twin-engine Cessna and was dragging her with him around the tail.

The goon pulled a gun from somewhere under his coat as he dragged Tricia with him to the trailing edge of one of the plane's wings. "I don't think so. You drop your gun, let us go, and I'll try really hard not to shoot you."

The gravelly voice had a Russian accent. That Viktor guy from Calder's place?

After a long hesitation, Quinn lowered his gun. "No need for that." He ejected the magazine, tucked it in a pocket of his coat, and then opened the chamber, ejecting the cartridge. He locked the chamber open and put the gun in another pocket. "There. Now you put down your gun and let Tricia go. I've called for backup. They'll be here in a few minutes; you're not going anywhere."

Dammit, Quinn. That's not going to help. Sierra checked Matt's status. He was kneeling on Goon #1's back and shoving the guy's face into the asphalt. He wasn't going to be able to help. She picked her way behind Viktor to the opposite wing of the twin Cessna.

Viktor gripped Tricia's arm with one hand and rested his gun hand on the plane's wing, which was conveniently under his chin. "How about I just shoot you and take Tricia with me."

"Look, let's talk about this." Quinn stepped closer, then hesitated when he saw Sierra. She gave him a thumbs-up as she reached the trailing edge of the Cessna's other wing and signaled to him what she was planning with a pantomime gesture.

Quinn gave her a nod so slight she wouldn't have seen it if she hadn't been watching for it. He focused on Viktor. "We can figure this out without anyone getting hurt."

The crack of a gunshot echoed against the metal wall of the hangar. Sierra gasped, the world at a standstill for a moment when she saw Quinn holding his upper arm, blood oozing between his fingers. He was still on his feet . . . he locked his gaze with her for a split second. She understood the message: *Stay put, I'm okay, get this guy.* She nodded and gritted her teeth. If something happened to Quinn, she'd kill that Russian gorilla herself.

"I won't be so generous with the next shot," said Viktor. "Back off and let me go with the woman, and you'll never see me again."

Sierra removed the control lock and shoved the aileron down, knowing the other aileron would slam up.

Viktor yelped as the aluminum surface caught his chin and cracked his head back.

In a flash Sierra ducked under the tail of the plane and pulled Tricia away from her dazed captor. He reacted, swinging his gun hand toward Sierra. She lowered her shoulder and drove him into the thin trailing edge of the wing. God, like hitting a truck.

Viktor grunted and grabbed the collar of her coat. Quinn shouted her name. Sirens filled the air behind the roar of a jet takeoff roll.

Tricia grabbed at Viktor's gun hand, keeping it pointing into the air, but that didn't help Sierra get loose. Sierra stomped on his foot, then tried to drive her knee into his balls, but he was too tall for her to get enough power into her thrust to hurt him.

Tricia hung on as he tried to free his gun hand. "Do something!" she screeched.

Sierra shifted and jammed the heel of her snow boot into his instep. That got his attention. He leaned forward, and Sierra dropped to the ground, pulling him with her.

Before Viktor dropped his full weight on Sierra, Quinn shoved him to the ground beside her, introducing the goon's face to the tarmac. He stomped on Viktor's gun hand.

Viktor yipped and let go of the gun as a marked Airport Police Department SUV pulled to a stop near the Cessna. A tall officer jogged over and yanked Viktor's hand from under Quinn's boot to slap cuffs on his wrist while Sierra took Quinn's proffered hand and rose to her feet. "You okay?" he asked.

"Yeah, I'm good." She had to kiss him because she needed it. His lips were warm and reassuring and settled her nerves. "What about you? He shot you."

"Just grazed me." He showed her the bloodstained hole in the arm of his parka.

Sierra turned him until the light gave her a better look. "Just grazed? Are you kidding? You're bleeding, and it looks like you're going to need stitches. We've got to get pressure on that. Where's the first aid kit in the cruiser? I'll—"

Quinn placed his bloody hand on hers. "Sierra, relax, I'll be fine. Tricia?"

Tricia brushed blood from her lip and pulled her coat close. "Yeah, I'm okay." She touched the swelling cut on her cheek and sucked in air. "God, this is gonna hurt tomorrow. Thank you, whoever you are."

"Let's just say Hartsburg was worried about you," Sierra said.

Tricia's lips pressed into a tight smile. "If he'd listened to his quality people in the first place ..." She shook her head. "This whole thing turned into a mess. I don't know how they found me."

"Good question. Are you sure you weren't followed?"

"I don't think so."

"What about your phone?"

Tricia rolled her eyes. "I watch TV. I turned it off."

"Do you have GPS in your car?" Sierra asked.

"Oh my God. Can that be tracked?"

"I'm not sure, but I know someone who might." Sierra made a mental note to ask Weezy about that the next time she saw her. Another APD SUV was parked where she'd seen Matt take down the other goon. Matt came around the SUV, still breathing hard, and joined them. He had a fresh bruise on his cheekbone and a scratch on his chin.

"Hey, nice tackle," Sierra said.

"Thanks." Matt said. "Second-team all-conference linebacker at Straight River High." He pointed behind them with a thumb. "Nice job with the other one."

"Well, let's go back inside where it's warmer." Quinn turned to lead them back to the terminal. "Matt, find out how Pen and Weezy are doing with Leighton. And let them know we've got Tricia."

Chapter 33

Hawke/Gina/Hartsburg

Hawke sat at the edge of the ad hoc group in Pen's condo, observing the frenetic activity. His revelation of the threat to Reverend Leighton had gotten their attention, but the phone call from Hartsburg to the woman they called Weezy had created a frenzy.

As Hartsburg pleaded for help to save Tricia, Hawke ruminated, rolling the situation over in his mind. *Gina has sent her muscle after Hartsburg's lady friend, and, undoubtedly, Biggs is on his way to dispatch Reverend Leighton. But where is Gina? Where would I be?*

Oblivious to the helter-skelter in the room, scowl lines creased his forehead as he tried to conjure the location of the slippery Greek.

But of course! Her plan has only one other loose end—Hartsburg. Gina is at Hartsburg's cabin to assure that the fish doesn't wiggle off the hook.

As Pen gave directions on who was to go where and do what, he slipped out the door to his waiting limousine. By his calculation, it was a three-plus-hour drive to Hartsburg's north woods retreat. He ordered his driver to make it in two.

*   *   *

"Do you really want to add murder to the long list of crimes you've committed?"

Gina leaned on her cane, calmly looking across the desk at a trembling Hartsburg. His hands shook as he tried to keep the pistol trained on her.

"If you shoot me, what will you gain?" she asked. "It won't save your crumbling company or bring back Tricia. It won't save your reputation. It will just get you another prison sentence . . . a very long one."

"But . . . but . . ." sputtered a red-faced Hartsburg. "We had a deal . . ."

"And Tricia endangered that deal by trying to run," Gina interrupted, her voice on edge. "If you don't do anything stupid, and play your part tomorrow at the board meeting, we will bring her back to you . . ."

The gun barrel drifted downward, no longer pointing at Gina.

". . . and you two can have a long life together . . . on whatever island you want to live."

Hartsburg shakily sat down in his chair. "How can I be sure of that?"

"You can't, but if you don't resign and vote me and my slate of directors to the Voyageur board, you'll never see her again."

The color faded from Hartsburg's face. He held the gun, but she was in control.

"You will only benefit by cooperating," Gina continued after letting her words sink in, "so why don't you put the gun down, and let's have a little of that bourbon on your back bar. We'll both feel better."

Hartsburg's head made little nodding motions as he appeared to process what she'd said. With slow, deliberate movement, he placed the pistol on his desk.

"I'm trusting you," he said.

His hands were still twitching as he poured bourbon into two cut crystal glasses, handing one to Gina. She raised the glass to make a toast. He didn't respond. "I'm trusting you," he repeated, an air of authority returning to his voice.

"I need something to eat," she demanded, ignoring his words. "I haven't eaten since breakfast. A man of your stature must have some epicurean delight in his pantry."

Hartsburg, annoyed, shrugged and turned in the direction of the kitchen, followed by Gina, the triple beat of her walking stick and high heels on the marble tiled floor the only sounds in the cavernous cabin.

"What would you like? I can make you a roast beef sandwich," Hartsburg offered.

"How American of you."

Gina sat on a high stool at the expansive kitchen island and watched him cut two slices off a leftover roast. She checked her watch: 9:30. Biggs should have called by now. So should Viktor and Maksim, for that matter. For the first time since she'd arrived at Hartsburg's cabin, she began to feel uneasy.

"Mayo or butter?" he asked as he placed two pieces of bread on a stoneware plate.

"Horseradish."

"Don't have any. Tricia's allergic."

"Then mayo." Gina looked at her watch again. "Where's the bathroom?"

Once in the bathroom, she locked the door, then dialed Viktor. No answer. The Russian thug hadn't set up voicemail on his burner phone, so she couldn't leave a message.

She tried Biggs. The call went immediately to voicemail.

"Everything okay?" Hartsburg asked as Gina hobbled back into the kitchen.

"Of course," she snapped.

"I don't think so," came the silky, accented voice from the opposite doorway.

Both Gina and Hartsburg spun around.

"Hawke?" a surprised Hartsburg blurted.

"You!" Gina shouted simultaneously.

"You were expecting someone else?" Hawke said coolly.

"What are you doing here?" Gina queried.

"I have come to collect my three million dollars," Hawke replied.

"There's no loan, so there's no fee," Gina replied. "I don't owe you anything."

Hartsburg stood, immobilized behind the center island, watching the drama unfold. "Let's call it a finder's fee for putting you in a position to take over Voyageur," Hawke said, unruffled.

"I knew about Voyageur before your feeble little attempt to save his ass," she said, pointing at Hartsburg. "I owe you nothing!"

"Ah, but you do," Hawke answered. "First, you have broken the unspoken code of honor by which we—you and I—survive and thrive. And, you have taken a safe, lucrative financial transaction and turned it into a high-risk potential bloodbath. Worst of all, you have tried to double-cross me *and* Mr. Hartsburg . . ."

"What do you mean, she double-crossed me?" Hartsburg interrupted.

"Ms. Apate has co-opted Ralph Calder's device and is using it to execute Reverend Leighton, to eliminate the last opposition to her takeover," Hawke explained. "But she doesn't want the company. She wants the device. She intends to expand its range and its scope so that it can be used to blackmail anyone with any kind of cardiac implant device."

"What?" Hartsburg shrieked, turning to Gina. "Is that true?"

"Don't believe that lying bastard," she replied.

"She intends to liquidate Voyageur and pocket millions from the sale of its patents," Hawke said.

"Shut up, you fucking liar!" Gina shouted, lurching toward Hawke.

"And, worse for you and Tricia," Hawke continued, "after killing Leighton and weaponizing Calder's device, she cannot afford to leave witnesses."

"You conniving bitch!" Hartsburg screamed as he lunged for Gina, a carving knife in his hand.

Although larger and stronger, Hartsburg was no match for the former EYP agent. Deftly, she blocked the knife with her cane and side-stepped his attack. As he spun to charge again, she slid the cane head from the shaft, revealing a nine-inch blade. Hartsburg's assault ended abruptly as an upward thrust of the dagger tore through his belly and sliced into his heart.

Gina, breathing heavily, pulled the dagger from Hartsburg as he slumped to the floor. She turned toward Hawke, who was still standing, unmoved, in the doorway across the kitchen.

"You are a dead man," she said, taking a step toward him.

"I am aware of your expertise in the art of Silat," Hawke said. "Do not come any closer, madam." He removed his gloved left hand from his coat pocket, holding a gun. Hartsburg's gun.

She stopped. "How did you get . . ."

"I came only to collect my fee," he said, ignoring her question. "You have solved that problem for me." He nodded toward Hartsburg's body and the expanding pool of blood in which it lay. "But, alas, you have created a larger problem. I do not wish to spend my remaining years looking over my shoulder. Nor do I wish to live in a world that you hold hostage because you possess Calder's instrument of death. Therefore, I must call the authorities to have you arrested for the murder of Mr. Hartsburg."

"I will kill you now, or I will kill you later," Gina snarled as she rushed Hawke, waving the dripping dagger.

The gun recoiled in Hawke's hand. The 45-caliber slug made a sizable hole in Gina's forehead and a much larger one upon exit. The impact snapped her head back, and she fell backward over Hartsburg's body and lay sprawled on her back, the dagger still clutched in her hand.

Hawke paused, considering the scene, then walked across the kitchen and, careful to avoid the blood on the floor, kneeled and placed the gun in Hartsburg's right hand. Curling Hartsburg's index finger over the trigger, Hawke pressed the finger and a second bullet discharged, burying itself in the wall behind Gina's body. His hand would now contain plenty of gunshot residue.

He stood and checked the room for cameras. Finding none, he looked down at Hartsburg. "Your life was filled with opportunities," he said aloud. "It is a pity that you squandered them."

His gaze shifted to Gina's body.

"I abhor violence," he murmured, "and the commandment says, 'thou shalt not kill.' For you, however, I am gratified to have made an exception."

Chapter 34

*O*ne *last night in this miserably cold place*, Hawke thought. He was glad to have been seated near the fireplace. He scanned the room from his table, observing people coming into the restaurant, chuffing and shivering despite their bulky coats and knit hats.

Thank God for absinthe. He took a sip of the warm, licorice-flavored liquid and let it sit on his tongue for a moment to feel the burn. He considered the remains of a fish filet lying on his plate, a thing they considered a delicacy here called walleye. Acceptable, but he preferred sole.

He retrieved his phone from a coat pocket to summon his ride, but hesitated, looking up as a noisy threesome entered the restaurant.

Such an interesting coincidence, he thought as Matt Lanier, Sierra Bauer, and the airport cop they called Quinn settled into seats at a table. Hawke smiled as he paraphrased a famous line from the movie *Casablanca.* "*Of all the gin joints in all the towns in all the world, they walk into mine.*" He set his phone on the table without making the call.

All three had been hostile in their earlier meetings, but if they were all here, could Weezy be far behind? He was intrigued by the rather odd-looking cyber-security whiz, envisioning her on the dance floor at The Moog. He caught the waiter's eye and ordered Pernod, eschewing the flaming spectacle of absinthe preparation. He would wait.

A few minutes passed and Pen Wilkinson wheeled through the door, followed by Weezy.

Serendipity.

*   *   *

Matt had secured a table at the Capital Grille, away from the street, after agreeing to meet Sierra and Quinn, and possibly Pen and Weezy. Sierra and Quinn arrived first. After exchanging handshakes and hugs, the trio settled into chairs and ordered drinks and snacks. A long, awkward silence ensued.

"Well, aren't we a bunch of charismatic crime-fighters," Sierra said at last. "We can't even think of anything to say."

"Matt never says a lot," Quinn pointed out.

"Any good musician will listen more than talk," Matt responded.

They were interrupted by the arrival of Pen and Weezy, both red-cheeked, wearing heavy coats, scarves, and mittens.

"Hey, guys," Pen called out. More hugs and handshakes followed.

Coats were removed, and chairs were rearranged so Pen could roll up to the table. More drinks and snacks arrived.

"We're all here," Sierra announced.

"And we did it," Weezy said, taking a sip from a smooth pinot noir.

"Pretty much," Pen agreed. "We've got Tricia free, Calder in jail, Apate's thugs rounded up, and the FDA is looking seriously at the 4750."

"What happened at the VCS board meeting yesterday?" Sierra asked.

Pen sipped from her glass of Chardonnay. "It was weird. According to Nancy Nguyen—who's back on the job, by the way —neither Hartsburg nor Gina showed up for the big showdown, and nobody could reach either of them. So the board named

Reverend Leighton acting chairman while they find out what's going on."

"Something happened up at Hartsburg's cabin," Quinn said. "I've got a buddy who's a deputy up in that county. The local authorities have imposed a complete news blackout, but my friend told me there was a huge amount of 'police activity' up there. I don't know what happened, but it's clear that even if Hartsburg and/or Gina are still alive, they're either in custody or on the run and subject to arrest, if they can be found."

"And who knows what the hell happened to Hawke?" Matt remarked, taking a gulp from his Guinness. "I assume he's in no legal jeopardy."

"Not as far as I know," Pen said. "But he was actually pretty helpful to us."

"Despite being a world-class sleaze," Weezy said.

Pen shrugged. "Maybe because of it."

Sierra took a breath and said, "We succeeded. But let's not forget the people who didn't make it: Alice Holmgren, Dr. Danilson, Lois Calder. And who knows how many deaths were caused by the 4750 defect? We need to remember them." She raised her glass.

The others followed suit. "Hear, hear."

After a brief, somber silence, Weezy set her glass down. "What is everybody going to do now?"

"How do we follow a project like this?" Sierra asked. "We got to act out our very own version of an Avengers movie."

"A low-budget production," Quinn said to laughter.

Sierra turned to Matt. "How about you, Maestro?"

Matt considered the question. "Number one is to restart my career, now that I've completed the rehab on my hand." He raised his left hand and wiggled his fingers. "Playing the alumni farewell concert with Dr. Dan was a decent start, but I'd love to make *great* music again someday. Number two: return to Castle Danger and rebuild my life. There's a woman there who just might be the one. And her kid's as cute as hell, too. Number three: The next time I stumble across a conspiracy, I'll run away as fast as possible, ears plugged, eyes closed, mouth shut. Two fiendish plots in two years—I've had enough."

Everybody laughed.

"Weezy, what about you?" Matt asked. "Are you going back to Silicon Valley?"

"No, home to Boston. Grunt work finding hackers for MIT."

"You don't seem too excited by the prospect."

She shrugged. "It will be fine. Part of me is anxious to get home. You know, the familiarity, the family. The comfortable, super-bright people at MIT. But—"

Everyone waited.

"But it won't be as exciting as this was. I really felt . . . *alive*, working with you guys. Who knows—maybe this business will be a chapter break for me."

"Your professional life is in high gear," Sierra said. "Maybe you need to pay a little more attention to your personal life."

Weezy blushed, trying not to look at Matt, as everyone chuckled good-naturedly. "Maybe I should," she said quietly. Pen sent her a fond smile across the table, and Weezy took another sip of wine.

Matt turned toward Sierra and Quinn. "How about you guys?"

Sierra answered, "What's the only rational response to sub-zero temps, conspiracies, and near-death experiences?"

Quinn grinned. "To leave town."

"Give that man a prize." She turned to the group. "Which is why we made our reservations this morning for the Hawaiian vacation I've been threatening to take Quinn on. Two weeks of warmth, ocean, and palm trees."

"And," Quinn added, "no Russian goon squads or bodies in airplanes."

"That, too," Sierra agreed. She turned to Pen. "What about you, Counselor?"

Pen twirled her wineglass thoughtfully. "Nothing earth-shaking. Just doing what I do. After my last case, up here, I thought I'd had enough of billionaires. But in a few days, I'll be heading down to Florida—a guy supposedly has a job for me. I don't know what the project is, but he's a billionaire, and there are rumors that he wants to run for president."

"Whatever the job is, we have total confidence that you'll have Mr. Moneybags eating out of your hand."

"Or behind bars," Quinn said. Pen laughed, and so did everybody else.

Pen leaned forward, reaching for her glass, and froze as she saw a figure strolling toward them.

"You've got to be kidding me," she muttered.

*   *   *

Hawke watched, lingering over his Pernod as the group got settled and ordered drinks. Although he couldn't hear their conversation, there were smiles and laughter. He envied their carefree camaraderie. In his line of work, you either ate alone or, when there was business to be transacted, you had your head on a swivel.

After several minutes, his Pernod glass empty, he called for his car, then strolled across the dining room into the bar.

"I am afraid my invitation must have been lost in the post," Hawke said to the flabbergasted five. "Consequently, I have only a minute or two I can stay."

The group responded with a collective groan, followed by:

"*Really?* Hawke?"

"Go away!"

"What are *you* doing here?"

Hawke dodged two balled-up cocktail napkins launched in his direction. Amidst the stammering and stuttering of the seated group, he continued, "To put a little bow on your party, you might like to know that Mr. Hartsburg met an unseemly demise, but in so doing, he funded the Lois Calder Medical Device Oversight Institute with twelve million dollars he had stashed offshore. A bit of atonement, and enough to get it started."

"How . . ."

"What . . ."

"And, I am pleased to say, you need not concern yourselves with Ms. Apate any longer."

"What the—"

"How do you—"

Hawke held his hands up to silence the inquiries. "It has been a pleasure meeting all of you. Of the many people I have dealt with around the world, I must say that this little collective is as formidable as any." Then, looking directly at Weezy: "And if we ever meet again, I pray that it is on a dance floor in a more temperate climate."

He turned and walked out the door to his waiting limousine.

Acknowledgments

The authors would like to acknowledge the assistance and support of everyone involved in the creation of *The Kill Code Collective*. We are especially grateful to our families for indulging all the hours we put into this multi-year project. Thanks also to our editor, Jennifer Adkins, and our cover designer, Jun Ares. And thank you to Fay Wallin, Timya Owen, Jasmine Branum, Alicia Kozak, Allan Schwartz, and Colin Nelson. John thanks critique groups Crème de la Crime and Minneapolis Writers Guild, his fellow Midwest Mystery Works writers, and his perspicacious editor wife, Beverly. Julie offers a sincere thank you to her Writing Sisters, bonded by the craft, and from whom she has learned so much.

Authors' Note

Every work of fiction, including this one, includes a fine-print disclaimer stating that the book is, well, a work of fiction. In the case of *The Kill Code Collective*, we feel compelled to add this: "*And we really mean it.*" Events like the ones described in this book have, to our knowledge, never actually occurred. However, we can say that medical device companies are very concerned about the security and integrity of their products and have invested heavily in protecting them from threats of all types.

About the Authors

Brian:

Brian Lutterman is the author of *Incel*, a psychological thriller set in Minnesota, as well as a series of suspense-filled novels featuring Pen Wilkinson, a sassy, whip-smart, paraplegic attorney, described by the *St. Paul Pioneer Press* as ". . . one of the most intriguing new characters on the Minnesota crime scene." Brian has been a finalist for the Minnesota, Midwest, and Minnesota Author Project book awards. He is a former trial and corporate attorney and lives with his family in the Twin Cities. Visit his website at: www.brianlutterman.com.

Rob:

Born in the wine country of California, raised in a beautiful little Mississippi River town in Wisconsin, and educated in the Minnesota State University system and Harvard Law School, Rob Jung now lives the writer's life in suburban St. Paul, Minnesota. He is the author of psychological/paranormal thrillers and the producer and host of Minnesota Mystery Night, a live monthly event featuring some of the country's top crime writers, and Masters of Mystery, a syndicated radio show. His websites: www.robjungwriter.com and www.mnmysterynight.com.

Julie:

Julie Holmes started her writing career in elementary school, where her first book starred a young girl and unicorns. She now writes a variety of mysteries, from suspense to police procedurals (but no unicorns). As a former aircraft mechanic, her experiences are fodder for her Sierra Bauer series. Technical writer by day, novelist by night, she is member of MWA, Sisters in Crime (SinC), and is a past president of the Twin Cities SinC chapter. She hails from south-central Minnesota, where she lives in the country with her husband and a menagerie of pets. https://julieholmesauthor.com.

Chris:

Chris Norbury is the ungainfully employed, non-bestselling author of four novels. Each book has earned various awards most people have never heard of. All are set in his beautiful home state of Minnesota. His thrillers feature a musician hero who's too brilliantly stubborn to let the bad guys win. Chris has also written a middle-grade adventure inspired by his twenty years of volunteering with Big Brothers Big Sisters. He belongs to Sisters in Crime and the Alliance of Independent Authors. Chris lives and writes in southern Minnesota. Learn more at www.chrisnorbury.com.

John:

John Baird Rogers studied creative writing in college and at The Loft in Minneapolis. His experience in technology and biotech informs his stories, but his focus is on his characters and the voices that animate them. His four novels feature Joe Mayfield and Louise (Weezy) Napolitani. He gets critical assistance and immense pleasure from Crème de la Crime and Minneapolis Writers Guild and is a member of Midwest Mystery Works. He and his wife Beverly live in Golden Valley, MN. https://johnbairdrogers.com

The Midwest Mystery Works

Formed in 2019, the Mystery Works promotes the books of its members and those of others in the Midwest. The Works sponsors Minnesota Mystery Night, a popular monthly event featuring mystery and thriller authors from the Midwest and across the country.

Advance Praise for *The Kill Code Collective*

Although it's said that too many cooks can spoil the broth, *The Kill Code Collective* lays that old adage neatly to rest. Five thriller writers have combined their talents in the creation of this suspenseful novel, each contributing a character from their own body of work. It's a unique approach whose success is due in large measure to the amazing threads of technology that seamlessly weave the delightfully complicated story elements together. Although there were lots of fingers involved in stirring this particular pot, the result is a smooth, fast-paced, thoroughly enjoyable medical thriller.

—William Kent Krueger

Librarians and readers seeking a medical thriller mystery that rests on the shoulders of not just one, but many powerful characters, will welcome how The Kill Code Collective dovetails events, personalities, and conundrums to create a vivid probe into a defect which becomes a murder investigation.

Packed with satisfying twists and collective strengths that prove especially engaging as the problem-solvers introduce different strengths towards a greater effort, The Kill Code Collective is a thoroughly absorbing, completely unpredictable story. It benefits from many contributors who spin a fine yarn to build an unforgettable story.

—D. Donovan, Sr. Reviewer, *Midwest Book Review*